"I'm lost, remember?" Jordan grinned. "I don't know the maze."

Delaney had been playing with him, wanted to show him the possibilities of the corn maze for a date. But somehow, the maze had already done some magic, because this was a different Jordan.

He pretended surprise when they hit a dead end and had to return. At the next fork, he took the wrong path again.

It was deliberate. And she loved it. It made it seem like a real date. Like they were a real couple.

At the fifth dead end, she couldn't hold back a laugh. "You're terrible at mazes."

A smile tugged at the corner of his mouth. "I told you this wasn't a good date idea."

"I guess that depends on what your goal is for a date."

His eyes fastened on hers. "The goal isn't to solve the maze?"

She shook her head, never breaking their gaze.

He took a step closer. "What is the goal, then, Delaney?"

Dear Reader,

The past couple of years have been difficult on all of us: physically, financially and also mentally.

My heroine in this book struggles with mental health issues, and as a society we still often dismiss or belittle those battles. I hope if you experience something similar that you don't feel less and that you can reach out to get help. And if you're fortunate enough to not have gone through this struggle, that you will be gentle and kind to those who do.

Kim

HEARTWARMING

A Country Proposal

—

Kim Findlay

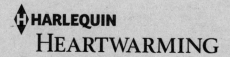

HARLEQUIN
HEARTWARMING

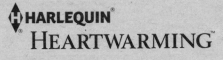

ISBN-13: 978-1-335-58492-2

A Country Proposal

Recycling programs
for this product may
not exist in your area.

For questions and comments about the quality of this book, please contact us at CustomerService@Harlequin.com.

Harlequin Enterprises ULC
22 Adelaide St. West, 41st Floor
Toronto, Ontario M5H 4E3, Canada
www.Harlequin.com

Printed in U.S.A.

Kim Findlay is a Canadian who fled the cold to live on a sailboat in the Caribbean and write romance novels. She shares the boat with her husband and the world's cutest spaniel. Bucket list accomplished! Her first Harlequin Heartwarming novel, *Crossing the Goal Line*, came about from the Heartwarming Blitz, and she's never looked back. Keep up with Kim, including her sailing adventures, at kimfindlay.ca.

Books by Kim Findlay

Harlequin Heartwarming

A Hockey Romance

Crossing the Goal Line
Her Family's Defender

Cupid's Crossing

A Valentine's Proposal
A Fourth of July Proposal
A New Year's Eve Proposal

Visit the Author Profile page
at Harlequin.com for more titles.

To those who work with food, and those who enjoy eating it.

CHAPTER ONE

THE MILL DIDN'T look like failure.

In fact, Delaney Carter had to admit it looked good. The last time she'd been here, years ago, it had been an ugly, abandoned lumber mill. Then her grandmother, Abigail Carter, had created a new revenue stream for Carter's Crossing by turning the town into a romantic getaway destination. In the past two years the town had been renamed Cupid's Crossing, and this building had undergone a massive renovation to make it an event venue for weddings and similar celebrations.

Now the former eyesore nestled into the hillside, blending with the early fall landscape, the longer side running parallel to the stream that passed behind it. Instead of a stretch of rusting metal, the wooden siding echoed the trees that were just beginning to show hues of yellow and red and orange among the green. The parking lot was covered with paving stones instead of gravel, and a portico welcomed people to the main entrance near the road.

Even the rear entrance, farthest away, had been renovated with new doors to match the rest of the building. Inside was the commercial kitchen she'd been assured was brand-new, everything top-of-the-line. She had no doubt it was designed to be perfect for a chef and her kitchen staff. Everything she could ask for. Hers, as of yesterday, to rule over for the next few months.

It was still failure. For a Carter, this wasn't enough. For her, it wasn't enough. For just a moment she wondered if she'd ever get back on her path, and her chest tightened.

Her brain scrambled through the familiar what-if scenarios. The ones that didn't end with her Manhattan restaurant closed, her partner in the hospital and Delaney back in Carter's—no, Cupid's Crossing. Her hands tensed on the steering wheel of her grandmother's car in frustration. What-ifs didn't matter. They weren't real. What was in front of her was.

She unclenched her hands enough for the knuckles to no longer show white and slowed her breathing. Her stomach twisted and she shook her head, trying to clear it. There was no way to turn back time. She was here. Here to do the pity job her grandmother had given her. She'd head up the kitchen for the Mill, the position available when they lost their original chef last week, one Rudy Dunstan. And while she was here she would figure out how to recapture her life. Her real, successful life.

Enough whining. She grabbed her shoulder bag and picked up her carefully packaged knives in their waxed canvas carryall. She opened the car door and stood up, breathing in the clean air.

She didn't want clean air. She wanted exhaust fumes and sweat and garbage. But this was what she had.

A quick glance around the parking lot showed that her organic produce supplier, OPD, wasn't here yet. Rudy had set up the arrangement, and Delaney now needed to take up the knife, so to speak. If OPD wasn't here, she wasn't late. She crossed to the rear entrance, determined to be the professional she was. She couldn't let her standards down just because she was no longer the owner of a hot new restaurant in New York City.

The code she'd been texted turned off the alarm, and the key opened the lock. For a moment she paused, hand on the doorknob, unwilling to enter and embrace this as her new reality.

The knob felt strange under her hand, but she turned it and stepped inside, shuddering. Windows let the light land over counters and appliances, all she'd expected. She set her knife bag down on a countertop and slowly pulled the purse off her shoulder.

She was cold. And her head felt like it was drifting upward. Was she coming down with something? She held up a hand only to find it trembling. The door latched behind her, and her stomach cramped. Her body told her she was in danger. She had to get out of this place. She looked around to find the source of that fear and felt dizzy.

She didn't remember leaving the building. The next thing she knew, when her stomach stopped twisting and her breathing was no longer shaking her chest, she was outside, sitting on the ground. She had broken nails, and her head still felt light, her thoughts chaotic and out of control.

What just happened? She'd never felt anything like it before. Was something wrong with her? She really feared there might be.

JORDAN EVERTON HAD to force himself to turn his truck into the parking lot of the Mill. He couldn't stay stopped on the county road forever, blinker on, so he braced himself and tapped the accelerator.

Once safely off the road, he let the truck idle. The Mill didn't look anything like the building in which his mother had died all those years ago. She'd been an employee there, but somehow left the office she worked in and was killed by falling debris in a closed-off section of the mill.

His father had already been trying to sue the Carters based on an old property claim. The accident had convinced his father that there was merit in the claim, and that his mother had been murdered, despite all evidence to the contrary. The results had upended Jordan's life.

He refused to indulge the painful memories. That was the past, and he wasn't going to dwell in it. The Mill bore little resemblance to its former life as a lumber mill beyond the basic shape. Didn't much matter. He knew it was the same place.

His dog Ranger whined beside him, picking up his mood.

"I know, boy. I signed up for this. Doesn't mean I like it."

His grip tightened on the steering wheel as he slowly drove down the length of the building to the rear entrance. He didn't need to dawdle. Just find Rudy Dunstan, the chef who'd placed the order, deliver the produce he had in the back of the truck and get a signature. Then he could go back to the farm and indulge on his own any guilt he felt about doing business with the place where his mother had died.

There was a car near the kitchen door, a Prius. Good. Dunstan must be here, so this would be quick. He had about two days of work to finish up before sunset, so maybe he could get a good portion of that done.

He backed the truck in, so the tailgate was facing the doors. The Mill was closed, but at least he knew his guy was around here somewhere. Probably working inside. He opened the driver's door and stepped out, waiting for Ranger to jump down after him.

He tugged the tailgate down, grabbed the first box and swung toward the doors to the kitchen. There was a buzzer, and he pushed it once he'd set down that box. He grabbed the second and returned to the door.

It was still closed.

Was there a problem? Maybe the buzzer didn't work?

He knocked on the doors, hard enough to create a loud echo inside the building. He hesitated, torn between wanting to empty the truck and be gone as soon as possible, and a looming feeling that something was wrong, and he might have to load everything up again.

Then he heard Ranger whine.

He turned. Ranger was staring in the direction of the stream that ran along the back side of the building, head tilted toward something out of view. Jordan listened again, making sure no one was coming to answer his knock, and followed Ranger around the corner.

At first, all he noticed was the stream, rushing closely alongside the Mill. Then he saw a pile of clothing, or maybe some table linens, heaped against the wall. He made out the shape of a white chef's jacket, wrapped around a person.

This must be his missing contact. Was Dunstan okay? He moved forward to check.

He'd never met the man, but the hair he saw was long and dark, pulled back in a French braid. And the hands, gripped tightly around the person's knees, were slender, long and smaller than he expected.

He shook his head. Not Dunstan. A female chef. And something was or had upset her.

He scanned the area, not finding any visible threat. Ranger was focused on the person huddled against the wall, so he didn't sense any immediate danger, either. Jordan squatted down in the narrow space in front of her, making his body smaller, less threatening. Ranger stepped closer, nose out, sniffing at the bundle of woman. They were frozen in place for a moment, and then the woman lifted her head and reached out her hands for Ranger's ruff. She threaded her fingers in his fur, gripping tightly as Ranger moved closer and sniffed again.

Jordan remained locked in position, balanced on his toes, hand down to steady himself when the surprise hit.

He knew this face.

It was older. The soft roundness of adolescence had firmed into a sharper jawline, higher cheekbones. There was a furrow between the brows, and lines around her mouth. But the eyes, deep blue with dark winging brows, were the same. The pink lips familiar, the straight nose unchanged.

Her head moved up, and those blue eyes locked with his. Her mouth dropped open, and she shivered. Then she tucked her head into Ranger's side, almost burrowing into the dog.

Jordan felt light-headed, his chest pounding. He'd never wanted or planned to see Delaney Carter again; never wanted to revisit that heartbreak. He should never have signed that deal with the Mill. Nothing good came from dealing with a Carter.

His dad was right.

DELANEY GRIPPED TIGHTLY to the dog's fur, grateful to have something to cling to. None of this could possibly be real. If it was, something was seriously wrong.

She'd thought, hoped, for a few minutes, that things were getting better. That whatever had happened when she went in the kitchen was over, an aberration, maybe the start of the flu, something she understood. She was getting back to her normal, her body feeling like hers again. No more panicky gasping for breath, her limbs responding to her commands. But then she looked up and saw Jordan Everton, and she knew she was in a dream or more likely a nightmare.

There was no way one of her greatest hits on the all-time Delaney mistakes list was here at the Mill.

Sure, his family farm was in the area. But even if he'd stayed on that farm, there was no way he'd set foot on the Mill property. There was nothing that would spur him into doing business with the Carters. And his dad—he'd have been the first suspect if there'd ever been a fire at the Mill. He hated her family.

No, she just had to accept that none of this was real. And if it wasn't, was there any possibility that the past two months weren't, either? Maybe she still had her restaurant, and her partner was uninjured?

What an incredible thought.

The dog whimpered as she accidentally tugged too hard. She eased her grip and turned her hands flat to pet him. Her. It.

She cracked open an eye to look at the animal. He was large, mostly German shepherd in appearance, but with a leaner build, a rounder muzzle, enough to show he was mixed in his breeding. She didn't care. Right now he was something she could cling to. She knew what a dog was, what a dog felt like. This was real.

Deep breath. Her lungs worked properly, and her stomach was no longer churning. Another breath. Even her brain began to feel like it was hers again, controlling her body, her movements feeling like her own once more.

Okay, whatever had happened, she'd deal with it. She was in her familiar chef's coat, so she was working. Maybe…maybe she'd find herself back at the restaurant in New York, the shooting a nightmare.

She really wanted that to be true. But she was sitting on dirt, not concrete. She could hear rushing water, not traffic, and there were none of the scents of garbage and car exhaust that she would breathe in if she was in New York.

Another breath and she looked up. And saw Jordan again.

Not the Jordan she knew. This was a man, not a teenager. He had a full beard and shaggy hair over a large, muscled frame. But those eyes—she'd know those eyes anywhere.

They were staring at her in horror.

She finally had it figured out. She'd somehow ended up in purgatory. Purgatory, with the boy who'd broken her heart.

JORDAN HAD NO idea what was going on here, but he had two immediate problems to work out. First, a truck load of produce. It didn't take much in the line of math skills to put together the Prius and the chef's coat and add it up to the unwelcoming total that Delaney Carter was supposed to receive his produce, not Dunstan. There was no one else here, and he wasn't sure if Delaney was up to it.

That was the second problem. This wasn't the Delaney he knew. Unless something drastic had changed her personality, she wasn't someone to huddle behind a building in obvious distress. He had to talk to her, find out what had happened to her and if she was okay. He might be unused to social conventions these days, but he wasn't going to leave her here like this.

His dad would tell him this served him right for getting involved with the Carters. The man was safely away in Florida right now, so he shoved thoughts of his father out of his head.

"Delaney." His voice cracked. He hadn't spoken her name in years.

She looked up at him warily. She wasn't afraid of him, was she? Even with what had gone down back in high school, he'd never threatened her or her family.

"Are you okay? Did something happen to you?"

He wanted to roll his eyes at himself. Obviously, something had happened. She was holding on to his dog like he was the last life jacket on the Titanic.

"Jordan? You're real?"

His mouth opened and closed. Did she often see things that weren't there?

"Pretty sure I am."

She glanced around their surroundings. From here she'd see the stream and the trees climbing the hillside behind the mill.

"So not purgatory."

He frowned. She thought of him and purgatory together. Didn't make him happy, but he was pretty sure she'd be in his purgatory as well.

He kept his voice calm and flat. "You're at the Mill. Do you know why you're here?"

He couldn't see any sign that she'd hit her head, but he wouldn't necessarily if the bump was hidden beneath her hair. What was going on, and what should he do?

She closed her eyes and gripped more tightly onto Ranger. Jordan thought he saw the dog flinch and felt for him. Still, Delaney seemed to need Ranger, so he waited, relaxing when her fingers did as well.

"I'm taking over for Dunstan in the kitchen. He got another job last week. I just agreed to work here two days ago."

Just as he'd suspected. He wondered for a moment if the Carters had deliberately not told him of the switcheroo, knowing he'd never have agreed to supply the Mill if Delaney was working there, but he refused to allow the idea to take hold. His father was paranoid enough about the Carters for both of them.

'You came here to work." He tried not to let any of his frustration come through, though he was tense enough to want to shout his protest.

She nodded. "I've got a delivery coming from OPD—" She broke off and scrambled to her feet. "What time is it? They should be here. I hope they didn't leave."

Her hand was still on Ranger, and it was trembling, slightly.

Jordan slowly rose to stand in front of her. She moved back but was trapped by the wall of the Mill. Jordan stepped away, hands up, doing his best to look harmless.

"Don't worry about OPD."

Her gaze slid from him to the corner where the parking lot was just out of sight, then to the trees and back to him. Jordan couldn't back up much more without risking falling into the stream, and he didn't think anyone could ask that of him. He turned and walked backward toward the parking lot. Ranger stepped forward to follow him, and Delaney kept her hand on the dog, with the result that the three of them moved together.

Jordan wished reinforcements had shown up while he'd been around back with Delaney since he had no idea what he was doing right now. The lack of audience meant no one watched him step around the corner of the building, arms up in front of him, with

Ranger and Delany following. As if Ranger was a weapon Delaney was holding on him.

Jordan hoped Delaney would relax when she had open space around her, but her gaze flicked to the door to the kitchen and back to him and then Ranger, as tense as when she'd been hiding behind the building.

Another glance around the parking lot. Her gaze stopped on his truck.

"Is that...? Is that OPD?"

He understood her confusion. The truck had Stoney Creek Farm on the doors.

"Yes, I'm OPD." He wasn't going to explain to her that he'd set up OPD, Organic Produce Delivery as a dummy company between Stoney Creek and the Mill so that his dad wouldn't realize that Jordan had agreed to become a supplier. The man might see the sale to OPD in the books, but at least nothing with the name of the Mill on it.

The farm bank accounts and records were down in Florida with his father. They had a joint account up here that Jordan used to deposit farm profits into, as part of the deal they'd set up.

The deposits into that account would show OPD, not anything connected to Carter's Crossing. He didn't want to mislead his father, but he needed the Mill's business.

He didn't need to share any of that with Delaney.

A glance at him, one at the truck and then the door of the kitchen. She took a breath, straightened to her full height and nodded.

"Excellent. Sorry to delay you. Let's get that food in the fridge."

Her voice was shaky, but she was saying the words Jordan wanted to hear. Organic produce was more delicate than regular and the less time in transit, the better. As well, he wanted to get back on the road. He needed time to come to terms with Delaney's being back. Jordan looked at Ranger, as if the dog could somehow explain the change in Delaney. She was all business now, despite the fact that she hadn't let go of Ranger.

"Okay," Jordan agreed. He wanted his food received, processed and the payment coming in. That was his only reason to be here. If Delaney could do that, then he'd leave. Happily.

He took another look at her.

No, he wasn't going anywhere. She was still gripping Ranger.

She took a step toward the door, shoving a

hand into her pocket. Her brow furrowed, and she patted the other pocket. Then the first one again. Her gaze ran over the ground.

"Lost something?"

"The keys. The door locks automatically, unless the latch is…" She walked quickly to the door, hesitated and then gave it a shove.

Nothing happened.

Delaney pushed on the door. Jordan came up beside her and shoved as well. Nothing.

"Do you have your keys?"

"Of course, I had them when I—"

Her voice trailed off.

"Delaney, are you okay? Did something happen? Did anyone…do something?" Aside from the dirt she'd picked up sitting on the ground, she looked alright.

Delaney pushed futilely against the door.

"No, nothing happened. I—"

She bit her lower lip.

"I came here. I had the keys in my bag. I remember pulling them out and then…"

Jordan's fists tensed as he waited to hear the end of that sentence. Something had to have gone down for her to behave like this. Something bad.

Her hand trembled on Ranger's shoulder again and tightened on his ruff.

"I unlocked the door, went into the kitchen and then... I ran out of the building, and I don't know why."

DELANEY COULDN'T LOOK at anything but the door. The stupid locked door. She hated that this had happened to her, hated that she had to tell someone and hated that she was telling Jordan Everton, of all people. But what else could she say? She was here to do a simple job and she was failing at it.

Now that she was thinking clearly again, or more clearly, the only explanation was that she'd rushed out of the kitchen, leaving her purse with her keys and phone in the kitchen, behind the door that was now locked. Jordan was here to deliver the organic produce they needed for the kitchen, and she couldn't even open the stupid door.

She fought back tears. She had a job to do. She couldn't break down and cry. Not now, not here and not in front of Jordan.

Deep breath. She could do this. She'd handled a restaurant in New York City. This... This was just a blip.

But in her head, she kept hearing *Failure*.

She turned, pulling on a smile. She couldn't look at Jordan, not directly again, so she focused on his earlobe.

"I'm sorry, Jordan. I've left my keys and phone in the kitchen."

Who else had keys? Mariah, Grandmother... but Grandmother no longer lived in Cupid's Crossing, and Mariah had gone someplace. She couldn't remember exactly where, but it meant that Delaney had come on her own. She didn't know who else had keys, since she'd just left her apartment to her roommate and driven up from the city yesterday. She'd stayed the night with her brother Nelson and Mariah, his wife, but no. She was not telling Nelson.

She wasn't sure what Jordan thought of all this, but the embarrassment of meeting him and looking anything but a successful, confident version of herself was almost worse than locking the key inside.

"Is there a spare key somewhere?" He didn't sound impatient, which he had every right to be. He was here to make a delivery. She was supposed to be a professional.

"I'm sure there is somewhere, but I just got here yesterday, so I don't know where it is."

She directed the words to his earlobe again

and tried for a conciliatory smile. She was sure it was just another on her list of current failures.

"If it might be a while, I should take my stuff back to the farm, then. Are you… What are you going to do without a phone or keys?"

Ah, yes. The Mill was about a mile outside Cupid's Crossing. Nelson's place was even farther out of town. Without a phone or car keys, she was stuck at the Mill, until someone came here with an extra set of kitchen keys.

She could walk to town, but who would she look for once she was there? She hadn't been here except for short visits since she was in high school.

"I…well…" She had planned to spend the day prepping the food her supplier, Jordan, apparently, brought, going through the schedule of events for the Mill, and the menus and recipes for those events. She didn't think any of the staff were coming in until tomorrow.

And she had to do something about whatever had happened to her in the kitchen. For that, she needed access to the internet and Dr. Google. And a phone.

She could probably find some kind of help in town, but word would get around. People would see her wandering around and Grandmother would hear. Nelson and Mariah would hear. That meant even her parents in…was it Kazhikstan?…would hear that she wasn't handling her job.

Or she could further embarrass herself in front of Jordan and ask him for help. The upside there was that she might get through this without any of her family finding out. Rock, meet hard place.

"Delaney?"

Shivers went up her back as that part-familiar, part-strange voice said her name. Her fingers clenched, and she realized she was still clinging to the dog. The chances were good that this was Jordan's dog. And right now having this dog around felt good, tipping the scales in her decision.

"I need to ask you for a favor, Jordan. I need access to the internet. Do you have that?"

"Not here. I don't have a smartphone, just an old flip phone." He stared down, as if he thought she'd judge him for his lack of the latest technology. Right now she was in no place to do that.

"Is there someone you can call?" He didn't sound happy. Why would he? She was a Carter and the Evertons hated the Carters.

"I don't have any local numbers memorized." She had them as contacts, but she didn't call them often, preferring to email.

Jordan let out a long breath. "I have a laptop and internet at the farm."

What if his dad was at the farm? He might chase her off with a shotgun.

She forced another smile. What choice did she have? "Could I come with you, then? Just till I get this straightened out. Um, if you're going back. If it's not too much of an inconvenience."

What if he had planned going into town to do some errands? It would be a lift at least.

"I need to get this food somewhere safe, so it looks like I have to head back to the farm." She risked a glance at his face, but he was staring at the boxes of food that were set by the door. His hand was rubbing the back of his neck. "You can ride with me, and we'll work something out."

A wave of relief almost made her sag in place or throw herself on his chest to thank him. More than looking professional or doing her job, right now she wanted to get away from the Mill. She'd known coming here was a step backward; she just hadn't expected it to be like this.

"Thank you, Jordan. I appreciate it. I'll help move your food."

He shook his head and turned his attention

back to her, and she was caught by those brown eyes. For a moment they were in high school again, and those eyes had seen her; seen her and appreciated her.

Well, she thought they had. That was her mistake. He'd seen a Carter; that was all. She swallowed and turned toward his truck, the dog still under her hand.

Not even ten o'clock in the morning, and this was already a horrible day. Not the worst, but it was ranking right up there.

"The passenger side is open. You and Ranger can get in while I load these up."

Ranger? Oh, the dog. Right. She caught the handle of the truck door, finally releasing the dog. When she pulled the door open with a re-sounding creak, the dog leaped into the seat. Delaney climbed in after him, and he made room for her without protest.

She pulled the door closed behind her and leaned her face into the dog's fur. She'd like to hide here for the day. Maybe the week. Until the world made sense again, and she knew what she was doing.

She'd come to Cupid's Crossing to start her career over. To take the first baby steps to regain some of the success she'd finally earned. If she couldn't even do this, what did she have left?

CHAPTER TWO

JORDAN SLID THE last bin into the back of his truck. He'd checked, and the produce was fine so far. Fortunately, now that the calendar had tipped into September, there was a reduction in the stifling heat of upstate New York in August, and the cool touch to the morning breeze had helped keep his food fresh.

He wasn't pleased to be returning everything to the farm. But he didn't have much of an option. Leaving it outside the kitchen door indefinitely would be disastrous.

He glanced into the cab of his truck and watched Delaney, sitting by Ranger. She had a hand on the dog again. He didn't understand what was going on here, but Delaney wasn't doing well. He must be the last person she'd want to ask for help, not after the disastrous ending to their short-lived high school romance, but he was the only one around.

Why he felt like he should help her deal with whatever this was, he had no good answer. For a couple of months back in high school he'd thought he was in love with her, and that she cared for him, but he'd been terribly wrong. He didn't owe her anything. The only connection between them was the heartbreak she'd given him. But still, he was taking her to the farm.

Thank goodness his father wasn't here. If one person could destroy his plans for the farm, it was Delaney, if his father ever learned about her visit.

He opened the driver's door and looked across the bench seat at the two heads watching him. Both seemed to be asking him something. *What was going on?*

He had no answer, so he slid in behind the wheel and started the truck.

It was a quiet ride to the farm. Delaney stared out the passenger window, hand on Ranger, and Ranger sat, watching first Jordan, and then Delaney. Jordan was relieved to see the Stoney Creek Farm sign and signaled his turn.

There was a gate across the drive. He got out and pulled it open. He flipped over the wooden sign that said Closed and left the other side saying Open visible to anyone coming in. Above it were the words Stoney Creek Farm, under, Fresh Organic Produce, Hiking Trails and Corn Maze. He needed to do some work on the corn maze, and this disruption to his day wasn't going to help him get to the maze any quicker. This was almost his last season to get his funds together.

He turned back to the truck. Delaney was still staring out the passenger window. He wasn't sure she realized they'd stopped.

He got back in and drove up the driveway to park beside his retail and storage building.

When he opened his door, Ranger moved to follow him but was held back by Delaney's hand. He saw her start when Ranger tugged against her grip, then she let the dog go. She looked around as if she hadn't noticed where they'd been driving.

Jordan let out a breath. "I'll show you where the computer is, then I'm going to put this food away."

Delaney nodded and slipped out the passenger door. He led the way over to the two-story stone farmhouse and around to the back.

He pulled open the screen door. The inner door was still open. Maybe he should lock up when he left, but he'd never had anyone try to steal anything. Usually, Ranger gave warning of new people arriving.

The back door opened into the kitchen, once they stepped through a small coat area. Jordan toed off his boots and headed through the kitchen to what had been a dining room. Since he and his dad were the only people to eat here anymore, and his dad lived in Florida now, Jordan had set up his office in the former dining room. A desk, a file cabinet, a laptop and a couple of chairs.

He could hear the dog behind him, and Delaney following. He leaned over the computer, jiggled the mouse till the machine woke up and typed in the password.

The screen flashed on, internet browser already open to where he'd been researching wildflowers and bees—different options to expand the farm's diversity and cash flow. Nothing there that should be of interest to a Carter.

His father would tell him he was foolish. That he couldn't trust a Carter. There was a lot of truth to that, but he didn't extend his paranoia to believing that Delaney had faked the distress she'd shown when he found her and pretended to lock her keys in the Mill just so she could check out the tabs on their computer.

His dad would carefully clean up the browser history whenever he left his computer. Jordan refused to share his paranoia. Hopefully, within the next year he could buy his father out. He could let what remained of that mostly one-sided feud with the Carter family wither from lack of attention.

Feuds didn't cover costs like property taxes or maintenance, so Jordan didn't want to be part of them. He just wanted to be left alone.

"The speed's a little slow, but you should be able to find what you need."

He stepped back from the desk, too aware of Delaney's presence. He needed to keep his distance. He didn't want her to think he was checking on what she did, or that he had any interest in her. Still, he watched while she sat down at the desk and ran the cursor over to a new tab. He returned to the kitchen and ran a glass of water, which he set beside her.

"Need anything else?"

Her startled gaze met his, and memories of the girl he'd loved in high school made him want to reassure her she'd be fine. He wanted to take care of her, as if they were still important to each other.

And all of that was a good reason to get away from her as soon as possible.

When Delaney shook her head, he got out of the house as quickly as he could. He had produce to take care of. A farm to manage. He didn't need to take on anything connected to Delaney as well.

DELANEY SAT ON the hard wooden chair, browser open on the laptop in front of her. She tapped in her email home page and her address. She bit her lip, wondering if she remembered her password. She had a list of them on her phone, but her phone was in the kitchen at the Mill.

She could have asked to use Jordan's phone, back while they were at the Mill. He might have Mariah set up as a contact already. Not Nelson, she was sure. But she didn't want to tell Mariah that Jordan had found her sitting on the ground outside the Mill, and she hadn't been able to think of a good explanation for why her keys, phone and bag were all in the kitchen there. In an email, she could ignore questions and just get the answer she needed.

Mariah would obviously ask what had happened. Delaney had heard something outside. And run to check it out, letting the door slam closed and lock behind her? Was that as incredible as the truth?

If she was lucky, there would be a spare key somewhere, and she could get back to the Mill before anyone else found out she wasn't in the kitchen there doing her job. Except Jordan knew. She'd worry about that later.

The second password she tried let her in. She emailed Mariah, saying that she'd accidentally locked her phone and keys in the kitchen, and was there a spare available. She didn't try to explain. She could work on a plausible story later.

Then she searched for a particular email, to provide the contact information of someone she'd never thought she'd need to reach out to. It popped up, and she stared at it.

Was she going to do this?

Yeah, she had to. She had to figure out what had happened to her this morning. It was something she'd never experienced before, and she feared it had to relate to the shooting at the restaurant.

She didn't want that to be the cause. If it was... If it was, it might mean she couldn't do her job. Not right now, and maybe not for a long time. But as much as she hated to admit it, it was the only explanation that made sense.

After the shooting, which had left her business partner Peter injured and ended the dream the two of them had worked so hard to bring to fruition, they'd agreed to have a counselor available for all the staff. Bad enough that everyone ended up losing their jobs—it seemed like offering a helping hand for the mental stress was the least they could do.

Delaney hadn't been at the restaurant when

the shooting happened. But the counselor had insisted on talking to her. Delaney had promised she was fine. The counselor had sent one last email, urging Delaney to let him know if she needed help.

Delaney didn't need a therapist to tell her she wasn't responsible for the shooting. Obviously, it was the guy with the gun who was the problem. But she was the one who'd fired him, so the guilt was well deserved.

And yes, it had been a terrible thing. Fortunately, no one was killed, but Peter was still in physical therapy, and that was on Delaney as well. No one else had been seriously injured, but for her to think she was another victim because she'd had to close the restaurant was ridiculous.

She didn't need the counselor and had thanked him politely for her concern.

Really, Delaney had gotten off pretty easy. But still…she'd started to feel bad when she went into the kitchen at the Mill. Her body felt weird, parts of her felt almost ill and her brain had disassociated from her body. It had never happened before, and this was the first time she'd been in a kitchen to work since the shooting, so maybe there was a connection.

She needed to know. She hoped the man

could tell her how to put this behind her. It shouldn't be that difficult, surely, since Delaney hadn't been on site. Peter was the one who'd been shot, and he hadn't mentioned any problems beyond the physical, so why would Delaney have any?

But maybe she needed a little help so she could get her career back on track.

JORDAN GOT THE produce put away in the cooler in the storage room behind his retail space. Since he was late to start his day, he heard cars coming down the drive as he placed the last of the produce in the coolers. He walked back out to see if this was someone who needed his attention.

The old machine shed had been renovated into two sections: storage in the back, and retail at the front, where he sold vegetables from the farm and beverages for the hikers. He needed to restock the storefront. He hadn't had a chance before he headed to the Mill, but the people getting out of the SUV were dressed in shorts and boots.

He waved at them.

"We're okay to hike here, right?" one woman asked.

Jordan nodded. There were three marked

trails, each starting at one side of the former paddock, now parking lot. This time of year people liked to see the leaves changing as they rambled through the hilly sections of the farm. "The trails are marked. Please stay on the trails. There's some poison ivy to watch for on the blue trail, and the creek is on the red one."

The woman nodded, and her friends checked their water bottles before they headed for the blue trail.

Maybe he should sell cortisone cream. People didn't listen to his warnings half the time.

He opened the door to his retail space and checked it over. The potatoes and onions were fine, but he had to get more corn in. Which reminded him the corn maze needed some maintenance soon.

With a sigh, he went into the back to restock the produce that had required refrigeration overnight. He checked the supplies of water and pop and sports drinks he kept for thirsty hikers and put up the sign instructing customers to call his cell number if they needed assistance. He had corn to pick, as well as beans and peppers. He didn't know if the Mill was going to take the food he'd tried to deliver today, and if they didn't, he'd need to find another place to sell it. Fast. It wouldn't last long. Not only did he need the money, but he also hated the idea of wasting food.

Another car pulled in, this time someone looking for produce. He answered questions about tomatoes and peppers until the people had finished their purchases. By this point more hikers had arrived, and another car of shoppers.

For a Monday, this was a rush hour.

Watching the car pull out, with two bags of vegetables in the backseat, he tallied the hiker vehicles, three, and considered his best move.

The corn maze could wait—he didn't have to open it up for a couple of weeks. The hikers coming back might want to buy something, but that was a maybe, and the crops in the field were more of a sure thing.

Delaney appeared from the back of the house.

There was his biggest problem. Both to his peace of mind, and to his plans for the farm if Dad ever found out.

He had sunglasses on, so he could watch her without her being aware. She was walking quickly, more confidently. Hopefully, that was good news. As in, she was ready to return to the Mill, and he could deliver his produce. He ignored the twinge of disappointment that thought gave him. He had no business being disappointed in spending less time with Delaney.

He waited in silence till she reached him.

"I've got good news, and good news." Her smile was bright, but maybe a little forced. He waited some more.

She gave a nod. "There is a spare key at the Mill, so I can get my purse and phone and, well, get to work."

Her hands were tensed into fists.

"And I did some research, and probably what happened was just a panic attack, so nothing to worry about."

Jordan frowned. That did not sound like good news to him. He'd seen her, outside the Mill. There was no *just* about what she'd gone through. Did he have the right to tell her? Was it any of his business? Maybe not, but surely, as a decent human being he should say something.

"I'm not sure panic attacks are as simple as you think. You looked pretty upset outside the Mill. Maybe you should just get your keys and take a break today. Go back tomorrow."

She froze. Her lips pinched.

"A panic attack isn't *real*. I wasn't sick or in a medical crisis. I just panicked. I have things to do, and now that I know what I'm dealing with, I can handle it."

That would depend on what brought on the panic attack. Maybe it was a one-time thing. Maybe, well, he didn't know. But Delaney was moving on, ignoring his concern, so there wasn't much he could do.

"I need to get back to the Mill. You can bring your order."

He considered. It would take time to load the produce up again, and he wasn't sure things were going to work out on that end as well as she expected. There was a decent chance he'd be bringing it all back again. Also, he was needed here now.

Just then another car pulled up.

Delaney turned and frowned.

The car parked and a man got out, wearing flip-flops.

Not a hiker.

"I need to take care of this." Jordan wasn't sure if he should be grateful for the interruption or not. If he told Delaney he wasn't sure she was going to be able to handle his order, she might get upset.

He headed to the shop, nodding to the new arrival, who was carrying some canvas bags.

Jordan unlocked the door and held it open. The man came in, and Delaney followed him.

It was soon obvious that this was a chatty customer.

"I saw your ad on the town website, so decided to drive out and take a look. This is all organic?"

Jordan nodded.

"I know everyone wants corn this time of year, but I'm all about the peppers. These do look nice. How long are you open? This season, I mean. Because I'll be back if these are as good as they look. Oh, I could use some more onions. Do you have pumpkins?"

"In October, yes."

"Of course, that's when you'd have them. Oh, what the heck. How about a half dozen ears of corn anyway? Since I'm here."

Jordan was glad for the business, but he was distracted by Delaney, moving quietly, checking the produce, the drinks in the cooler, and watching him with a strange expression. Jordan did his best to ignore her, ringing up the man's purchases and taking his payment.

"Thank you." The customer smiled as he left with his bags full of organic, really organic, produce. Jordan closed his till and turned to Delaney.

She was biting her lip.

"I'm sorry. I didn't consider that you had a business to run. I assumed the Mill delivery was your priority for the day. I can't expect you to be my taxi service."

Which was absolutely true, and he deserved her to recognize that. He needed to take care of his farm.

But since Mariah hadn't been available to help her when they were at the Mill, he strongly suspected that the only person she had to call was Nelson and no way did he want Nelson on his farm. Especially with Delaney here with him. That was too close to high school again.

"I can take you back there. I won't load up the food, unless you're using it today. I can bring it for you tomorrow morning."

Delaney looked through the window to the parked cars.

"They're hikers. They probably won't buy anything anyway. I'll just leave a note that I'm gone for a while."

Delaney bit her lip. "I'm sorry to be so much trouble. You're right. I probably won't start any food prep today."

Jordan just jerked his head toward the truck. Delaney followed him out the door, and he turned to write *Back in an hour* on the chalk-board he'd set up there for just that purpose.

He crossed the parking lot, his work boots loud on the gravel. He couldn't hear Delaney behind him, but he could feel her presence. Not a good thing. Getting her back to the Mill was the smart play.

A large portion of the farm's profits were going to the purchase of the farm from his father. It had been hard to pin the man down and set up their arrangement. His dad wasn't attached to the farm, not like Jordan, but he was wary and Jordan had had to push before his dad would agree to sell. Jordan was investing every bit of his energy and cash to meet that dollar amount before his father could change his mind.

The man was paranoid to the point where Jordan worried about him. All the farm paperwork went to his father in Florida, which the man blamed on the Carters. He thought the Carters would be able to access their records if they were local. Jordan had long given up trying to make his father understand that the Carters didn't obsess over the Evertons.

Having a Carter on the farm was a problem, if his father ever found out. But since his visits back were shorter and rarer every year, that shouldn't happen. Jordan wouldn't see him here till after Thanksgiving, and that was still a long way off.

They were quiet on the ride back to the Mill. Ranger sat between them, and Jordan noticed Delaney's hand reach for the dog again. Ranger turned to him, as if to say, *not this again*, as her grip tightened every mile they traveled. She was tense and grew tenser as they got closer to the Mill.

Her hand was so tight on Ranger's fur when he signaled the turn into the Mill parking lot that he was tempted to apologize to the dog. He was glad he hadn't brought his produce. Delaney wasn't going to be able to put this panic attack behind her as easily as she thought she could.

He'd give her points for trying, though. He pulled the truck to a stop outside the kitchen doors. He could almost see the pep talk she was giving herself, but her hand was trembling as she opened her door. He got out as well, because if she needed help, he should be ready.

"There's a box here, with a code. There's a key inside."

"Want me to get it for you? I could also go in, make sure everything is okay in there."

Delaney drew in a deep breath. "No, I've got work to do. I'll be fine."

"I'll wait, in case there's a problem."

She shot him a glance but headed toward the public entrance at the front, under the portico. Jordan stayed where he was, giving her space. Ranger sat beside him, looking as worried as he felt.

"What are we gonna do?"

Ranger pressed against him.

Delaney walked back. She had a key in her hand.

"Should all be good." She was trying, her voice determinedly cheerful, but her hand wasn't steady, and her smile was more of a grimace.

"I'll just wait to make sure it works before I take off."

Delaney nodded and went to the kitchen door. She stood for a moment, and then put the key into the lock and turned. There was a click, and she pushed the door open.

Jordan waited to see how she'd respond. He didn't know what had happened last time, so he wasn't sure what he was waiting for. Delaney walked in, and the door swung almost shut behind her.

Silence, except for the sound of the stream running behind the Mill, the occasional bird and the rustle of an unseen animal that had Ranger perking up his ears. Then Ranger turned his head back to the door of the Mill and whined.

Jordan shot over and pushed it open. Delaney was huddled on the floor, shuddering and struggling to breathe.

Ranger went to her, and she immediately wrapped her arms around him. Jordan looked around, certain there must be something to trigger Delaney's response, but nothing was apparent. It was a commercial kitchen, big and clean. The only things out of place were a handbag, Delaney's he assumed, and another bag, which had her name on it. There was a phone and a set of keys by the bags. Otherwise, the place was quiet and immaculate.

Obviously, Delaney wasn't going to be working here today, and just as obviously she couldn't stay here on her own. He picked up the keys and phone and dropped them into a pocket in the handbag before throwing it and the other bag over his shoulder. Then he crouched down in front of Delaney again.

He wasn't sure he should touch her, so he tried calling her name, quietly.

"Delaney. Hey, Delaney. Are you okay to walk? I could carry you."

Despite her height, he'd noticed that her clothes were loose. He suspected she'd lost weight recently and wouldn't be surprised if this was connected with whatever was happening to her now, but it meant he could probably pick her up easily.

She didn't respond, so he risked a gentle touch on her arm.

"Delaney. Let's get out of here."

Ranger nosed her face and she shuddered. Then nodded.

"Should I carry you?"

A shake of her head. She moved a hand from Ranger and started to push herself up. Jordan kept a loose grip on her arm, just in case.

"I've got your stuff, so let's get back to the truck."

He needed to get back to the farm, and she needed to be away from the Mill. Once they were through the doorway again, he glanced at her car, but no. She wasn't ready to drive.

Outside, she drew long, shuddering breaths.

Jordan let his hand drop, since she seemed to be steadier.

"I'm… I'm sorry…"

Jordan didn't know anything about panic attacks, but he didn't think Delaney had done anything deliberately. She didn't need to apologize.

"Don't worry about it. I don't think you're up to driving. Can I call someone for you?"

She jerked her head, obviously not wanting her brother or anyone else she could call to know what was going on. She wouldn't be able to keep this secret for long, but right now she needed to be someplace she felt safe. That appeared to be wherever Ranger was, so it looked like he was taking her home.

"Do you want to come back to the farm?"

It wasn't the smartest call, but he didn't seem to have any choice.

Delaney nodded, quickly and jerkily.

He opened the passenger door of his truck, and like previously, Ranger jumped up, followed by Delaney. She wouldn't meet his eyes.

He passed over her handbag and the other bag he'd picked up, setting them gently on her lap. Then he got back in the driver's seat and started up the truck.

He had no idea what they were going to do once they got back to the farm. He just knew that he still had a soft spot when it came to Delaney Carter, and that she needed help. Right now he was all she had.

CHAPTER THREE

THE TRUCK RUMBLED down the drive and pulled to a halt in front of the house. Delaney rubbed her hands over her face, still unsure what she should be doing—about the Mill, about these panic attacks—multiple now—or even what to do once she got out of the truck. She had to do something. She couldn't sit here with Ranger providing comfort for the rest of the day. Though it held a lot of appeal. She didn't want to make decisions, deal with whatever was going on in her brain, deal with family and pressure and...

The door opened beside her. Jordan. Being much more decent than she would have expected considering their past and her last name.

"I don't know about you, but I'm hungry. Just let me change the sign and I'll make us something. Go inside if you want."

Okay. She could do that much. Just go inside and wait, and someone else would deal with things, at least for a while.

Ranger jumped out after her, following Jordan, but Jordan shook his head, and Ranger stayed with her. She didn't blame the dog. She wouldn't want to be with her, either, if she had a choice. But if Jordan was letting her have Ranger's company, she would take it. The feeling of his fur grounded her, and he asked nothing, just provided a feeling of safety. Maybe she should get her own dog.

No, she couldn't, not with her schedule. If she still could do her job. She was clutching her knives and her purse. And still standing beside the truck. She gave herself a mental shake and moved to the back door of the farmhouse.

This time she took a good look at where she was. The house had lovely bones. Two stories, gray stone, with a front veranda and a small porch outside the back door. There were a few bushes around the house, all needing some pruning. Delaney hadn't had anything to landscape for years, but she remembered Grandmother's house here in what had been called Carter's Crossing then. Abigail's property, with the flowers and shrubs, had always been beautifully maintained.

She opened the screen door and could walk right in. Jordan didn't lock up. She frowned.

It was one thing if he was alone here on the farm, but he had people coming all the time to his store. She could hear the sound of tires on the gravel. Someone was arriving now, so she hurried inside.

The chances were good it wasn't anyone she knew, but she didn't want to risk it.

The kitchen was old-fashioned. The appliances were clean, but dated, and the finishes dark and worn. Jordan's mother had died when he was in high school, so it had probably just been his dad and him since then, and they didn't seem to worry much about decor.

She dropped her purse and knife bag on the wooden kitchen table. She looked over to the laptop in the next room. She should check for emails—but she had her phone now, or did she?

Yes, it was in the pocket of her bag, with the keys for her car and the Mill. She didn't remember putting them there, so Jordan must have. She sat down and picked up the phone, dread spooling in her stomach.

A couple of missed calls. A text from Mariah, asking if she'd found the key. A few emails relating to the New York restaurant.

She let Mariah know she'd found the key but couldn't think of the words to explain what had happened once she'd gone into the kitchen. She didn't try. She texted her thanks and left it there. Then she put the phone back in her bag. Ranger's perking up beside her let her know Jordan was coming.

When she looked up at him, he was rubbing his hand on the back of his neck. He'd done that before.

"So I guess me making you something is a little odd…since you're a chef and all."

People reacted this way. Sometimes they appeared to expect her to critique what they made, and sometimes they wanted her to make the meal instead. She hoped that wasn't what Jordan was looking for, because she was afraid to try making anything right now.

He huffed a breath and opened the fridge. "I don't have a lot. Some eggs and cheese… omelets?"

She forced a swallow and said, "That would be lovely. I'm sorry to be such a nuisance."

He shrugged and grabbed butter, the eggs and cheese and some ham.

He pulled out a heavy cast-iron pan from the bottom drawer of the oven and set it on the stove. After turning on the burner, he cracked eggs into a bowl. He cut a pat of butter and dropped it into the pan, then started chopping the ham into pieces.

More tires sounded. He angled his head to look out the window over the sink, and grimaced.

"Sorry, gotta go."

She nodded, but he didn't see, already slamming through the screen door. Ranger followed and she had to hold back a call for the dog. It wasn't her dog. She couldn't demand he stay with her.

With a start, she noted the smell of the butter browning. She stood up, body moving almost without her brain involved. She turned down the heat and reached for the bowl of eggs.

Then she paused. But there was no shaking, no panicked response. Her muscles were moving on autopilot, and she welcomed the familiarity.

She poured the eggs gently into the pan and opened drawers till she found a spatula and a grater. She dropped the ham onto the firming eggs and grated cheese over top. There was salt and pepper handy, and she was ready to plate the omelet almost before she recognized what she'd done.

The cupboard beside her had stacks of worn dishes. She slid the warm eggs onto the plate, stomach grumbling at the familiar odor. She hadn't eaten this morning, and her digestive system appeared to be happy at the prospect of food.

She reached for more eggs and cracked them into the bowl. By the time Jordan came back into the kitchen, the second omelet was landing on another plate.

He paused; surprise written over his face.

She turned and raised an eyebrow. She hadn't done much—just two omelets, but it had worked wonders for her confidence. She hadn't lost her cooking skills. She had problems, but here, in this old-fashioned kitchen, she could prepare food.

"Apparently, not all kitchens are a problem for me."

Jordan nodded. She set a plate on the table and gestured for him to sit.

"Thank you."

Delaney shrugged. "You left the burner on, and when I smelled the butter browning, I got up, and I just…cooked."

Jordan sat down. "That must have been reassuring."

Delaney brought her own plate to the table and sat across from him.

"Definitely. But there's something preventing me from working at the Mill."

Jordan shrugged. "Might as well eat and then worry about it."

Which was good advice. She followed it, enjoying the simple food. The eggs were farm eggs, the cheese regional, not mass-produced.

"This is really good."

Delaney ignored the hint of surprise in Jordan's voice. She hadn't shown herself to be a competent and capable chef. He probably hadn't been following her career, didn't know where she'd studied and that she'd started her own restaurant in New York.

"You had good ingredients."

Jordan snorted. "Still doesn't come out like this when I use them."

She smiled, and Jordan's gaze met hers.

"Um, thanks. It's good to know I haven't lost all my skills."

There was the sound of more tires. Jordan stood up. "Sorry, I should check on this."

Delaney watched him go, Ranger following on his heels. She had time to finish her own meal and do most of the cleaning up before Jordan returned. His omelet was cold, but he didn't seem to take notice. He might not care much about what he ate, or maybe he was interrupted frequently enough that he was used to cold food.

That latter thought sparked an idea in her head.

Jordan crossed to the sink and stood beside her. "You don't need to clean up."

"It's the least I can do. You seem to be pretty busy."

A frown crossed his face, and this close, she noticed the signs of fatigue: shadows under his eyes, a weariness in his stance. Her idea expanded.

"People coming to your shop take up a lot of your time. Do you have other things to do?"

A long sigh escaped him. "I have produce to get off the field, and I'm late to get the fall peas in. Next week there's more to plant, and the corn maze to work on."

Guilt hit her. How much of his day had he wasted on her when he had so much else to do? And that strengthened her resolve. This idea was something that would help her, no doubt, but it would benefit Jordan as well. If he could just get over the past, and that whole Everton/Carter thing and let her do it.

"Can I talk to you for a minute? Just a minute, I promise. Five tops."

Jordan looked at her, then nodded. He pulled

some cold water from the fridge, poured it into a glass and sat back down at the table.

Delaney hoped no cars drove in till she had a chance to get this all out there.

"I have an idea that might help both of us."

Jordan leaned back and crossed his arms. At least he hadn't said no right off the bat.

JORDAN WAS GLAD to see a spark in her eyes, but he was wary of what Delaney's idea might be. She was a chef. She didn't know squat about farming. But even if he had to squash that spark, he didn't have time to train her. And he couldn't afford to hire help until he'd bought the farm from his father.

His father wanted to buy a boat in Florida to expand the fishing charter business he helped his brother with. The only asset his dad had was the farm. Jordan had asked to buy the farm from his dad, instead of it being sold to a stranger. His dad had agreed to that if Jordan could save up enough money to allow him to invest in the fishing boat. Then his father would sign over the farm and it would belong to Jordan.

They hadn't written anything down, but Jordan's uncle had been part of the conversation, so his dad wouldn't forget. Jordan would have felt better with something on paper, but his father was touchy about anything related to the farm. His father was touchy about a lot of things and getting worse as he got older.

The farm was the one place in the world that felt like home to Jordan. The first place he could remember feeling secure. It was the last place he'd lived with his mother. Jordan knew how to farm, but not much else. He worried that if he didn't get the money soon enough, his dad would find another buyer, in spite of their agreement.

One thing that would definitely end the arrangement was if his father found a Carter here. Fortunately, he was not expected to return for weeks yet. He always called Jordan when he left to make sure Jordan had a room ready for him. The man had no friends up here, so there was no chance he'd find out about Jordan's visitor today.

Delaney sat down across from him, her fingers making patterns on the tabletop.

Her nails were cut short, some broken, and her hands looked like they'd seen a lot of use. They weren't the pampered hands his father would expect of a Carter, but if she was working as a chef, those hands would have taken a lot of abuse.

"I have a problem, obviously. I was supposed to work at the Mill, but that's not happening. I need to figure out what the problem is and what I can do about it so I can get back to work."

Jordan grunted. Nothing he could do to help with that.

"I don't know what's going on with me, but one thing that's obvious is that this place doesn't trigger the, er, the attacks." She waved a hand toward his stove, and his eyes narrowed.

"You need help, and I need a calm place to get myself figured out. I thought if I was here to take care of all the things those people drive in for, then you could do your other work without interruptions."

He waited to see where she was going with this. She couldn't possibly be suggesting what it sounded like.

"If you'd let me stay here, for a bit, I could help you, and make meals—I can do that really well."

His mouth opened and then he shut it again. *Stay here?*

He thought she was going to suggest she could work for him during the day and ask him to pay her, and that he couldn't do. There was little enough profit in the farm. But stay here? With him?

His father would have a heart attack. And it would be the end of the arrangement to buy the farm.

Delaney had her hands clasped together in front of her.

"I can't afford to pay for help." That should stop her.

She shook her head. "No, I'm not asking for you to pay me. I'm good for now—I was going to work at the Mill to help them out, not because I need the money."

Jordan swallowed. He had to make her go. If his dad found out…but then, if he had help, could he get more work done, get enough profit out of this season to finally buy the farm? Maybe before his father came back in November?

He rubbed the back of his neck again. It would be such a relief to know the place was his.

Jordan sighed. "But you're a Carter."

"Your dad isn't here, right? Is he going to be?"

Jordan uncrossed his arms and ran a hand through his hair.

"He usually comes up after Thanksgiving, but he's in Florida till then." Or until he heard about a Carter on his farm.

"I won't stay that long. I can't. I have things I need to do." Something crossed her face, something sad and more. He wondered what it was, and how bad it had to be that staying here on his farm as an unpaid laborer was preferable.

"Jordan, I have no right to ask, but please, can we make this work? I can't work at the Mill, obviously, not right now, and I have no idea what I'm going to do. I just need some time and a safe place to work things out. I'm not going to stay forever—I have commitments and obligations back in New York. I'll do whatever I can around here. I'll clean the house or the chicken coop or weed your produce, *anything*."

Having Delaney stay here was ridiculous. No way should he be entertaining the idea. But he was. There was real urgency in her voice, need in her eyes. And in spite of everything, he wasn't immune to her.

"What about your family?"

She was a Carter after all. He wasn't sure if Abigail Carter was around. Since she'd started dating Mariah's super-rich grandfather—Carters always fell on their feet—she wasn't always in Cupid's Crossing the way she had been. But Nelson was here. His hands balled into fists at the thought of Nelson Carter.

Delaney shook her head in frantic refusal. "No, I can't ask Nelson for help. Not now, when everything is—" She flapped a hand to describe her panic attacks today and whatever else was going on with her.

"Are you two still…?" Back in high school, back when he and Delaney had shared everything, she'd told him how she felt like she was always in competition with Nelson. But now?

"I love my brother, but I need to get myself together before I talk to him about all this."

Apparently, some things stayed the same.

"I don't have chickens." It was a feeble attempt at a rebuttal.

The sound of tires on the gravel didn't help his case any. He stood up to see if this was someone who needed his attention. Delaney, no longer wearing her chef coat, followed him.

The couple who'd driven in wasn't here for the hiking trails. They'd come for produce. Jordan opened the door to the store. He moved behind the counters, checking how the inventory levels were holding up. It had been busy this morning, and he'd made two trips to the Mill, eating into his workday.

He didn't normally talk to customers unless they asked for assistance. Delaney had followed the couple in, and he guessed she wanted to show him that she could add value if she stuck around.

"What are you looking for today?" she asked the couple, smiling brightly.

The woman smiled back at her. "We wanted some corn. It's so good this time of year."

"Absolutely." Delaney nodded. "How do you prepare it?"

And Delaney went to work. They discussed boiling versus grilling, husks on or off, and Delaney added some ideas to enhance the flavor. Then the woman asked about preparing potatoes, and by the time the couple left, they'd bought the corn, potatoes, onions and had noted down a recipe for beans. Which they'd also purchased.

Delaney smiled them out the door, and he braced himself with arms crossed to face her again.

She scanned the room. "Who certified you as organic?"

He blinked, not having expected the question. "Nofa."

"You should have that displayed prominently. And you don't charge enough."

His hands moved to his hips.

"Excuse me?"

"I saw your invoice from OPD, before…well,

before. Based on what you charge the Mill, you should charge more here."

"Then I'd lose customers."

Delaney shook her head, all traces of the panicked woman from the Mill gone. "You have a limited quantity to sell, so you need to maximize the price. People pay more for goods that are worth it, and believe me, I've seen more than my share of vegetables. Yours are good."

The compliment warmed him. He worked hard to grow the best crops he could. But he didn't like being schooled on his business. By a chef. And if she was wrong, he'd lose money that he needed.

"You're not changing the prices."

They both paused as the implications of that statement filled the room.

"If I promise not to change the prices, can I stay?"

Her eyes were pleading. They reminded him too much of that period in high school when she'd ask him for one more kiss…just a few more minutes together.

He'd never been able to refuse her back then.

He knew he'd regret it. Somehow, this was going to blow up in his face. But he could use the help, no denying it. And he'd always been a sucker for Delaney Carter.

Until she'd been done with him.

He nodded, but vowed to himself that this time he would be wary. He wasn't going to end up with another heartbreak thanks to Delaney Carter.

DELANEY'S KNEES THREATENED to buckle from relief. She was shocked by how badly she wanted Jordan to say yes.

Not because she wanted to spend time with him. Definitely not that. She'd learned her lesson back in high school. But this time he wasn't using her because her name was Carter. She was offering because she needed this break.

The past two months had been horrific. A nightmare. Now that she had to stop and take a breather, she could understand, a smidge, that maybe the counselor was right. Maybe this was more than just being too busy and stressed. Maybe the events at the restaurant had affected her.

If she was here on the farm, she had a chance to avoid stress, if not busyness. She didn't mind bartering some labor for the chance to take a break. Apparently, she needed that. She needed time, and a safe place, to find out how to get past these panic attacks so she could get working again. At least here she'd have something to do beyond worrying about her future.

"Thank you. If you show me how to handle your till, I can take care of the store until whenever you close, and you can focus on your other jobs."

He nodded, a little more happily as that idea settled in his head. Sure, she was doing this to help herself, but she was helping him, too. It was a win/win situation. If his father wasn't here, the two of them could get along, right? As long as his father didn't find out.

Jordan showed her the till, and where he kept the extra produce stored. There was a price sheet behind the counter. Delaney bit her lip but didn't comment.

"I'm good. I'll just go get my phone so I can make some arrangements." She needed her car, and clothes and toiletries. She wanted to work that out with Mariah, not Nelson. "What do the hikers pay?"

Jordan went still. "Nothing. They sometimes buy drinks or produce to take home."

Delaney's mouth dropped open, and then she slammed her jaw shut when she saw Jordan's glare.

He had no idea just how much he needed her

help. And he was going to get it. She'd more than repay him for his assistance today. He'd get the Carter touch.

CHAPTER FOUR

DELANEY TRIED TO come up with a cover story to tell Mariah but couldn't think of anything that was remotely convincing.

I got to the Mill but was just too exhausted to handle being the executive chef. And was too exhausted to drive Grandmother's car, which is still parked there. And the only place I can get any rest is at Stoney Creek Farm.

Yeah, that wouldn't raise questions. Especially when Nelson found out. Then it was just a short step to her parents finding out. She'd lost ground after closing the restaurant, and she couldn't let them know what had happened today, at least not until she figured it out herself.

I got to the Mill and had an extreme allergic reaction to something there. Had to get a lift with Jordan, and I can't come back. No, I've never shown signs of allergies previously. No, you don't need to get someone in to check the place out. I'm sure it's just me being allergic.

It was going to have to be the truth. Or a close facsimile.

She double-checked that no customers were in sight and hit Mariah's number.

"Delaney! Did you get the key? Everything going all right?"

Delaney took a firm grip on the phone. "Yeah, about that. It's not going so well."

"What's the problem?"

Delaney had come to know Mariah after Nelson got engaged to her in a strange, fake relationship-turned-real proposal that was supposed to be a promotion for Cupid's Crossing. That proposal had been part of the launch for the town to become a romantic destination, the name changing from Carter's Crossing to the new Cupid's Crossing. It had been the reason for Mariah to come here, setting it up, but Nelson was the reason she stayed. Mariah was family now and the way Mariah was wired, her first instinct was going to be to try to solve this problem.

Delaney didn't think she would be able to. If there was an easy solution, Delaney would have found it for herself. Still, it would be nice…

"I had a panic attack."

Silence for a moment before Mariah spoke. "You're okay?"

Breathe out.

"Yes. But I can't work at the Mill."

More silence.

"Is this related to needing the spare key? What happened?"

"I went into the kitchen, and I don't even know how to describe it, Mariah. It was so scary. My body didn't feel right, and my head felt like it was floating and—"

Delaney stopped her babbling.

"I ended up running out the door and left the keys inside. Jordan Everton came to deliver an order, and he took me back to his place. I reached out to someone who'd been helping us with counseling after…after the restaurant. And it sounds like I had a panic attack. I had Jordan drive me back to the Mill when you told me where to find the spare key, but it happened again."

"What can I do?" Mariah went right to the point.

"You'll need to find another chef. And hopefully someone can meet Jordan with his food tomorrow."

There were some clicking noises in the background.

"Got it. Now, what about you?"

"I've talked Jordan into letting me stay here for a bit. I made him an omelet."

"Oookay."

Delaney realized she hadn't explained well.

"I was fine in his kitchen. So it's not cooking that's the problem. I just can't work at the Mill, for some reason. Jordan has more work than he can handle right now, so he agreed I could stay and help out in return. I don't think it will be long, but I know you can't be without an executive chef, and I can't give you a definite return date."

Carters did not let people down, so she had to let Mariah do whatever was necessary for the Mill. Delaney had caused enough problems.

"If that's what you think is best."

Delaney nodded, even though Mariah wouldn't see. "Now the big ask. I need my clothing and toiletries and I need you to tell Nelson and keep him away. And make him keep this a secret."

Mariah snorted. "I can get you your things, no problem, but Nelson? You've got me confused with a superhero. I don't have that kind of power."

"Can you try your best? There's some history between Jordan and Nelson and Jordan is doing a big favor just letting me stay here. I don't want to inflict Nelson on him."

"That must be quite a story."

Delaney considered. Yeah, it was a story, involving Jordan's dad and the mill, and Jordan's mom dying. She didn't think any of them had let it go. She wasn't sure why Jordan was helping her, to be honest. Maybe he felt bad for what he'd done back in high school? She didn't want to question him in case he changed his mind.

"Someday I'll tell you what happened. Thanks, Mariah. I appreciate this. Best sister-in-law ever."

"That would carry more weight if I wasn't your only sister-in-law, but I'll do what I can. Take care of yourself, Delaney, and let us know if there's anything else we can do."

"I will. And I think maybe for the first time in a while, I am taking care of myself."

Delaney clicked off the phone. Knowing Mariah, her things would be here today. Whether she could control Nelson was another issue. Maybe they'd luck out and someone would have a vet emergency, keeping her brother busy till late in the night.

It wouldn't keep him busy enough not to notice Delaney wasn't at his place, and he'd want to know why.

Older brothers had an overdeveloped protective instinct. As had been only too obvious back in high school when it led to expanding the feud Jordan's father had with the Carters to include Delaney and Nelson and Jordan. Or maybe Nelson was just the catalyst.

Nelson had found out Jordan was using Delaney to try to get information on the Carters and the mill situation. Then he'd faced down Jordan. When Delaney had tried to find Jordan and make him explain, she'd run into his father.

Mr. Everton had been brutal, confirming Nelson's story, and breaking Delaney's heart. Jordan did owe her for that.

Not that she hadn't moved on.

A car pulled into the lot and Delaney looked out the open door, hoping for something to do, a way to be useful. But the people who stepped out were wearing hiking gear.

She went out to greet them anyway.

"Hello. Welcome to Stoney Creek Farm. Going hiking today?"

The men nodded. "That's okay, right?"

Delaney stretched out a smile. "Of course.

If you need drinks, or some fresh organic produce, stop by on your way out."

They nodded. Delaney watched them start down the trail, unsure whether they were nodding to shut her up, or if they really wanted to stop by.

Jordan was passing up a golden opportunity. He could charge just for parking. Get reimbursed for the wear and tear on his property. She wondered if he maintained the trails, doing it for free.

Would hikers pay for parking? Or maybe they could donate something toward keeping up the trails?

There was a sign listing the rules for using the trails in the parking lot. It would be easy enough to install a box, with a sign that suggested people could donate money for the trail maintenance. If everyone gave a dollar or two, it would add up. She'd seen quite a few people stop in today, on a Monday. With Carter's— no Cupid's Crossing attracting visitors from places like New York City, there would potentially be a lot of people wanting to use Jordan's trails, and they might not be able to buy corn or carrots to take with them when they left.

She made a note on her phone. She was going to help Jordan succeed in spite of himself, to ensure she helped him while she was stuck here. Now, what else could she do?

It was a relief, being able to concentrate on his work in the fields, and not be distracted by hikers and customers. Selling the farm's produce provided his income. He got better prices from the people stopping by than he did from the restaurants he'd contracted with, but sales were smaller and it would take time to build them up. Time, his least available commodity.

He'd checked on Delaney a couple of times. Not that she'd know; he'd just swung by the house so he could see if there were any cars. Once, he'd seen a woman who came by most weeks leaving with a second bag of produce. That wasn't normal.

Perhaps Delaney was going to help his sales while she stayed. Maybe the gamble would pay off. He was useless at upselling, or whatever it was called. He could answer questions about his food when people asked, but he didn't like to engage in conversations. He knew he should, but he didn't know what to say.

As the sun fell in the sky, earlier now that it was September, and his stomach let him know it wanted food, he stretched and put his tools away, ready to call this part of the day over.

He needed to think about dinner. Not just for him, but for Delaney as well. He might be willing to live on a boring diet of sandwiches and eggs, but he didn't think she would.

He bit back a smile. Going from whatever big, fancy kitchens she'd been working in to his sparse one. That was a big step down for a chef, let alone one of the Carters. But the smile dropped as he thought of how he'd found her, how she'd reacted to the kitchen at the Mill. She had been in trouble.

He was being selfish. He should have insisted she work on that problem before anything else, like selling his corn. Even if there was still a hurt from high school, when she hadn't trusted him. Hadn't believed him.

Probably she just hadn't cared about him the way he did her.

He washed his dirty hands in the sink behind the produce building, throwing water on his face to cool down and clean off whatever dirt had landed there. If part of the reason he took extra care today was Delaney, no one had to know but him. And Ranger.

He was nodding at the dog to come with him to the house when he heard tires on gravel. He hadn't told Delaney about closing the gate and flipping the sign to Closed. He'd best do that before they discussed dinner or how her staying here was going to work.

It wasn't someone wanting corn who was in the parking lot. The vehicle was a white van that said Carter's Crossing Veterinary Clinic on the side.

Nelson Carter. Jordan's pace picked up. One Carter on the farm was more than enough.

He came around the corner of his house to find Nelson standing on the porch, banging on the front door. Mariah stood on the ground behind him, arms crossed. Jordan wasn't sure where Delaney was, but she hadn't come out to see her brother. Jordan knew she didn't want to talk to him, so this was his chance to get rid of Nelson for her, and he was going to enjoy it.

"We're closed." Jordan strode up.

Nelson turned and scowled at him. "I'm here for Delaney."

"We're closed. You aren't welcome here. This is my property and I want you to leave."

Nelson growled and stomped down the steps to where Jordan was standing. Mariah grabbed Nelson's arm and tugged on him.

"Nelson," she warned.

He glared at Jordan. "I'm not here to buy lettuce or cucumbers. I'm here to take my sister home."

Jordan pushed his anger down. "Well, it's a good thing you don't want lettuce or cucumbers since they're not in season and I'm not a grocery store. And the last I checked, your sister is an adult who can make her own decisions, so unless you have a legal document to back you up, you need to leave."

Nelson snorted and turned to yell at the house. "Come on out, Delaney. We'll take care of you."

"Don't bully her."

Nelson switched his focus back to Jordan and snarled. "Me, bully her? How did you get her here, and what are you trying to prove?"

Mariah shoved her weight into Nelson, making him step back to keep his balance.

"I told you what happened. Delaney couldn't drive, so Jordan brought her back here. And she asked me to bring her clothes so she could stay. Back off, Nelson. You promised to let me handle this."

"That was before I knew where Delaney was. She's not going to get better here."

"Not your decision, Nelson."

Jordan liked having Mariah on his side.

Nelson almost growled again. "Mariah, you don't know the history here. This isn't the first time he's tried to manipulate Delaney. The

Evertons have a grudge against the Carters, and they'll use anything or anyone against us."

The bitterness of the injustice crawled up Jordan's throat.

"I've never used Delaney, or anyone else." The words came through clenched teeth.

"Oh, come off it, Jordan. You admitted as much."

Jordan wanted to hit Nelson's smug face. It was that day, back in high school, the same lies, the same Carter arrogance. He'd managed to get the farm truck and gone to meet Delaney, in secret, since their families were in a legal battle over Jordan's mother's death. Delaney hadn't shown up; Nelson had. And accused him of using Delaney.

He'd only been doing his best to love her then. Now he was letting her stay at his place, risking his father finding out, because she needed a safe place. Nelson was completely out of line, again. This time Jordan wasn't backing down. It was time to clear up the past.

He drew in a long breath. "No, I didn't. What I *admitted* was mailing a letter for my dad."

"Yeah, a letter to the lawyers who were trying to sue us. The ones that killed the deal with the investors who might have kept the mill going and kept the town alive. They'd been spooked by the accident, but your dad saying it was deliberate was what made them back away."

Jordan's knuckles turned white as he fought to keep this from becoming a shouting match.

"I had nothing to do with that," he said as calmly as he could. "And those lawyers you're so stuck on were also handling the fallout from my mother's death. Remember? At your mill."

A silence followed his words. Jordan wasn't sure how much Mariah knew about what had happened, but there was enough surprise on her face to tell him she didn't know the full story.

Nelson rubbed his shoulder with one hand.

"I'm sorry about your mother's death. It was a terrible accident. But it *was* an accident."

"I know."

Nelson froze, hand on his neck. "Your father said it was deliberate."

"My father also believes that the old claim he dug up in the attic about some hundred-year-old dispute about lumber rights on our farm is valid. I don't believe everything he does."

"I thought you were with him on the claim. Why did your mother work at the mill, if not to try to get information about that?"

Jordan looked down. "For money. My dad was spending everything he could on tracking down that bogus claim, and we needed money. She convinced him to let her work there by telling him she'd look out for information, but there wasn't any. She just wanted to make sure we had enough to eat."

Heat washed over Jordan's face. Embarrassment. As if not having money, or a rational father, was his fault. His weakness. He saw the sympathy in their eyes, and he hated it.

"Why didn't you say anything?"

Jordan looked over their heads, part of his brain noting more color in the trees on the hills.

"What, to my dad? Yeah, not likely."

"I meant why didn't you tell us?"

Jordan's gaze snapped back to Nelson. "Oh, yeah. Tell my friends? You and Dave? The ones who believed I was spying for my dad? The ones who stopped hanging out with me after my mother died and my father embarrassed himself saying it was the mill's fault? Those friends?"

Nelson's head dropped. "Okay, yeah. We weren't much help. But Grandmother had some investors who were looking at the mill, and the accident spooked them. Then, when your dad started making those accusations, well, it seemed better not to get too close to you, in case they thought we believed your dad. That was a crappy thing to do. I'm sorry."

Jordan swallowed. The apology felt good. Like something he'd needed. An acknowledgment that they had had a friendship, and that Nelson and Dave had let him down.

"Yeah, it was."

Nelson shook his head. "But you were sneaking around with Delaney. That wasn't cool."

Mariah jerked.

Years of buried anger were right at the surface now. "It was okay for Dave to go out with her, but not me?"

"You were sneaking around with her. You didn't talk to me about it. And I thought you were using her."

"You had the right to approve anyone she wanted to spend time with? You would have given me your blessing, after you stopped hanging around with me? I wasn't using her. I told you I knew my dad was wrong."

"But you admitted you were. That's what you told Dave and me."

"You said I was!" Jordan roared. "You found that stupid letter for the lawyer in my backpack and called me a traitor and said you only were my friend out of pity, because your grandmother told you to. Then *you* said I was using Delaney to spy on your family, like my mom had been spying at the mill, and that *yeah* I said in response? That was sarcasm, idiot. Heard of it?"

Suddenly, Delaney came charging around the corner of the house. "Was that what happened, Nelson? When you told me Jordan had bragged about using me?"

Nelson stepped back. "Delaney, he said that and I—"

Delaney skewered his chest with her finger. "You told me you'd talked to Jordan and he told you he'd been using me to get information on the mill. You said he didn't want to see me anymore if I wasn't any good as a source."

Nelson stepped back.

"I thought I was doing the right thing."

"Well, you weren't!" Everyone flinched at the volume Delaney was projecting. "You broke my heart because you were an arrogant know-it-all and you were wrong, Nelson."

Nelson put up his hands, either to placate Delaney or keep her from drilling her finger in farther. "I know, Dee. I'm sorry. I'd heard Grandmother on the phone—the investors were out because of Jordan's dad. Then when his neighbor, Maisie, told me he was sneaking around with you, and you were supposed to meet him, well…"

"You decided it was up to you to step in and make a mess of everything? Not your business, Nelson."

Mariah was rubbing Nelson's arm, soothing him.

"I know. I know I messed up. But I'm trying." His expression was pained, enough that Jordan thought he was sincere.

"You know, Nelson, I might be more sympathetic if you'd bothered to explain. But right now I just can't. I've got enough of my own stuff to try to deal with. Goodbye."

Delaney pivoted and stalked back to the farmhouse.

Jordan was almost shaking with reaction to this baring of truths from the past. Like Delaney, he just couldn't deal with Nelson.

"You should leave now." He pushed the words past stiff lips.

"I've got Delaney's things, the stuff she asked me to bring over," Mariah said. "Why don't I give you that and we'll get out of here. Tell Delaney I want to know how she's doing."

"But—"

Mariah put a hand over Nelson's mouth.

"They've got a lot to deal with. You've just dropped something big on Delaney when she's already struggling. Right now you need to leave her alone."

"But here?"

Jordan's hackles rose. He'd have said something hurtful if Mariah hadn't spoken first.

"Nelson, it's not your call. You need to do some processing as well. If Jordan cared about her back then, then you have no reason to think she won't be safe here. You've done enough. We're going home."

Jordan's molars were grinding, but he kept further words back.

"Tell her to text me!" Mariah shoved Nelson over to the van, where he slid open the side door. She carried over a couple of suitcases and a duffel bag to Jordan. He nodded. Then she pushed a reluctant Nelson into the driver's seat before getting in the passenger side. Jordan watched them drive away, listening to the sounds of the van getting fainter.

He rubbed hands over his face. Now he knew why Delaney had never spoken to him again, never answered a letter or a call. All because of one word he'd said, when Nelson cut the ground out under his feet. It was a mess, and he didn't have time to deal with it. He turned, ready to chop wood for an hour or two to vent his frustration, when he remembered his guest.

She would need food. Probably. He should eat as well, since there wasn't going to be any break in the farmwork simply because Jordan needed a mental health day.

He turned to the house. He had no idea what to say to Delaney, or how to act with this new information. But he didn't have the option of ignoring her, either, not when she was staying in his house.

He didn't seem to have many options at all right now.

CHAPTER FIVE

DELANEY WAS AFRAID to look at Jordan when he came in.

She was *so* angry with Nelson. Nelson, who always felt that he knew best. Who had decided that he could dictate who she wanted to spend time with without even asking her. Who'd hurt Jordan, taking one sarcastic comment and using it to force the outcome he wanted. It had changed her, both in the career path she'd followed and in how she defined her value to people.

Nelson, who she'd been competing with all her life, and who now knew she was in trouble. She just wanted to find a place to hide and never come up for air.

Unfortunately, she wasn't in her own apartment in New York. She was in Jordan's house, sitting on a chair in his living room, unsure if she could stay, and if she couldn't, she had no idea where to go except to Nelson's.

Jordan's footsteps stopped and there was a

thump. She risked a glance and saw her suit-cases, dropped on the floor beside him at the foot of the stairs. That meant he was letting her stay, right? She almost shuddered with the relief. She was not herself today. She wasn't in control, and she didn't know how to handle life like this.

"So." Jordan wiped his hands on his jeans. "I can take these up to your room and then find something to make for dinner."

She *was* staying. The relief was overwhelming. "I can make something. I said I'd do that."

He looked at the doorway to the kitchen.

"I didn't take any meat out of the freezer. Today was a little…"

She nodded. "Yeah, it was. And that was because of me. If you don't mind me nosing around your kitchen, I'll see what I can do with what you have."

His shoulders eased. "That would be good. Thank you."

He leaned over, picked up her bags and went up the stairs.

Right. Let's see what she had to work with. It would be like a challenge on a cooking show.

Jordan didn't have a lot, but she found spaghetti, butter, parmesan and pepper. Everything she needed to make *cacio e pepe*. And it should be easy enough to throw together a salad from the vegetables Jordan had on hand. She ran over to the store and grabbed an armful of fresh produce.

When she opened the screen door, awkward with her arms full, she found Jordan standing in the kitchen, staring at the food she had on the counter.

"I grabbed some veggies. Is that okay?"

He stepped out of her way. "Of course. I need to go close the gate."

She set the veggies on the counter and did the math in her head. "This will take about twenty minutes."

He nodded and left.

Except for her knives, which she wanted to hug to her chest, the utensils Jordan had in his kitchen were underwhelming. But she found comfort in the familiar rhythms of cooking. Her brain wandered to a what-if... What if she was at the Mill? But she shook those thoughts out of her head. Whatever it was about being there that had brought on the panic attacks, she wasn't prepared to deal with it. Not right now.

She took a moment to send another email to the counselor she'd brushed off after the shooting, asking if they could maybe have a video chat. Obviously, Delaney needed help.

Jordan walked in through the kitchen as the water in the pot came to a boil. He kind of grunted that he'd be back, and she heard water running after he climbed the stairs. He came back down in clean jeans and a T-shirt, his hair and beard damp, just as she was plating the pasta.

"That smells delicious."

Delaney wrinkled her nose. "It's packaged parmesan, so…"

"Delaney."

She looked up at him. Was that a trace of a grin on his face?

"I'm the guy who bought packaged parmesan, so don't worry."

She relaxed. They'd probably need to discuss the whole fiasco that Nelson had caused back in high school at some point, but he wasn't angry with her, and that was good enough for now.

They ate in silence. Delaney watched Jordan out of the corner of her eye, hoping he liked the pasta. She'd claimed she could prepare meals but would he like what she cooked? And why was she, a chef who'd faced critics in New York City, on tenterhooks over what a farmer from upstate would think?

He ate quickly, like a man who didn't have

time to savor his meals. Once he'd cleaned his plate, he met her gaze.

"That was excellent. Thank you."

The words warmed her. "Glad you enjoyed it. Um, where would I find other food—the freezer?"

"It's in the cellar. It's not very nice down there, so if you want me to get you what you want…"

Delaney stood. "You haven't seen some of the kitchens I've worked in. Unless you have rats and cockroaches and vats of old grease, I don't think you'll even hit my top ten list."

A frown crossed his brow. "They have things like that in restaurants?"

"Not in good ones. But I've been in some bad ones. Is it okay if I take a look around?"

Jordan waved a hand toward a door at the back of the room. "It's all yours."

Delaney set her plate in the sink, and curious, opened the door and felt for a light switch.

The basement consisted of rough stone walls, a concrete floor and a couple of light-bulbs swinging from chains on the ceiling. Washer and dryer by a concrete laundry sink. Chest freezer, and shelves with preserves and canned goods.

Delaney lifted the top of the freezer. She

recognized the waxed paper bundles as coming from a butcher. Chickens in bags. Other meat, looking to be locally sourced. She let the lid close and checked the shelves, squinting in the limited light. Preserved vegetables and fruits, some legumes…

She could work with this. She was looking forward to it.

She went back up the stairs, switched off the light and found Jordan finishing the dishes.

"I meant to do that," Delaney protested.

He turned. "You cooked. Only seems fair. Did you find what you wanted?"

"I haven't seen any animals on your farm, but that looks like locally butchered meat."

Jordan nodded. "A neighbor. I let him graze on one of the fields I'm not using, and he gives me some meat."

"And do you preserve your produce?"

Jordan snorted. "No, don't have the time, even if I had the desire. I give the Fletchers on the next farm over any extra produce I have, stuff that's going to go bad, and they preserve it. Give me half."

Delaney wondered how difficult it would be to do some preserving while she was here. She wasn't going to push Jordan yet. She'd settle in for a day or two, find out how things went, and then she'd offer her suggestions.

"I thought maybe I could make soup tomorrow? And biscuits? I didn't see any yeast so I can't make bread."

Jordan's mouth opened, and then he swallowed. "You make bread?"

Delaney shrugged. "I'm not a baker, but I've done my fair share."

"I'll get you yeast if you want to make bread."

Delaney held in a smile. So Jordan had a weak spot.

"Sure. I'll thaw some chicken for soup tomorrow. What time do you get up? When do you eat breakfast?"

"I can have a bowl of cereal. Don't worry about it."

Delaney didn't push, but she was determined she was going to do this right. He wouldn't regret having her here, not when it came to the food at least.

"And when should I open the gate, start things going?"

Jordan looked away. "I don't have a set time. When I'm ready, I open the gate, flip the sign."

Delaney had no idea how he managed to keep the business going with such lax routines.

Her thoughts must have shown on her face.

"When it's just me here, I have other things I have to do as well. Like, tomorrow morning I'll need to take that stuff back to the Mill. Mariah messaged that someone would be there."

All of Delaney's smugness crumbled at her feet. Jordan at least could manage his job without having a panic attack. All her plans and ideas were for nothing if she couldn't execute them, and right now making soup for Jordan and selling some produce seemed to be all she could handle.

She should ride to the Mill with him in the morning. She didn't have to go inside. She could just get the car and bring it back. But the thought of going there again—just the idea that she might get that nauseated, light-headed feeling, lose control of herself again, had her breath coming in shallow gasps and her palms sweating.

Jordan was watching her, but he didn't say anything. She didn't know what thoughts were going through his head, but he didn't blame her for his extra trips, or suggest she should go with him tomorrow.

No, thanks, she'd stay right here. If she had a chance to talk to the counselor tomorrow, then maybe she could make plans for dealing with the panic attacks. Get a timeline, figure out when she could get her life and job back on track.

"Why don't you open the gate and flip the sign when you head out and I'll manage things here?"

She could do that. It wasn't much. Wouldn't impress anyone. But at least she was doing something.

JORDAN KNEW SOMETHING was bothering Delaney. He didn't know if she was more upset about the panic attacks, or what her brother had said. He knew he should talk to her. Clear up any misunderstandings left after Nelson's bombshell. Make sure they both knew exactly what had happened back in high school.

He just wasn't up to it right now.

That altercation had upset him as well. The anger at Nelson was familiar. But finding out the details? Confirming that Delaney had stopped speaking to him because of her brother's lie? He'd wanted to find her, ask her what had happened, but his dad had taken away the truck keys and told Jordan if he left the farm to never come back. Any attempts he'd made to contact her surreptitiously had received no response.

"I'm gonna take Ranger for a walk." Not that

the dog needed extra exercise, but Jordan had to do something, and staying here with Delaney wasn't going to help. He needed to get his own head screwed on straight so that he didn't do something to upset her.

He let himself out the back door, Ranger following.

He strode back toward the corn maze. Something about wandering through it, the pattern familiar, soothed him.

His mind wanted to sort through the what-ifs. What if he hadn't had that fight with Nelson and Dave? What could have happened with Delaney? Would they have had a future? Was there anything for them now?

There was no point in following that train of thought. They weren't the same people anymore. His life was here, on the farm.

The first years of his life had been nomadic. His father always had a big idea, some grand scheme, and the family kept moving to chase that. He was certain he'd make it big, make a fortune. Instead, his mother had worked at dead-end jobs, keeping food on the table and a roof over their heads. His father had nominally babysat him, but he was always planning, scheming, meeting people. He didn't pay a lot of attention to a small boy.

It was hard to make friends and impossible to keep them when they moved around so much. Then his grandfather had died, and suddenly they had a place where they could stay. A place that was clean, and where Jordan was free to roam. To claim. Something about the farm pulled him. It welcomed him. It was home.

For the first couple of years, his mother homeschooled him, and he'd had hours to wander the farm, getting to know every inch of it. He loved it. But his father didn't keep jobs, still looking for the opportunity that was going to make him rich.

When Jordan was old enough to attend high school, he'd suddenly been thrown back into the public school system, and his mother had found a job at the one employer in town—the Carters' mill. His parents fought, verbally, but Jordan would escape to the woods and fields. He hadn't understood the realities of what was going on with his father. His parents' relationship had never been easy. But after his mother died, it was like his father had lost his last grasp on reality when it came to the Carters.

With Dave and Nelson turning on him, Jordan no longer had friends, and when Delaney cut off contact, it had been even worse. No one in town was happy with his father and his claims against the Carter family, and Jordan was his son. Everyone assumed he supported his father, and they were pariahs in town. It had been a relief when they moved back to Florida. His uncle had a place near the coast, and Jordan had gone to college while there.

After he graduated with a degree in agricultural science, he returned to the farm, which had been mostly abandoned for the previous four years. Once he'd breathed the air, walked the fields, he'd relaxed for the first time since he'd left. Jordan settled in, but never went into Carter's Crossing. He made relationships with people in Oak Hill, a town farther away, but those people didn't have the investment in the Everton/Carter feud that people in Carter's Crossing would still have. He was almost a hermit, but he bought supplies, had an evening at a bar, found some acquaintances there.

His father came back to New York occasionally. Jordan's uncle took an annual trip to visit his old army friends after Thanksgiving, so his father would land back on the farm. He no longer was pursuing a claim against the Carters, but his animosity continued unabated. Jordan knew his obsession wasn't healthy, but he wasn't equipped to deal with it.

The first couple of years his father had come up with ideas about how to improve the farm. After he'd invested scarce resources in a project only to lose interest and lose all the investment, Jordan made a deal with him. Jordan would manage the farm and buy it from his father. He wanted to be sure his father didn't sell the place to finance another scheme.

He'd been surprised when his father agreed. Surprised but grateful. He'd always wondered why the farm had never been sold to finance one of his dad's many ventures in the past. Two years ago, when his dad wanted to join his uncle chartering deep sea fishing trips, they'd nailed down the details, at least verbally. Now he just wanted to lie low and keep his father calm until he finally had the deed in his own name.

Delaney shouldn't be here long, and his father would never find out.

If he could finish up this season with some bounces going his way, and if no major expenses popped up, he hoped to have enough money stashed away to at least get a sale registered. Enough to cover that fishing boat. Depending on what boat his father chose, Jordan might still be paying him a year or two down the road, but it would mean the place was his.

He got to make the decisions. He could play it safe. Make sure the farm wouldn't be lost.

What was happening with Delaney and Nelson wouldn't affect him in the long-term. This was only a blip. Delaney would return to her normal life, and he'd return to his.

There was no reason to find that depressing. Sure, he'd been in love with her back in high school, but that was a long time ago. It was over. And he wasn't disappointed to find her already gone to her room when he finally got back to the house. It was actually a relief, since he needed to get to bed, get some sleep before another long day.

He couldn't be blamed for what thoughts his subconscious came up with in his dreams.

MARIAH MET HIM at the Mill the next morning.

"I didn't know you were going to be here." Jordan didn't want to put her out and was embarrassed to see her after yesterday's showdown. He wasn't sure if she knew what to look for if she was checking out his produce, either.

"I'm here to welcome the new chef. He's late."

Jordan opened the tailgate of his truck and paused, not sure if he should unload.

Mariah noticed what he was doing.

"Go ahead and unload. I told him to be here

to check your shipment out, and since he's not, he'll just take what you give us."

Jordan didn't like the idea that he was being used to teach the new chef a lesson, but he was behind on his work, even with Delaney covering the shop today. He nodded and carried the first box in through the door Mariah had propped open.

It wasn't hard to identify the cooler, so he unloaded the first box and went back for another. It didn't take long to finish. Mariah was tapping on her phone, probably working on world domination while she waited for her new hire.

Jordan didn't envy the guy when he finally showed up.

He passed her the packing slip. She signed off. "You're not going to check it?"

She looked back up at him. "I'm trusting you on this. If anything is wrong, our new chef will be responsible, since he wasn't here. And I have better things to do. I've got the wedding this weekend to organize, and preparing the meal is not my responsibility."

Jordan shrugged. He knew he'd brought what was ordered and it was in good condition. His gaze landed on the Prius, still parked in the lot.

"That's Delaney's car. If someone can pick up the keys and drive it to the farm, I'll make sure to drive them back."

It would take more of his time, but he'd seen the panicked look in Delaney's eyes when she'd thought about coming for it herself.

Mariah glanced over at the car and tapped something on her phone. "Got it. I've sent through the authorization for your payment. Tell Delaney I'm not sure when the car will arrive, but sometime today."

Jordan looked around for Ranger before remembering he'd left the dog with Delaney. He didn't expect any problems on the farm, but if she had another panic attack, the dog might be a help again. He slid in behind the wheel and started up the engine. It was a relief to have made the delivery, but now he had a long list of things to finish up. He puttered to the entrance of the Mill to turn on the county road and braked as a sports car spun into the lot.

Probably the new chef. He was almost tempted to stay to watch the showdown with Mariah but reminded himself he should check on Delaney.

A short while later he pulled into the farm, noticing a couple of cars in the lot. Mariah had warned him that as the leaves turned, he'd have more people wanting to hike the trails and capture the colors.

He thought of what Delaney had said, that he should at least charge for parking. Problem was he couldn't always be here, checking on who drove in. He wouldn't charge people coming to shop, and how would he know which cars had paid? What if a hiker bought produce? What if someone came to buy a particular item, and he didn't have any on hand—did he charge them? It was easy to come up with ideas, but they didn't always work.

Jordan had grown up with a parent big on ideas and failing badly at follow-through, so he was slow at innovating. At the end of the day the farm operation was all on him, so he made sure he could handle it on his own before he took the leap.

The money would be good, but it wasn't worth the extra hassle.

Delaney stepped out of the house as he parked the truck.

"Everything go okay?" she asked.

He went to the back of the truck to grab his bins. "Yeah. All safely delivered. Mariah's gonna make sure we can get your car over here."

"Oh." Her expression was blank. "I guess that's good."

Jordan nodded, because he couldn't imagine it being a bad idea. Her car would be safer here.

He stacked up the empty bins and lifted them out of the truck to return to the storage area in back of the shop.

"So Jordan."

He didn't pause but heard Delaney coming after him. He didn't like that tone of voice. The wheedling, I-want-to-ask-you-something voice. Was she going to talk about prices again? He needed to sell his food, not risk it going bad while he gambled on people being willing to pay more.

He dropped the bins in the shop and turned, finding her almost chest to chest with him.

"What is it, Delaney?"

"I had an idea, about the store."

Yep, sounded so much like his father. But he was an adult now, this was his place and he got to make the decisions.

"I'm not changing the prices."

She rolled her eyes at him. Actually rolled her eyes. He crossed his arms, ready to refuse whatever she asked.

"Someone came in while you were out, and I made some suggestions to them while they were looking at the produce. And that's when

I thought, why not have some recipe cards? Give people ideas, maybe get them to buy some more stuff."

"I'm a farmer, Delaney, not a chef."

"I know, but I could make them up and—"

"And how long are you going to be here, making up recipes and talking people into buying more stuff? What if you put out recipe cards, and then a month from now, or next summer, people ask for them? I don't have the time or skill to take on something like that.

"You wanted to help, so just sell people the stuff they ask for so I can do my work. That's all you need to do. This isn't your concern."

What he'd always wanted to tell his dad— but had never been able to. He knew he'd been brusque, maybe even rude, but he'd apologize later. He shouldn't take it out on her, but he didn't need her to improve things. Maybe this wasn't good enough for Carters, but it was good enough for him.

He slipped past her and headed out to the corn maze. Some mindless cleaning up of the paths was just what he needed right now.

CHAPTER SIX

No, SHE WASN'T letting this go. She thrived on challenge. Her parents had always pushed her. She'd spent a lifetime competing with Nelson for their approval. To open a restaurant in New York when she did? That didn't happen without pushing past a lot of naysayers.

For a moment thoughts of New York and the restaurant and the past two months slipped into her mind, but she shoved them aside. The shooting had been an aberration. Like the panic attacks at the Mill. But here on Jordan's farm she was herself again. Mostly. If she could be herself here, then she could get back out into the rest of the world and get her life back.

She'd done a lot of work on promotion and marketing for the restaurant, enough to know Jordan was totally falling down on the job. And she was going to help him in gratitude for this place to stay in spite of himself.

The idea made her more cheerful than she'd been in months. The restaurant had been stressful, leaving little time for fun. Showing Jordan she was right gave her a purpose and felt good. They would need to talk about what they'd learned from Nelson about his very active participation in their high school breakup. For years Jordan had been entrenched in her thoughts as the bad guy. The boy who'd played with her heart just to try to get information for his father.

Years later she'd started to wonder what he'd expected to learn from her, since she had nothing to do with mill business, but she'd hated to think about that time and shoved the thoughts aside.

In her memories he'd been a user and now she knew that was wrong. There was still some residual anger, but also burgeoning sympathy for what he'd been through, and curiosity about what might have been. Thoughts about Jordan were confusing, so she pushed them aside as well to consider the idea of offering recipes instead.

The recipes themselves would be easy to come up with. She'd need something fairly simple, not the kind of thing she'd create for a restaurant. It would need to work in a kitchen like Jordan's, with the tools he had on hand.

She'd want to incorporate as much of the current produce as was reasonable.

Jordan claimed he didn't want to offer something he couldn't continue. She'd be happy to promise to send him a recipe or two every month, with seasonal products, but he'd refuse right now. First, she'd show him the value of the idea, taking into account his objections, and then he'd have to agree that having recipes on hand was a great idea, even when she wasn't here.

What a ridiculous argument. As if it wasn't possible to have limited-time promotions or giveaways. She was pretty sure he just didn't want to accept her ideas, so she'd have to show him they worked.

She considered options as she started the soup. There should be a vegan/vegetarian option as well as something with meat. Limited ingredients, simple processes. But a bit of zing, something that would make it a recipe you'd want to save and reuse.

She was interrupted a couple of times by cars driving in, but they were all hikers. She asked if they wanted beverages, but they'd come prepared.

Hmmm. She didn't want to call them freeloaders, because it wasn't as if they were circumventing Jordan's revenue stream. He didn't ask them to contribute. But what if the shop had products like granola bars, maybe a high energy mix of nuts and fruits to take along the trails? So easy to prepare, and since the ingredients were a little pricey, people were used to paying a bit more for those kinds of things. Jordan could make a good margin on that.

She helped another shopper find produce and managed to upsell her when they discussed what she was making with her purchase. People came here with the idea of buying fresh whatever, but they didn't always have plans as to what to do with it. When Delaney offered tips in person, it absolutely worked. If she had recipes available, it would do much the same.

When there was a break from customers again, she went to the computer and typed up two simple, easy recipes. Then she printed them out, four per page, on some pieces of paper she found in the printer. If she could decorate the borders...but that wasn't happening now. After cutting them up into individual recipes, she put them in her pocket.

If she just offered them herself, it wasn't a commitment from the farm. She grabbed another sheet of paper to keep notes on what additional produce she sold when someone had a recipe. Data and facts. That was how to get past Jordan's prejudice.

He came back to the house around noon. Delaney had made another salad, but this time she'd added some of the chicken that was the base for the soup simmering on the stove, some hard-boiled eggs, ham and an assortment of vegetables. Enough to make the salad a meal. She added a couple of biscuits she'd tried with what she could find in the kitchen. The meal was ready and waiting for Jordan when he came in. She didn't know when to expect him, but assumed he had to come eat sometime.

He came through the back door and stopped when he saw the lunch laid out on the table. He rubbed a hand over his beard.

"Uh, thanks. I hope I didn't upset you earlier."

She moved her mouth in the facsimile of a smile. He hadn't upset her in the way she suspected he meant, hurting her feelings and making her cry. No, he'd upset her by treating her like she didn't know what she was doing, but she was taking care of that herself.

"No problem. Go ahead and eat."

He shot a glance at her, then the table. "Are you not eating?"

She shook her head. "I did some test runs

on the biscuits and ate the evidence. I've been snacking as I prepared. I'm good."

There was some movement of his jaw under his beard, but then he nodded and sat at the table. The sound of tires on gravel gave her the excuse to leave.

It felt like the paper in her pocket was a blazing beacon, but Jordan didn't run after her to tell her not to give out the recipes, so she smiled and greeted the customers.

The couple glanced at each other. "Do you have corn?"

Delaney smiled. "Lots of corn. Why don't you come in and see what we've got?"

They were retiring people, the kind who probably felt more comfortable in an anonymous chain store where they wouldn't get attention. Delaney went to the storage area in back, pretending to check for more corn—which Jordan must have picked at some point in the morning because there was lots available. She gave them space to look around.

When she returned, they had a half dozen ears of corn bagged up and were looking at some beans but stepped back when she reappeared.

"I don't know about you, but when the weather gets cool like this, I love making soup. I've got a pot on the stove right now, with those beans and I couldn't resist snacking on some while I was preparing them."

They looked over at the beans. "You put beans in soup?"

Obviously not freestyling in the kitchen, this pair. "Soup is great, because you can add anything to it. I've added some of almost everything in the store."

She bit her lip. Delaney knew the woman was interested, but maybe wasn't confident in the kitchen?

"I have my recipe here, if you wanted to try it sometime. I've been playing with it. Wouldn't mind some feedback."

"Oh, I don't know."

"Just take a look. See if it looks good. Do you eat meat?"

A quick nod. Delaney passed her the somewhat crumpled copy of the meaty soup option and stepped back in the cool storage room. She counted out two minutes and returned.

The couple had added a variety of vegetables to their corn.

"I'll give it a try. It sounds good."

Delaney smiled. "I hope you enjoy it." It wasn't quite the same thrill as serving someone food she'd prepared and watching them eat it, but it was close. And it was definitely an upsell for Jordan. This couple would not come back upset if there wasn't another recipe. But they would come back. That she was sure of.

Delaney added up their total and waved them off once they'd paid. She noted down the additional items they'd purchased, and the amount.

She'd proven their restaurant could be profitable, back in New York, with spreadsheets and projections and costs and sales. This was simple in comparison.

JORDAN WAS GONE when she got back to the house. He'd cleaned his dishes and left them draining in the drying rack. Delaney put everything away and checked the soup. She turned off the burner and went back to the laptop.

Her email was still open, and she checked the new messages. One was from the therapist.

She drew in a breath. She'd been able to forget, for a while, that she had her own issue to deal with. Working in the kitchen here, talking to customers at the store, she'd felt her normal, confident and capable self.

But she wasn't. Because she might be fine here, but this wasn't her life, and she wasn't her usual self once she left the safety of the farm.

The man offered a few suggestions for her, including referrals in the area. But right now she didn't want to go anywhere. She didn't want to risk another panic attack. She tensed up at the thought of leaving the farm.

He suggested talking to her online. She could do that. Tell him in more detail what had happened, find out what she could do about it. She'd have to ask Jordan for help, because right now she was on call for the store, and this online chat wasn't something she would interrupt.

She didn't want to ask for help or need help. But she was short on options.

She didn't know how long Jordan would let her stay, as much as she might help on the farm. She couldn't be here when his dad was, so there was definitely a limited time frame. Either she risked another panic attack with an in-person visit, or she got Jordan to cover for her while she went online.

Asking Jordan was the easier option. Not very brave, but this was where she was at now.

JORDAN RETURNED TO the farmhouse when the sun was low in the sky. He was tired, but for once he felt like he'd actually made real progress. As he pulled open the screen door to let

Ranger in, the most delicious aroma reached his nose.

That soup had smelled good at lunchtime. Now it was something else.

Delaney was at the sink, rinsing off a plate. She turned as she heard him come in.

"Hey. How was your day?"

It was like something from a television show, someone waiting for him and asking him about his day. He couldn't remember that happening, not since his mother died. It was unsettling.

"Got a lot done, since I didn't have interruptions. Thank you." He hadn't been as nice as he should have been earlier, so he could work on being a bit more polite.

"Ready to eat?"

"Just let me wash my hands."

She stood aside and started to ladle the soup into bowls. His stomach rumbled and her eyes met his, laughter crinkling up the corners.

"I'm a little hungry." His body was letting him know that this was preferable to the slap-dash food he fed himself. He was always too tired or busy to cook much.

He returned to the table and noted the differences. Not just the bowl of appetizing soup in front of him, or more of the biscuits on a plate. There were napkins, and a jar with flowers.

Where had they come from? The silverware seemed to shine brighter, and there was a bread plate set out. Even the butter looked different.

Delaney sat down across from him. "I hope you don't mind. I have a hard time not setting up a frame for the food."

"No, that's fine." He'd jumped on her about the recipes, and that hadn't been kind. She didn't understand how the farm worked. But if she wanted to pretty up the table, it didn't matter.

He paused, unsure if there was anything else to do before eating. But Delaney picked up her own spoon, and he followed suit. He dipped the spoon into the soup and put it in his mouth. He tried to hold back the moan, but some weird sound came out of him anyway. Delaney's eyes shot to him. He swallowed.

"Um, that's good." It was more than good, but he didn't know how to express it. It was chicken soup, not haute cuisine, but there were layers and levels of flavor and he quickly fed himself another spoonful.

"Glad you like it." She had a little grin on her face, like she knew that he wanted to just tip the bowl up and get that fantastic flavor inside him as quickly as possible.

She picked up a biscuit and slathered some

butter on it. Her expression when she took a bite let him know it was also delicious. He did the same and his taste buds told him he'd been missing out on a lot. It was going to be a disappointment when she left. He reminded himself that she wasn't here for long, and he shouldn't get too comfortable with her food. Or her company. Somehow that kind of thing was always for other people, not him.

Once the first edges of his hunger were smoothed over, and he'd had…what, he'd had four biscuits? He remembered that he'd been raised with manners.

"How was your day? Things okay out there?" He nodded to the window facing the parking lot.

"It was pretty good. Not too busy, but I sold a fair amount. What other produce do you have still to harvest?"

He was surprised at her interest but could answer it easily enough. She knew enough about growing things to ask intelligent questions. Soon, he'd finished a second bowl of soup, and he felt better than he had in days. Weeks. Full, tired but not overwhelmed by all he hadn't done in the day. He normally was happy with just Ranger's company, but it had been nice to talk to Delaney over dinner.

She started clearing the dishes from the table. Jordan stood and walked to the sink.

"Oh, I can wash up," Delaney said.

Jordan shook his head. "You cooked. I clean."

She frowned but nodded. Didn't matter. Jordan had already started. Delaney moved around him, putting the leftover soup in the fridge, stacking the dirty dishes beside him on the counter, and then picked up a dishtowel to dry.

"I just let them air dry overnight."

"I don't mind doing it. And I like coming into a clean space in the morning."

Jordan made note to leave things tidy for her. A meal like that was worth a bit of extra effort on his part. Living alone had made him cut a few corners when it came to the house.

It was nice, standing in the kitchen, working together. He hadn't realized that he'd missed being with people. It had been easier to stay in, not make the effort to go out and socialize, but that needed to change. Once harvest was over and the corn maze closed up, he had to reach out to his few friends, keep himself from becoming a hermit.

And there was another effort he should make.

"I want to apologize for some judgments I made about you."

Delaney turned to look at him, but he kept his gaze fixed on the plate he was washing.

"What do you mean?"

"I didn't know what Nelson had told you. Back then. I didn't know much, and when you wouldn't talk to me, or answer my messages, I was pretty angry."

Delaney put down her cloth. She took a long breath.

"Yeah, maybe we should talk about it. It just makes me furious. Nelson." He saw her shake her head out of the corner of his eye.

Jordan was washing the pot she'd made the soup in. It was the last thing he had to do, and he dropped it on the rack, pulling the plug and letting the water swirl out of the sink.

"I should have told him sooner. About us."

Delaney shook her head. "*I* should have told him. Whatever stupid thing Nelson had in his head as to who I spent time with was wrong."

Jordan turned, leaning back against the countertop. He crossed his arms. "He was my friend—" He stopped. "I thought he was my friend."

Delaney was staring at the pot. "He was such a— So sure of himself. I get it—my parents encouraged that bossiness, but that was so arrogant."

Her voice rose as she spoke. Jordan was sure that this control issue hadn't just popped up when Nelson found out he and Delaney were dating.

"When Zoey didn't show up for their wedding, I totally got it. I mean, I know Nelson was devastated but I didn't blame her. The rest of the family was really angry, but he hadn't listened to her."

Jordan frowned. "Zoey? Wedding?"

Delaney met his gaze. "You hadn't heard? Nelson was engaged, turned into a groomzilla, ignored his fiancée when she told him she had doubts, so she didn't show up for the ceremony. It was a big scandal. Nelson had to leave the vet practice in Richmond—Zoey's dad was a partner, and that's when he came back to Carter's Crossing."

The satisfaction Jordan felt on hearing that Nelson had gone through that was proof he wasn't always nice. It seemed like karmic justice that Nelson's overconfidence had cost him something.

"Mariah swears he's got over that—mostly. But it doesn't change what he did, to us. And I apologize as well. I wanted some terrible things to happen to you back then."

Jordan nodded. She'd gotten her wish, though

she might not realize it. He'd already lost his mother, and after this, he lost his friends and his first love. Then he and his dad had gone to Florida, so he'd lost his home as well.

"I'm trying to rewrite it in my head, you know? Like, you were so nice to me at the Mill, but I thought you should be mean, based on what had happened back in high school. I was angry that I had to be grateful to you. After what Nelson told me about you using me, I was suspicious of everyone I met. I was afraid that people were only interested in me because of my name and my family."

Jordan rubbed his hands on his jeans. He hated that he'd been part of doing that to her, even though he hadn't used her. But they'd kept their relationship a secret. He knew his dad would flip, though he'd told himself Nelson and Dave should be fine with it. Dave had dated Delaney and that had gone okay, but a part of him had been unsure.

Correctly, it turned out.

"What about you?" Delaney's expression was soft. Caring. Viewing him as a fellow sufferer. He wasn't comfortable with that. He didn't open up to people, because that gave them the chance to hurt you.

Some of that was a result of what Nelson

had done. Jordan had thought Nelson and Dave were his friends. He'd thought Delaney liked him, possibly loved him. And his belief in that had been shattered.

But he'd had a lot more going on. Losing his mother, leaving him at the mercy of his unstable father had been difficult. Here in Carter's Crossing, he'd finally felt some stability. Even if he hadn't been a popular kid, he'd had his home, and his mother who loved him.

But after she died, everything changed.

"It wasn't great." He admitted.

"What did happen afterwards, to you?"

"We went to Florida. My uncle lives there. I went to college. Dad, he didn't want anything more to do with the farm and Carter's Crossing." His father refused to call the town by its name. Made up his own angry versions. Nothing that he wanted to repeat to Delaney.

"But you came back?"

Jordan nodded. "It was the one place I felt was home."

His father said he didn't want anything to do with the farm or town anymore, but he'd come up sometimes, while Jordan was at school. Despite how things had gone wrong after Nelson's accusations, Jordan still loved the farm. He studied agricultural science and told his father he wanted to come back here when he graduated.

Jordan had worked hard to make the place profitable. And even though his father insisted he wanted nothing to do with the farm or town, he couldn't seem to leave Carter's Crossing alone. He'd visit a couple of times a year, and appear to be miserable, but he kept coming back.

But Jordan didn't want to talk about that.

"What did you do, after I left?"

Delaney looked away. "I was pretty upset, especially after talking to your dad."

"Dad?"

Delaney nodded. "I wanted to talk to you after Nelson told me you'd been using me. Ask if it was true. But your dad was at the entrance to the farm when I arrived, and he confirmed what Nelson had said."

Jordan gritted his teeth. That must have been when his father found out that he'd been seeing Delaney. But Delaney was still explaining.

"After talking to Grandmother, I went to a boarding school. She wasn't sure if your dad might do something to hurt me or the Mill. The whole history repeating itself."

Jordan nodded and then stopped, as the words hit home.

"History repeating itself?"

"Your dad and my aunt."

Delaney stood there, calmly, as if this was something he should know about. But it wasn't. And he suspected this might explain something vital about his father.

"What are you talking about?"

She looked confused. "Really? He never told you?"

CHAPTER SEVEN

JORDAN SHOOK HIS HEAD. He didn't know what she was referring to, but he wanted to know. His parents had never talked about anything that happened before they were married. Maybe there was some reason for this obsession his father had.

"Let's sit down." Delaney said. Jordan nodded and led the way to the living room. Couch, chair, TV and not much else. He hadn't had anyone but his dad here since he'd moved back.

Delaney curled up in the chair. Jordan sat on the end of the couch, leaning back against the arm to face her.

She pulled the tie out of her hair, letting the dark strands fall around her face. She looked younger, more like the girl he'd fallen in love with.

He didn't need to think of that.

She exhaled and rested her chin on her knees. "So, apparently your father and my aunt Claire dated back when they were in high school. You didn't know that?"

Jordan shook his head again.

"They were pretty serious. Aunt Claire talked to Grandmother about it, and Grandmother wasn't happy about them dating. It wasn't because he didn't have money. His dad was a truck driver who sometimes did deliveries for the mill. But Grandmother thought—"

Delaney trailed off, and Jordan braced himself. "What did she think?"

Delaney grimaced. "She thought he talked a lot about himself, and had a lot of big plans, but not a lot of concrete action. She told Aunt Claire she needed to be sure she really, really loved him because Grandmother thought that life with him would be difficult."

Jordan couldn't argue against that. Abigail Carter had a pretty good handle on what his father was like. He was mostly talk, and mostly about himself.

When Jordan didn't speak, Delaney continued. "Grandmother told me that Aunt Claire tried to talk to your father about it, and he accused Grandmother of being a snob and looking down on him. He told Aunt Claire to choose between him and her family. He scared her, so she chose her family. According to what Aunt Claire told Grandmother who told me, he said that he was going to show everyone when he was rich and could buy them all out."

She gave him a sad smile. "Then, after what happened with us and Nelson…your dad kinda scared me, and I was heartbroken, so when she asked if I wanted to leave Carter's Crossing, I said yes."

Jordan rubbed his face with his hands. There was a lot of new information to process. Jordan hadn't even known his grandfather was a trucker as well as a farmer. He'd never heard this story about his father before, but it explained a lot. His father's obsession with the Carters and trying to find financial success. But Dad always looked for shortcuts, and nothing worked out.

He wasn't sure how his mother fit into the story. She wasn't wealthy. And he'd never felt that his parents had a grand passion.

But wait. His grandfather, his paternal grandfather was a truck driver? Did he not just work the farm? Why not? His parents had never discussed their parents with him. He'd overheard a fight between his mom and dad where they'd whisper yelled about how his mom had been kicked out by her parents when she got pregnant. Jordan had known his pending birth was the reason for his parents' marriage. It wasn't until his grandfather died and they inherited the farm that he learned he'd had a living grandparent.

Maybe his father had a similar thing happen? Some reason he'd been banished from the farm? Maybe his mother and father had both been forced out by their families. It would explain why he'd never heard about this family history. He'd have to ask his father when he returned.

"A lot to think about, right?"

He lifted his head to look at Delaney. He wasn't sure how long he'd been lost in his own thoughts.

"Yeah. That explains a lot."

"I guess things wouldn't have worked out anyway."

Things? What things?

Delaney must have heard the unspoken question. "You and me. Even if Nelson hadn't stuck his nose in, your dad would have done something to stop us."

Definitely. It was a big part of the reason they'd kept their relationship quiet.

"I told you I couldn't tell him."

"I didn't understand till I talked to him. You were right. I thought maybe you blamed us, my family, for what happened to your mom."

Jordan shook his head. "I didn't blame you for anything."

He'd been lost after his mother died. Jordan spent most of his time either at school or working at the farm. He'd tried to keep his head down and attract as little attention as possible after his father started conspiracy theories about the Carters causing his mother's death.

Delaney had helped him through that difficult time. She'd let him talk about his mother and complain about his father. She'd listened to him, made him feel like he mattered. It had been devastating to know how little he had mattered, when she'd left him. Except, maybe he had, more than he realized.

Now, she was listening to him that same way...and no, he couldn't go down that mental path.

They'd had a magical two months together, full of stolen moments and secret notes and a lot more time spent waiting to see each other than being together, but it had helped him cope. Helped him look at the situation with some objectivity, so that he didn't go down the rabbit hole with his father.

"I'm not sure how I'd have got through those months after Mom's death without you."

She paused when he said that. "Really?"

He nodded.

"Thank you." She looked pleased. "I feel better, knowing that I did something good. It was a special time for me, too."

Was it real? He wanted to ask her. They'd been teenagers, yes, but had she meant it? Had she loved him?

He couldn't ask. If she said no, it would taint some of the few good memories he had. And what if she asked him? Would he seem pathetic if he admitted it was the best relationship he'd had?

He felt itchy, like his skin wasn't fitting right.

"I'm going to take Ranger out." Another evening, another escape from her. From her and the memories and the futility of wondering what might have happened if things had been different. If they'd been different people with different families.

It didn't matter. This was reality, and he needed to get himself and his messy emotions under control.

He stood, snapping his fingers to get Ranger's attention.

"Goodnight." Delaney said. He slipped out into the dark, the cool air soothing his heated thoughts.

DELANEY WAS RELIEVED that Jordan was back to himself the next morning. She'd taken the oatmeal she'd found and improved it with some spices and fruit. He thanked her and ate it appreciatively. It was reassuring to demonstrate she still could do her stuff.

She needed a broader range of spices and herbs and other ingredients. She could do so much better with just a few more options to work with.

"How do you get groceries?"

Jordan stood to take his bowl to the sink. "I go to Oak Hill. Are we out of something you need?"

She swiped a forearm over her face, pushing back some loose strands that had fallen out of her ponytail. She was flouring cubes of beef before braising them for a stew for dinner. She planned on a frittata for lunch.

"Not really, there are just a few things I'd like to have. If I could get some yeast, I could make bread, and some spices." What she could do with access to the wide range of seasonings she'd had back in New York. And she knew he'd shown interest when she talked about making bread.

"Your car should be here today, Mariah said. Do you want to go, or would you like me to?"

She wanted him to. She wanted to stay a little longer in this bubble where she felt safe. But Jordan had work to do. She had nothing to do but help him out and schedule time with the therapist. There was no good reason why she couldn't drive to a grocery store. She could do this.

"I'll go, but it means you're on store duty." She forced a smile.

Jordan watched her with eyes that seemed to see through the brave front she was trying to present. "I've got a delivery to make to Oak Hill tomorrow. I could drop you off, pick you up after I'm done."

She shouldn't see anyone she knew in Oak Hill, so no one would ask why she was there and what she was doing. She could give Jordan a list, but she'd rather choose what she wanted herself. And if she wasn't driving, maybe then she wouldn't have to worry about a panic attack?

"Who'd take care of the store then?"

Jordan shrugged. "I'd have to keep the place closed while I was making the delivery anyway. I try to go early, so I don't miss too many people."

She couldn't hide out here on the farm forever. She had to push herself, at least a little.

Surely, this wouldn't trigger another attack. "Okay, let's do that. I'll make a list of what I want, and you can tell me if you need anything as well."

Jordan looked at the cupboards and grimaced. "I'm happy to let you take care of the food. You're a good chef. Even with the limited stuff I have here."

It wasn't that limited. The selection of vegetables was amazing. But other things, like herbs and utensils were in short supply or missing altogether. She had a few ideas, things she'd like to try, inspired by the plentiful produce. She had to be careful, though.

Jordan did not take well to new things. At least, not the new things she'd suggested. She didn't expect him to accept all her suggestions, since she wasn't a farmer, but she knew food. She knew something about business and marketing. He had a knee-jerk reaction of saying no to everything.

She wasn't sure what all that was about, but she suspected his dad played a part. Her family had some issues, but Jordan's dad was in a different category all together. She remembered the things Jordan had told her about his home and his parents, back in high school when they'd shared everything.

It was a quiet day. She got the stew and frittata done. There were a few cars, mostly with hikers. It still bothered her that Jordan offered this opportunity to people yet didn't charge anything. It had to cost him time and resources.

Could she suggest a donation box? Would he take offense and shut her out? Probably. She marshalled up arguments while she worked in the kitchen. It wouldn't take much time. She'd offer to make the boxes herself, but it wasn't anything she'd ever done before, and she wasn't sure what would be required.

Nails? Glue? Wood for sure. Saws and paint and…yeah, better that she not try that herself.

The frittata, with another salad using peppers and beans from the incredible bounty of fresh organic produce was a success. Based on the amount Jordan ate, anyway. With the stew ready, Delaney went to the store to work on a grocery list for the next day while helping anyone who showed up to buy something.

A couple of cars drove in with customers eager to get what they wanted and then leave, giving Delaney no scope to upsell. She considered options like taking some of Jordan's produce to a farmer's market. Or even inviting other farmers to bring their produce here and provide a central location for people to buy farm goods. Maybe the people Jordan swapped with to get meat and eggs and chickens would be interested in doing that.

How did she broach these ideas to Jordan without him shutting her down before even considering them? The idea of a busy, prosperous farm made her itch to get things happening.

She was distracted by another car. A woman got out, looked around hesitantly, then made her way to the store. Delaney had propped the door open, since the day was mild, and she wanted to make the place as welcoming as possible.

"Good afternoon. Welcome to Stoney Creek Farm. What can I help you with?"

"I don't know. I need to feed my family, and I was hoping for something new to try. And maybe even healthy for them?"

Delaney had to refrain from dancing on the spot. This was exactly why her recipe idea was so good.

It wasn't until she was ringing up the woman's purchases, all items for the soup recipes she'd taken from Delaney, both vegan and carnivore, when she realized Jordan was standing in the doorway between the storage room and the store.

She shot him a glance. It wasn't easy to read his expression behind that beard, but she thought his jaw was tightly clenched.

"Thank you so much for your help, and for the recipes. I'll be back for more soon."

The woman left for her car, looking less careworn than when she'd arrived. Delaney watched her leave, all too aware of the man standing rigid behind her. Well, she'd helped a couple of people anyway, even if Jordan shut down the idea from here on out. But how could he just turn his back on an opportunity like this?

She turned to face the music.

"Go ahead, yell at me."

He glanced away; lips pinched.

"I told you not to give out recipes."

She crossed her arms. "You gave me a bunch of reasons why it would be a bad idea. And I respected that."

He met her gaze, hands on the door frame. "Oh, really? I could have sworn that woman thanked you for recipes."

Delaney pulled the somewhat battered slips of paper from her pocket.

"These are my recipes. *Mine.* I didn't claim they were yours, or part of the farm. I have a piece of paper behind the till listing the additional sales made because people wanted to try MY recipes. I was trying to collect data to prove to you this is a good idea."

Jordan snorted. Ranger looked at her from around his legs. "You've been here for two minutes, basically. You don't know anything about what I do and how this farm works."

That was all true. But she wanted to do something to thank him for letting her stay, and she had knowledge he could use. She couldn't just sit on her hands and do nothing to improve this place. She could make it better!

"What I know is that I'd like to help. And I know food. And what people do with it. That woman who just came in was looking for something different, something healthier for her family, but had no idea what she wanted. I helped her come up with a solution and that solution involved selling more of your produce. So why exactly is that a problem?"

Jordan shook his head as if clearing his thoughts. His chest was heaving, and he was gripping the door frame with white knuckles.

"Because it's easy to get big ideas. Easy to

get excited about them. But then you're gone, and there's no one to take care of your shiny new idea and then we've lost money and are on the move again."

Jordan stopped, eyes wide. He cursed and escaped out the doorway.

Delaney stared at the space where he'd been, mouth open.

She was obviously not the most well-adjusted person around, since she was hiding here, afraid of another panic attack without really understanding why they were happening. But Jordan had issues as well. That speech hadn't really been about her ideas. It didn't take much to realize it was totally about Jordan's father.

It explained why Jordan was so resistant when it came to trying new things. She was sure he had good cause. But if he didn't do something, he would be in trouble anyway. She'd have bet her fancy chef's knife that the hiking trails, the corn maze, even this produce store were essential extras because the farm needed more income and they were stretching him thin. Trying something new would be problematic just based on time. Add on whatever his father had done, and yeah, those heels would be well dug in.

Delaney didn't have to get involved. She could just throw up her hands and give up on any ideas about helping. After all, she wasn't going to be here long. She had obligations back in the city that she'd soon need to meet. She had no investment in the place, nothing she would gain from pushing Jordan's limits. She could just make meals, sell vegetables and watch the hikers head down the trails.

Jordan would be thrilled if that was all she did.

But she wanted to do more. She couldn't not try to make the farm the best it could be. To make her time here productive. It was in her DNA to push for success. Success for Jordan, and if she was honest, for herself as well.

Jordan had helped her. He'd given her this safe place to stay, even when he had good reason to want nothing to do with her. Thanks to that altercation with her know-it-all brother, she now knew that her heartbreak from high school wasn't because Jordan had used her. There were still hints of that boy she'd loved back in high school, hidden behind the guardedness. Hints that pulled at her.

She wasn't staying, either on the farm or in Cupid's Crossing. But she'd like to do something nice for that boy who'd made her feel so special back in high school. To thank him and apologize.

It wasn't going to be easy. Fortunately, Delaney was used to working hard. Jordan best prepare himself for what was coming.

CHAPTER EIGHT

JORDAN SPENT AS long as he could outside before going back to the house to face Delaney again. He couldn't believe that outburst. He didn't talk to people about things like that. It was personal and mostly history and he didn't want to see the pity in anyone's eyes.

Still, he owed Delaney an apology. He shouldn't have yelled at her, and he shouldn't have vented his frustration with his father at her. She wanted to help, to make things better. Then again, his father had always truly believed that his next idea was going to be the one to make them all rich. To impress the Carters? Maybe. It was depressing to think that might have been the motive behind the way his family had lived.

Ranger nosed at his hand, and he knew he had to go in. He carefully removed his boots and entered the warmly lit kitchen warily.

He didn't see her, which was both a relief and a disappointment.

Ranger was staring into the dining room, and he spotted Delaney sitting in front of the laptop. Ranger padded over and nudged her, bringing her to awareness of their presence.

"Oh, sorry. Um, just let me get the food on the table."

"Are you okay?" He hoped it wasn't his surliness that had upset her.

She rubbed her hands over her face. "I'll be fine. Just…just thinking about something."

"Was it what I said out there? Because I'm sorry. That…it wasn't about you, and I shouldn't have yelled at you."

Delaney stood and gave him a weak smile. Better than nothing, but he still felt terrible.

"If you think that's yelling, you should try some of the kitchens I've been in. Don't worry about it. It was something else."

She brushed past him, and he stood back to give her room.

Now that he wasn't looking for her, he could see that the table was set again. Something pleasant moved inside his chest. She wasn't angry with him. Well, not too angry. Not angry enough that she hadn't set up a table for the two of them.

Delaney moved a pot onto some kind of trivet he wasn't aware he had and stirred the contents with a ladle. An incredible aroma drifted out, and he was settling into his seat almost before he knew it.

"It smells wonderful. Thank you."

This time her smile was bigger and reached her eyes. She filled his plate with a large portion of the stew, filled with chunks of beef and vegetables. She set it in front of him, then filled a plate for herself and sat down.

Jordan took a bite, and barely held in a moan. He'd made beef stew before, but it had never tasted like this. He almost asked for her recipe, just so he could try to recreate this after she was gone, but he didn't dare.

Not after he'd yelled at her about recipes. Which he could admit now was stupid. This wasn't some crazy scheme his dad came up with that could cost him the farm. The long walk with Ranger had given him time to clear his head, separating his issues with his father from what Delaney was doing. This was a low-key marketing effort, that wasn't costing him anything beyond the paper it took to print up the recipe, and with results like this, not only would people be buying the ingredients, they'd come back for another recipe.

Definitely.

"I'm sorry, Delaney, and I was wrong."

Her head lifted up. She blinked, and then her expression cleared. "Oh, about the recipes?"

He nodded but wondered what she'd been thinking about. Her mind had been elsewhere.

"If you want to do that, I'd be—" He swallowed. "Grateful. It's a good idea."

She smiled, even bigger, and there was a sparkle in her eyes. "Really?"

He nodded.

She bit her lip, smile straightening out. "I could put the name of the farm on the recipes. Maybe if we got some nicer paper for the printer, things like that. So it would be promotion for the farm."

He paused, spoon halfway to his mouth. "Oh. Um…"

Her expression shifted to neutral. "It was just a thought."

He wanted to kick himself for doing that to her. "No, your idea is good. I just don't know exactly where to get that. An office store? Or is there some place to order it online?"

She put her own spoon down. "I bet you could get something good online. I hadn't thought about that part of it. I can check after dinner."

She looked happy and eager, and like whatever had been dragging on her was no longer on her mind, so Jordan nodded. "Okay, let's do that. Or you can search while I clean up."

"There's not much to do. I cleaned up as I went."

A quick glance showed how true that was.

"I don't mind washing up. I'd clean up a lot more than dishes for food like this."

She picked up her spoon again. "Well, it's good to know that all my training wasn't wasted."

He shot her a glance, but realized she was joking with him.

JORDAN WAS WHISTLING as he loaded up his truck in the early dawn light the next morning. He and Delaney had spent a good part of the evening debating over the best card stock to use for her recipes, and then she'd bounced ideas for content off him.

He wasn't a great help. All her ideas sounded delicious to him, despite having just stuffed himself on dinner. Delaney promised to use him as her guinea pig, and he was more than happy to offer himself and his stomach up for her experiments. It had been the most enjoyable evening he'd spent in…it was embarrassing to even try to count. Instead, he looked forward to whatever tonight's trial recipe would be.

He slid the last bin into the truck and closed up the tailgate. He pulled the truck up in front of the house and waited for Delaney.

She'd been quiet at breakfast. He didn't interrupt her silence. Having a warm breakfast made for him was a treat, and if she wasn't a morning person, he appreciated that she'd got up to do that. He noticed movement, and watched Delaney make her way around from the back of the house. He should tell her she was welcome to use the front door. He never bothered, because he was normally in work clothes, and it was easier to keep all the muck in one place.

He glanced down. He'd put on clean jeans and a flannel shirt, but farming was a dirty business, and he could see some smudges of dirt on his pants from packing up the truck.

Why was he worried about that? He slapped at the dirt anyway.

Delaney threw him a smile as she got in, but it didn't last. He kept an eye on her out of his peripheral vision as he drove down the drive, opened the gate and drove through, closing it again behind him.

Delaney didn't comment. She didn't seem to notice they'd stopped and started again. She stared out the passenger window, lost in her thoughts.

Jordan liked silence. He didn't appreciate people who intruded into his quiet contemplation to ask silly questions. People who thought silence was a void to be filled. This stillness shouldn't bother him. But he was worried. Was she quiet because she didn't want to make this trip? She hadn't been able to handle being at the Mill kitchen. Was she worried about being at the grocery store? Would she be okay?

Maybe he should go directly to the restaurant and drop off his produce, then go to the store with her. If Delaney felt better with him around (and that thought made him feel good) he could totally do it.

"Delaney?"

She turned towards him. "What? Oh, sorry. I was thinking. Not being good company."

Jordan frowned. "I do this drive all the time on my own. I don't need company." That sounded like he didn't want her there. "I mean, I'm glad to have company." That was almost a lie. Most company he didn't enjoy. "I mean, you don't have to talk if you don't want to."

Except he did want to ask her something.

"Just, would you tell me if you have a problem? I mean, if you don't want to go into the grocery store, I could do it. Or I could go with you, if you want."

There was a good reason Jordan spent most of his time on his own.

This time her smile looked real, not forced.

"I think I'm good but thank you. I'm a little spacey today, but it's not you, or the groceries or the farm."

That was a relief.

"I'm supposed to think of the things that make me anxious. And honestly, thinking about things that make me anxious makes me anxious."

He felt a smile pulling on the corners of his mouth, but he kept it hidden in his beard. He didn't want her thinking he was laughing at her.

"Maybe it would be better not to think about it then."

Delaney sighed. "I've been emailing a therapist. About what happened at the Mill. He's the one I've been talking to about my panic attacks, and next steps. Panic attacks are caused by anxiety. So, I do need to figure out what's making me so anxious if I'm going to move forward."

"I guess you have to at least try it then."

Delaney turned to him, determination on her

face. "I am, but I don't know if I'm getting it right. Some things are normal to worry about, right? How do I know what isn't? What makes you anxious? You know, a regular person."

Jordan snorted. He was no poster child for well-adjusted. But he wanted to help Delaney.

"The weather. Crop prices. My father." He hadn't meant to say that last one.

She considered him, then nodded.

"Okay."

He shrugged. "Not sure I qualify as a regular person."

"Not me either. Did you hear what happened in New York? At the restaurant?"

Jordan felt a chill lick over his skin. Had someone hurt her? Was this the source of her panic attacks?

"I don't have a clue what you're talking about."

She looked startled. "You didn't hear anything?"

It must have been something big then, but he was isolated on the farm. He certainly wasn't looking up the Carters on the internet.

She turned back in her seat, staring at the road ahead of her.

"Peter and I opened a restaurant in New York."

He made a noise in his throat.

She turned to look at him. "Had you heard that?"

He shook his head. And wondered about Peter. Was Delaney with him?

"I don't even know who Peter is."

"He's another chef. He's one of my best friends. We met at school, in Paris. And we made a pact to open a restaurant together. We worked really hard, and finally, finally we were able to do it. And it was going so well..."

If Peter had been responsible for whatever had happened to Delaney, Jordan was tempted to make a trip to the city just to find him. He could intimidate a chef, couldn't he? Farming was physical work, so he had some muscles.

"I had to fire a guy. A sous chef. He had a bad attitude, missed some shifts, so I had to, right?"

Jordan glanced at Delaney and saw her hands twisting in her lap. Her voice had been tight, the sentence going upward at the end as if she was unsure.

"Sounds like it."

"I shouldn't have." Her breathing had sped up. Jordan would have been willing to put money down that this firing was a source of stress, based on her posture and the tension in her voice.

"After I fired him, he came back to the restaurant with a gun."

The truck lurched to the right, and Jordan wrestled it back. "What?"

"Oh, I wasn't there. Don't worry about me. But he shot Peter, and a couple of staff and one customer were all grazed by bullets before he ran out."

He wasn't aware he'd done it, but his hand was on hers, gripping tightly, offering reassurance.

"Peter is still in rehab. It's going to take a while yet before he's back to anything like normal."

"That's terrible. You're okay?"

Her voice was dry. "Oh, I'm fine. I only got there after the police had our ex-employee in custody and there was no danger."

Her voice cracked. He'd have bet all the produce in the truck that she was revisiting that trip back to her restaurant. And she wasn't fine.

"It was in all the papers. It took a few days before we could even think of reopening, and during that time all the reservations were cancelled. A few ghoulish types wanted to come and be at the scene of the crime, but we didn't have the reserves to wait it out and try to make a comeback. As if anyone would have forgotten anyway."

Jordan made a mental note to look up everything he could find online. He needed to know, in case Delaney was leaving out anything important.

"Are you and Peter…"

Delaney shook her head. "No, he has a partner, a romantic one. We're just friends and business partners."

Jordan had no right to feel relieved about that.

"When did this happen?"

"A couple of months ago. I've been busy taking care of everything since Peter's in rehab. I don't want him to stress about it."

Instead, Delaney had been taking it all on herself. This must have been a big part of the panic attacks she'd had at the Mill.

"That's why you came back to help at the Mill when they needed someone?"

It didn't sound like she'd had much time off to work this through.

"It's not like I had anything better to do. And it was helping out the family, in a minor way. Mariah's made a big success of Cupid's

Crossing, so if I can't do my own thing, I can at least help her."

Silence fell. Jordan worked through what she'd said.

He didn't know much about the Carters, despite his father's fixation on them. He'd heard about how rich the family was, and how selfish and greedy they were.

Nelson and Delaney had been living with their grandmother, Abigail Carter, in Carter's Crossing while they were in school. He'd never met Delaney's parents or known anything about them. Which meant he didn't know what they might have done to mess her and Nelson up, the way his father had done to him. Because everyone thought their lives were normal, until they found out differently.

Maybe there was a reason Nelson had behaved like he had, back in high school. Jordan wasn't going to give the guy a pass for what he'd done, but maybe even the Carters, with their money and their history in the town and the way everyone looked up to them, had their own troubles.

"Is your family upset that you're not at the Mill right now?"

"My parents don't know yet, unless Nelson told them."

He didn't talk to his father, rarely called between visits, but he'd thought he was unusual that way.

"They'd understand though, right?"

Give Nelson his due, he hadn't taken issue with Delaney having a panic attack, as if that was something to look down on her for, just that she was at Stoney Creek Farm.

"They'll be disappointed." She sighed again. "But I'll deal with this, get back to New York and Peter and I will start again."

She sounded determined, but not exactly happy about that.

Not his problem he reminded himself. But he had to wonder if Delaney wanted to go back or was doing it for other people. Like Peter.

But what did he know about her? He'd been close to her for a short time in high school. That had been almost fifteen years ago. He had no idea how she would have grown and changed, and what motivated her now. Even if she didn't want to rebuild her restaurant, she didn't want to be in Cupid's Crossing either.

Still, he watched her carefully as he pulled into the parking lot of the grocery store in Oak Hill. Made sure she appeared relaxed as she picked up the reusable shopping bags they'd brought with them. Watched her walk into the store, and finally out of his view.

Then he waited a few more minutes to make sure she didn't try to call him on his phone to say she needed help. He put the truck back in gear and made his way to the restaurant to drop off his delivery. He kept the phone close.

CHAPTER NINE

DELANEY DIDN'T FIND everything on her list.

She'd been making some unkind comments. *Really? Is white pepper that obscure a thing?* She had to remind herself that this wasn't New York City. She didn't need to reinforce stereotypes of New Yorkers. She'd thought, since she'd lived in Carter's Crossing for so many years, that she belonged here, in a way.

Her attitude did not.

If she was going to create recipes that Jordan could give his customers, she needed to work with what was available in local grocery stores. Like a challenge on a reality TV show.

It took her longer than she'd expected to find most of the items on her list. She was glad, looking at the produce available, that most of what she had to use would be from Jordan's farm. Much better than what the store carried. She was used to having the best food options available to her with a simple phone call.

She looked around the store, checking the

other shoppers, making sure no one was watching her. Her hands clenched the cart. Was that the start of another panic attack? She relaxed her hands, and was able to finish shopping, but she hated having to worry about doing such a simple activity.

Jordan was waiting when she finally pushed her cart outside the doors of the store. He'd parked along the store front and eased forward till the truck was beside her.

He shot her a sharp glance, checking that she was okay, and she hated that. She'd been raised to be strong, self-reliant and ambitious. The fact that someone felt they needed to make sure she'd been able to handle a trip to the grocery store irritated her. She had to work to keep from snapping at Jordan.

It wasn't fair. Jordan was doing a lot for her. But that just annoyed her further.

"Find everything?" he asked as he set the bags in the back of the truck.

"I made do." Hanging on to her sunshiney, everything is fine persona was becoming too difficult to keep up.

Jordan paused. "If we're ordering the paper online, maybe we could add some of the things you couldn't find here. Depending on what it is, of course."

She hadn't thought of that, and that made her crankier. "It won't help people who are limited to what they can find here, will it?"

He watched her climb into the truck. She wanted to yell at him. He didn't need to monitor everything she did.

He swung up into his own seat. "Guess you're right."

Yes, yes she was. About a lot of things he wouldn't give her credit for.

Jordan didn't speak again as they left Oak Hill. Delaney stared out the passenger window, trying to will her irritation away.

"Did anything happen at the store?"

Delaney turned to see Jordan focus his attention back on the road, but he'd obviously been watching her.

"No, nothing 'happened' at the store. I didn't break down. It was fine."

She waited. He didn't say anything else. "Why did you ask?"

She knew she was provoking him to say something to make her mad. She wanted to be angry. No, she was angry. She wanted a target.

Jordan shrugged but didn't answer.

"Go on, say it. You want to know if I panicked."

Jordan shook his head. "If that had happened, there'd have been a big fuss at the store. You just seem upset."

"Why would I be upset? What could I *possibly* have to be upset about?"

Jordan carefully kept his attention on the road.

"I know you have a lot of things to be upset about."

"You know, do you? You know so much. You know I've had panic attacks. And you know I don't want to be around Nelson. I'm fragile, right? You have to be careful around poor Delaney."

"That's not—"

Delaney cut through his attempt to speak. The anger was pouring out, searching for fuel to keep the fire blazing. "I know things you don't know. And I'm not afraid to try something new. *I'm* not a coward. I'm working on this."

"Are you saying I'm a coward?" Even through the beard she could see muscles ticking in his jaw. Yeah, he wasn't happy about what she was saying but she wanted someone else to be the weak one this time.

"Just saying you won't try anything new at the farm. You wouldn't admit recipes were a good idea until I proved it to you. You won't try to get money for the use of the hiking trails. That seems like you're afraid of something."

Jordan's knuckles were white on the steering wheel. A part of Delaney wondered what she was doing, pushing him like this.

"You don't know anything." His voice was a growl.

"I know what I see."

"You don't know my dad. You have no idea what he's done." His lips had almost disappeared, they were so tightly clenched.

Delaney's anger sagged; the burst of adrenaline gone. Because he was right. She didn't know his father, only as a problem for her grandmother, and something of a joke around town. When it came to his relationship with Jordan, she only knew what he'd told her, and she suspected that wasn't everything. Gerald Everton was the root of the blow-up that had happened in high school, causing the rift between Jordan and her brother, and ending her first love.

She'd been hurt for so long that she hadn't considered that he might have been hurting as well. That shamed her. She didn't want to be so self-absorbed that she ignored the problems other people had.

Was she like that?

"I'm sorry." She said it quietly, no energy left. "You're right."

"All his big ideas did was mean mom and I had to move to a new place every year. Mom would have to find a new job, because none of dad's ideas ever panned out.

"When my grandfather died, and we moved up here to the farm it was the first time we stayed still *ever*. It was the first place where we had something that was permanent. The only place. Mom never let him mortgage the farm, so it was ours."

Delaney kept her eyes on the road. She didn't think his face was something she deserved to see right now.

"After mom died." His voice cracked. "And everything that happened, we couldn't stay here. We went back to Florida. My uncle had a settlement from his work and he'd bought a place. I went to college, and dad did… I'm not sure what all he did. But when I graduated, I told him I was coming back up here.

"He came with me and had a bunch of big ideas for the farm. Heirloom cattle was the first one. When I was away working on an organic farm, finding out how to apply that to our property, the cattle got sick and since he didn't bother to look after them, most of them died. By then, he was busy on his next idea, the corn maze."

"I'd planted that field with something else, but he plowed right over it, and I couldn't handle it anymore. I told him I was done. I couldn't watch him destroy the farm, the one good memory I had."

Jordan gripped the steering wheel as if he might lose the vehicle if he eased off.

"He said he wasn't cut out to be a farmer, so he'd leave me to it and go back to Florida. His brother bought a fishing boat and they thought they'd do fishing charters. I didn't care, I just wanted him to keep his hands off the farm.

"Whenever he comes back now, he always has some big idea, but I've talked him out of anything else. I'm not going to lose the farm because of his crazy idea of what's the next big thing. It's mine. I'm not risking it."

They were at the farm now. Jordan braked, then got out to open the gate. Delaney got out as well. Jordan picked up the gate and shoved it to the side of the driveway. He didn't look at her.

She flipped the sign to open. "I'm going to walk back. Unless you want me to call Nelson and get out of here."

Jordan got back in the truck and drove

through the open gate. He hadn't said she had to leave, so she wasn't going to push it until he had time to cool down. She had a lot to think about. She started to walk down the driveway.

WHEN SHE MADE it back to the farmhouse, Jordan and Ranger were gone. The groceries were sitting in the kitchen, perishables still in their cool bags. Delaney was able to get everything put away before she heard a vehicle in the drive.

She stepped out, saw another group of hikers exit the vehicle. She waved, but they didn't pause for more than a quick wave back.

Jordan needed to make some money out of this. She had a better understanding now of why he didn't like new ideas and changes and why he was so risk averse. But her idea was safe. Risk free. The problem was how to approach it after what he'd said. And after her outburst.

If she tried to talk about it now, would he just ask her to leave?

She chewed on the problem for the rest of the day while she made up the newest recipe cards, still on plain white paper for now. She sold produce and shared the recipes with customers while she still worried about it. She experimented with a version of Shepherd's pie and decided she had to try to introduce this idea and hope he didn't kick her out.

Jordan was working himself to the bone to keep his home, the only place he felt safe. She was dealing with anxiety but had a whole network of friends and family she could reach out to. Jordan didn't. She didn't want to leave, because that feeling of safety that Jordan found here was something she'd experienced as well, but she needed to help.

The Shepherd's pie was done, keeping warm in the oven when she heard Jordan come in through the back screen door. There was a pause, and she wondered if he'd hoped she was gone, or if the food made up for her presence. It did smell good.

He paused in the doorway.

"Hi." Delaney swallowed. "Hope it's okay I'm still here."

He looked at the ground. "I owe you an apology."

"I owe you one as well."

He looked up at that.

"I was upset." Delaney met his gaze. "Not at you, but I took it out on you. And I attacked you and that made you angry. Think it all falls on me."

Jordan shook his head. "No, I can take the responsibility for my own words. I'm just not used to sharing some of these things. It makes me...itchy."

She didn't deserve this kindness from him. "I kind of feel like that too. Can we call a truce then? Maybe remember we're both not used to this?"

Jordan rubbed his chin. "Okay, if I can have some of whatever smells so good."

"Absolutely." Delaney felt the smile stretching her face, which might be excessive, but she was so relieved that she could stay longer with Jordan and Ranger in this little bubble they were in. She needed to do better, so that she didn't risk it again.

That made her understand Jordan a little better. But she had to do something, something productive with her time here.

Getting food on the table while Jordan washed up gave them a chance to get over the awkwardness. He sat at the table, complimented the food with his first bite, and asked how the store had done. Conversation flowed from that.

As had become the norm, Jordan insisted on washing up. Delaney had started bread dough rising, and kneaded it down, placing it in the fridge to rise overnight. She wanted fresh bread for morning.

Jordan watched her intently. "That's bread."

She grinned. "Told you I could make it. The cooler temp of the fridge will slow the second rise. Once it warms up to room temp again, I can bake it and we'll have fresh bread for breakfast."

Jordan looked at her, eyes wide. "That's amazing."

She fought a grin. "Not that amazing, really, but I'm happy if you think so. And, while I've got you in a good mood, can I talk to you?"

Jordan looked wary but nodded. She led him into the living room.

"Can you cover the stand tomorrow for about an hour?"

His shoulders relaxed, and he sat down in a chair. "Of course. You're not tied here. You're a volunteer, so it's up to you to set your hours."

Delaney curled up in a corner of the couch. "No, we have an agreement. Watching the store is my part. I pushed my way in, so I need to do what I said I would."

"I appreciate that but take as long as you need. Do you want the afternoon? The day?"

Delaney ran her finger over the arm of the couch. Her cheeks warmed. "No, it's just an hour. I'm doing a video session with a therapist. About the panic attacks."

She didn't look at him, but his voice was warm. "Then take your hour, or however long, and if you need some time after to process, do that."

That he'd be this nice, after she'd blown up at him today made her feel horrible. "It's at one, about the time you'd normally be here for some lunch anyway. I can have something ready for you."

She felt Jordan's hand on her fidgeting fingers. "Delaney, it's okay. Taking care of yourself is the first priority. I did manage to get by before you were here. I won't starve."

Her gaze shot up. He shrugged. "But your food is much better, so I'm not going to turn down anything you make."

"Thank you—I appreciate that. And there's something else I wanted to say. Can you just hear me out—I don't want you to get mad."

Jordan looked wary. Fair enough. Anytime someone said they didn't want you to get mad, you were pretty much guaranteed that they were going to say something that would make you mad.

"I had an idea, and please, believe me, I

heard everything you said previously. But this could help you, and I'd like to do that."

Jordan leaned back, but his arms were crossed again, and resistance was there in every line of his body.

"I think you should be getting some kind of recompense from the hikers. I know, what I said before about the parking isn't realistic. I get that. Really."

He jerked his chin. A nod, probably.

"But I also think people would consider it fair to pay you something for the privilege of using the trails. I don't think they all even consider buying something from you. If they're visiting Cupid's Crossing, they might not be able to take fresh produce home with them."

Jordan hadn't changed his position, but neither was he interrupting her. About as much as she could ask for.

"I don't want to come up with a crazy idea, see it halfway through and forget it. In fact, I can do the initial startup labor and after that, it's minimal."

His eyes had narrowed. He wasn't sold.

"Okay, the initial layout of cash would be about twenty dollars, and I'll pay that, and if the idea doesn't work, I won't offer any more of them."

She'd bought supplies to make trail mix bags for hikers, her next suggestion, so this idea better work.

"What is this incredible idea?" The sarcasm was heavy, coming from the bearded man across from her. Still, sarcasm wasn't a no. And he hadn't walked away or told her not to keep talking. If you didn't listen to the tone, it was just a question.

"A donation box."

"A donation box?"

So far, so good. No immediate arguments.

"On the post, underneath the trail rules sign. A box that people can put money in, under a sign that says donations for maintenance of the trails are appreciated. A box could only cost about twenty bucks, right? And I could print up the sign and cover it in plastic for starters. It would just mean checking the box at the end of the day to see if any cash was in there. Not a lot of work, and I'll do it as long as I'm here."

She stopped, noting that her hands were twisted in her lap. Her stomach was a little swoopy. But she wasn't panicking. Probably because this wasn't connected to her professionally. Even for Jordan, it wasn't going to be thousands of dollars.

Jordan was sitting in the same position, but

he wasn't looking at her. He was staring past her. Considering her idea? He hadn't jumped in to say no. Not yet.

He'd agreed to hear her out though. Maybe she had to tell him she was done.

"That's it. That's the idea."

His eyes flicked toward her, but he didn't speak. She flexed her hands, making them lie flat. She glanced toward the stairs, wondering if she should just go up and read till it was time to sleep. She wanted to get up early to take care of the bread anyway.

He probably needed time to think about it. Come up with arguments against her suggestion.

"I've got some wood in the tool shed."

She looked back at Jordan. His arms weren't crossed any longer.

"I don't know that you're right, that people would put money in the box if they didn't have to. But I can make the box if you make up the sign."

Delaney felt her head nodding. Her relief was all out of proportion to the stakes. It wasn't her farm, she wasn't staying here permanently, and it wouldn't be for much longer. Surely a session or two with this therapist should be enough to get her to a place where she could leave the farm and return to being a professional chef.

He was leaning forward now, attention focused on whatever was going through his head.

"I can build the box while you're doing that thing tomorrow. It should be easy. A hinged lid with a slot in it. Sound right?"

She nodded again.

"And if no one puts any money in, it's no big loss. And you don't say anything to them, right? Otherwise it's not a fair test. Because the rest of the time, when you're not here, it's just if they bother to read the sign and decide to pay something."

She'd like to suggest a donation to any hikers she saw, but he had a point. Jordan certainly wouldn't give them a nudge when she wasn't here. But that was a good thing, not an idea that should bother her. It meant she was better, ready to return to New York.

She shook off that thought. "It's a deal." She took his hand when he held it out to her to shake. The palms were rough, calloused and dry. She felt guilty, because while she wouldn't say anything to the hikers, she was still going to try to make sure they didn't miss it, even if just by staring at the box until they caught on.

In any case, if one in ten people put a bit of money in, it would still be something. A start.

She had ideas, and not a lot of time to suggest them, so she needed this to work.

JORDAN WASN'T SURE if he wanted this idea to work or not.

It would be an easy enough way to get a bit more cash flowing in. And the clock was ticking on his arrangement with his father. But his suspicion of easy cash flows was long ingrained. He was pretty sure Delaney had more ideas. Just the thought of her wanting to make additional changes made his skin itch.

Jordan smoothed sandpaper over the box he'd built. It was rough, plain, a clear afterthought. It would need to be painted. He also had a flat piece of plywood, ready for the note that Delaney thought would jolt people into giving money to him.

He set down the sandpaper. It wasn't like he didn't have ideas of his own. The whole organic plan had been his, from start to finish.

Once the farm was his, once he had the security of a bank account balance to weather risks, then he could take a chance, try something new. Something that didn't have a sure return attached to it. Like adding animals. He'd like that, but after what his father had done to the cattle, he wasn't going to attempt that until the farm was his.

Jordan played it as safe as he could. He'd had the farm certified organic because there was a demand for that, and if the demand ceased, he could return to farming the way it had been done before.

Mariah had talked him into opening up the hiking trails last year, but that hadn't cost much beyond his labor, and it brought people to the farm to buy his produce. At least, that was the intention. The corn maze was there because his father had already spent the money, and Jordan didn't want to dig it all up when he'd lost the first crop anyway.

Mariah had more ideas that he'd turned down. He didn't think it would be as easy to say no to Delaney.

He wiped the box clean, carefully examining the joins, then tucked it under his arm to take to Delaney to inspect. He'd left her alone most of the afternoon. He didn't know how things had gone with the therapist, but he knew he wouldn't have wanted to be asked about it, so he gave her the space he'd have liked for himself.

The kitchen smelled amazing. The aroma

of fresh baked bread this morning had almost dragged him from his bed. He pulled in a breath. Something with chicken again.

He was going to miss this when she was gone.

Delaney turned to him when he entered the kitchen, and her gaze focused on the box. Her eyes widened, and she gave a big smile.

"That's perfect."

He set it on the table. Delaney wiped her hands on a cloth and walked over. Her fingers smoothed over the surface.

"I need to paint it before I put it up."

She looked up. "I could do that, if you leave the paint and brush out."

He let his eyes wander over her face, checking for any indication of whether the session had upset her. If it had, she'd recovered. A few days ago, he wouldn't have known, but he'd learned some of her tells now. Her hands were loose, her shoulders down. He relaxed.

"I'll do that. What smells so good? And thank you again."

Delaney shrugged. "I'm keeping my hand in. I've been putting the leftovers in your freezer, so you'll have meals after I leave."

There was no reason that should hit him, make him feel like he was scrambling for air.

He'd always known she'd be leaving. There was no more chance of a future for them now than there had been in high school.

"I'll wash up now." He escaped from the kitchen, needing to get himself under control.

He'd had a crush on Delaney Carter in high school, and that had been stupid enough. Reviving that crush as an adult was asking for trouble. He had to be smarter.

He wanted to help her, but if his father found out, Jordan would lose the most important thing in his life now, the farm.

CHAPTER TEN

TWO DAYS LATER, when Jordan came in from the field, he paused at the edge of the parking lot. Delaney's car was there but hadn't moved since Mariah had brought it over. There were no other cars, but he'd seen some during the day.

He looked at the house but didn't see Delaney in any of the lit windows. He was curious but didn't want her to know he'd started to believe in her idea. He walked quietly over to the donation box he'd set up on the post this morning.

He lifted the lid and saw nothing. He felt back into the corners with his fingers, since the light had faded, and felt nothing there.

Disappointment. He was disappointed that her idea hadn't worked. He shouldn't be. He didn't need her convincing him to try out any more ideas. But he didn't want her disappointed. Which meant he was stupider than he should be.

He went to the kitchen door, determined not to mention the box. No need for Delaney to know her idea was a bust, not yet. Maybe tomorrow would be different. He toed off his boots, enjoying the aroma of another wonderful meal. He was sorry for the reasons that had brought Delaney here, but he wasn't sorry that he got to enjoy her cooking.

He stepped in the kitchen, and almost got an armful of Delaney.

"It worked."

It took time for the words to make sense to him. His vision was full of Delaney, grinning ear to ear, bouncing on the spot in front of him, holding something out in her hand.

He finally looked down. A handful of dollar bills.

"What?"

She shoved the money into his hand. "I saw some hikers read the sign and walk away, but the next group reached into their pockets. I didn't see what everyone did, but there's thirty-five dollars here. That's more than the cost of the box, right? So it's working."

Jordan looked at the money in his hand, and then smoothed it out. He counted it. A ten, three fives, and ten one-dollar bills. Just like she'd said.

"Really?"

People didn't just give you money, not unless you worked for it. But they had. Delaney was right.

The joy on her face made him glow from the inside.

"People appreciate what you've done, and they're willing to give money so you can keep it up."

She was right. And maybe even more surprisingly, no one had stolen the money while it was sitting in the box.

"I admit that I was wrong. Though this was only one day."

She nodded, excitement unabated.

"Yeah, I know. But even if this only happened a few days a week, it would help, right?"

Anything would help. He found himself adding up numbers.

"It will. Thank you."

"Good." She whirled around. "Because I have something else."

Immediately, his body tensed up. He prepared to resist anything she said. He wasn't ready for this. Too much change, too short a time. He'd had a lifetime to build up his resistance.

Delaney was back in front of him, this time

holding a spoon in one hand, her other cupped below it.

"Try this?"

"Whaa—"

His question was cut off when she shoved the spoon into his open mouth. Then she slid it back out again.

He was almost afraid to close his lips, unsure what it was.

Her eyes widened. "It's okay. It's just trail mix."

Yes, trail mix fit. He crunched on the mixture, identifying nuts and coconut and seeds. There were other ingredients he couldn't name, but they all harmonized into one amazing taste.

He swallowed and met Delaney's anxious gaze.

"How is it?"

"It's good." He hesitated. "But why did you stick a spoonful of trail mix in my mouth?"

She tapped the spoon on her palm. "It's another idea I have."

"Force feeding people trail mix?"

A smile ghosted over her lips. "No, but you could sell this in the store."

Another idea. He wanted to say no. He bit his lip.

Delaney sighed and her shoulders dropped.

His instinctive response, to say no to something new, battled with his urge to make her happy. After a moment of struggle, the happy urge won out and he said, "Tell me about it. Just let me clean up first."

The light came back into her expression, and despite his worry, he felt good. He passed by the table, already set, the aroma of warm and welcoming food urging him on. He slipped up the stairs to the washroom, eager to see what today's dinner was.

Eager to see what had lit her up.

This wasn't good. But it didn't stop him.

She was at the table when he got back downstairs, a dish of pasta in front of both place settings. He sat down, and she waited for him to take a bite. It surprised him, the way she waited for his response each time, as if he was some important food critic who knew how to judge this.

"Delaney, if you weren't already a chef, I'd suggest you take it up as a career. This is really good…"

He trailed off as her face fell for a moment. He took a guess as to what had upset her.

"You're going to get back in a restaurant, I'm sure of it."

She shook off her distress. "Of course. And

thanks. It's been a nice break, just to cook for the fun of it. No pressure."

He wanted her happy again. So, surprising her as well as himself, he asked "What's this new idea?"

"It's connected to the hikers again. I wanted to come up with something that you could sell them. I mean, they can't really eat a cob of corn or a potato on the trails. But something like this—" She nodded her head at the end of the table where she had a couple of sandwich bags filled with the trail mix.

Objections tried to push out of his mouth, but he held them back.

"I know some of your questions but let me try to answer them. This is all stuff I bought at the store in Oak Hill, so you can get the ingredients. I can leave the measurements—the most important part is the seasonings, not the particular combination of nuts and seeds. You could mix up a batch once a week and sell it till it ran out.

"I can test it out this week, see if there's a demand."

She paused.

He flicked through the objections in his head, trying to come up with the least deflating ones.

"How will anyone even know to ask for it? The hikers don't normally come in the shop." That was a reasonable question, wasn't it?

"You can put it on your website. Also, I can put up a sign at the start of the trail, just to get the information out there. And maybe when they stop by the shop after their hike, they'll see it and buy it. I thought I'd have some to give out as a sample for now, to get people to try it."

He still had objections. Sure, it might not take a long time to throw the stuff together but putting it into little bags would be fiddly and time-consuming work. He could add it onto his list of things to do, but that list was already too long.

He wouldn't stop her from testing it out. He had no doubts, after seeing her talking to people about carrots and beans that she could convince people to try it, and he wouldn't deny it tasted good. Everything she made was good. And trail mix was easy to carry while walking, and probably just what people needed to keep up their energy.

But this wasn't his dream. It wasn't anything that made him happy, and that he found enjoyable. He loved the farm, the planting, growing, tending, and harvesting. Being outside, working with the soil, that was why he loved his life here. Mixing up food and selling it—that wasn't what he wanted. He didn't want to keep track of levels of nuts and seeds and stock up every week and order in the bags.

He appreciated that she was taking care to work with his risk averse propensity. But she didn't get what he wanted.

The hiking trails, the corn maze…the trail mix. It was just to get enough money so that the farm could be his. He didn't dream of a big farm, with dozens of employees making trail mix and soup and whatever else was on her mind. He liked his quiet. He liked a place that was just his.

He nodded, and told her to give it a try, but it was all an act. And underneath, there was a flutter of panic. He was losing control, and that petrified him.

OKAY, SOMETHING WAS WRONG. Jordan was not happy about the trail mix idea. Delaney barely tasted the Carbonera, giving Jordan sidelong glances as she tried to figure it out.

The donation box worked. She'd come up with an idea to collect revenue that wasn't going to take up his time or be impossible to sustain. Maybe it was too much all at once?

Maybe he needed time to adjust to these new ideas instead of her dropping them on him all at once?

The problem was that she only had so much time here. And she wanted to do what she could while she had the opportunity. It was important to her that she accomplish something while she was here. That she'd leave an imprint.

Her chest tightened and she froze, tried to relax. She closed her eyes and added this to the list of things that caused her to tense up. Next session with the therapist she'd have to mention it. Then she opened her eyes and focused on the kitchen, the food, and Jordan across from her.

Jordan complimented her on the dinner, and she smiled and thanked him while her brain spun.

Nelson, and then thanks to Nelson, Delaney, had hurt Jordan back when they were teenagers, and it bothered her. Yes, she'd been hurt as well, but she had the support of her family, and all Jordan had was his dad, and that man was too obsessed with his own pain to help Jordan. Probably Jordan had to be more of a parent to his father.

This was a way to make up for that. It wasn't

just for her. She liked Jordan. When they'd been seeing each other, back in high school, he'd been a refuge. A change from her competitive family, he'd been someone who liked her just as she was. He never pushed, never asked for anything but her presence. For those stolen moments they'd been together he had provided an oasis of calm, a chance for her to relax and believe she was enough.

Just like he was doing now.

There'd been something sweet and innocent about that time. Learning to kiss, learning to function with those bubbles in her stomach whenever she was with him. Feeling a sense of possibility, and love.

When Nelson burst into her room, telling her that he'd intercepted her meeting with Jordan and that Jordan had admitted he was using her, she'd been devastated. It was too easy to believe that once again she was a Carter first, not Delaney. That no one would love her just for herself.

It hadn't just been a heartbreak. It had broken her belief in herself. She hadn't realized it at the time, but ever since, she'd been striving to be accepted. She'd gone to boarding school, and worked hard at her classes, but she never could get grades like Nelson did so easily.

"Delaney?"

Jordan was looking at her with a worried frown. She blinked, returning to the present and the farmhouse.

"You okay?"

"Yeah, just lost in thought. Did you need something?"

"I just asked how you ended up being a chef. I don't remember that being something you wanted. Back…"

She hadn't known what she wanted to be back then. At fifteen, there'd been a lot of family pressure and she'd been afraid to make the wrong decision. She certainly hadn't thought of being a chef. More likely a doctor, lawyer, engineer. Jordan wouldn't know what had led her to this path.

"I used to enjoy being in the kitchen. Before we moved to stay here with Grandmother, I hung out in our kitchen at home. Helped our housekeeper making cookies and things like that."

"Your parents didn't mind?"

"They didn't know." They'd been too busy with work and networking. Delaney didn't want to think about her parents' opinions right now. She still could feel the sting when they'd asked why she was so clingy, why she wasn't more like her brother. She pushed the painful thoughts aside before her breathing choked up again.

"Then later, after I left Carter's Crossing, when I was home from boarding school, they had a party and the caterer hurt herself during the meal. I'd been hanging out in the kitchen again, watching what she did, and since there was no one who could step in, I did. Everyone was complimentary and something clicked."

Jordan was watching her intently. It was flattering, that someone was interested in her story.

"I'd been struggling in school."

Jordan raised his eyebrows.

"Not like failing. I got okay marks. But Nelson always did so much better. I was never going to do as well as he did. And I thought, this is something I can be good at. Something different. A totally different kind of job that wouldn't mean competing with him. He'd just got into the University of California veterinary school. I wasn't going to do as well as him at university, but this…

"My parents helped me get into culinary school in Paris. And I was really good at it.

So… Peter and I came back here and worked in New York, and well, now I'm here."

In spite of everything, she still wanted to cook. Food made sense. Food brought people together. And food was a totally different path from her brother, or her parents, or cousins and aunts and uncles. One where she could stand out on her own.

Food was still something she could do. Just not at the Mill. And her therapist wanted her to figure out why that was. Delaney was also supposed to share with people about her panic attack, as much as that thought chilled her.

She looked at Jordan, who'd stood up to clear his plate and wash the dishes she hadn't been able to take care of previously. He insisted on doing that each evening. He didn't want her to do everything.

Maybe it was difficult for him to accept help. It was for her. Maybe he didn't like her coming up with ideas and plans for the farm when he felt it put him in her debt.

Maybe if she talked about her panic attacks, and shared like she was supposed to, tested it out with Jordan, maybe that would help him see that she didn't think she was superior, or judging him.

Because years ago, he'd accepted her. And while she'd thought all this time that he'd been using her, she'd been wrong. If Jordan Everton thought she was weak or a failure, it wouldn't matter, would it? She wouldn't see him again after this interlude. But if he thought she was still okay, maybe other people would to.

"Um, Jordan, could we talk?"

Jordan looked at her over his shoulder as he rinsed their plates in the sink.

"You want to talk?"

She heard the reluctance in his voice. He didn't want to talk, so that trail mix thing had done something.

"It was my therapist's suggestion."

His expression, his posture, everything changed. Tension gone, ease restored between them. He nodded. "Okay, I'll just finish this up."

Delaney boiled water for tea and put some baking on a plate to take into the living room to nibble on while they talked. And to distract her. The change in Jordan convinced her this was the right move.

As much as she hated the idea, she had to open up, and he was the person she was most comfortable to start that with. Because his opinion didn't matter, right? Or maybe it was because this place, the farm, was a place she felt safe. She wasn't sure why. Maybe because this was temporary, or maybe because there wasn't any pressure with Jordan. Whatever, this was a happy place for her right now.

Delaney curled up in the chair in the living room, and Jordan sat on the couch. He stayed quiet, waiting for her to lead. She wasn't used to that. In her family, there was always a push to control the conversation, to take charge, to make sure things went the way you wanted.

She rubbed her palm over her forehead.

"This sucks, you know?"

Jordan passed her a piece of the zucchini bread she'd made. "Life often does."

She broke off a corner of the bread and put it in her mouth. It was good. Maybe just a touch less vanilla next time, but maybe she was being too picky. She loved baking, and she needed to get back to it professionally. And to do that, she had to say these things.

She swallowed.

"I'm supposed to work on my triggers, what causes a panic attack."

She kept her eyes on the bread in her hand.

"And I'm supposed to tell people that it's happened. Not hide it."

A pause. Jordan's voice was quiet. "Which of those is more difficult?"

She shot him a glance. "The second."

"Why?"

Delaney sighed and set the bread back down. "Because it's a weakness. A failing. Carters aren't supposed to have breakdowns."

Jordan's brow creased. "Are panic attacks the same as breakdowns?"

Delaney shrugged.

"I don't know. But I hate having to tell everyone. I didn't ask for this!" Her voice was loud and she struggled to rein in the emotion.

"No one does. Your family will understand you're going through something, though, won't they?"

Delaney felt her breathing speed up. "I don't know. I mean, grandmother was widowed with four small children when she wasn't much older than me, and she managed the mill and raised her kids."

"She had help though, didn't she? Probably people to babysit the kids and other people working at the mill."

That wasn't the point. "But she didn't break down."

Jordan frowned. "You didn't either. She didn't have to face someone with a gun."

"Neither did I! So why am I the one struggling?" Delaney rubbed her forehead again.

"I don't know. Because you feel guilty?"

She shook her head. "Because I'm not strong. I'm not a good Carter."

"What!"

Delaney flinched. "Why are you yelling?"

"Why would you think you're not a good person because you had a panic attack?"

Delaney waved her hands around in frustration. "I didn't say I wasn't a good person, it's just that I'm a Carter and we need to be better."

Jordan stood up. "Delaney, I'm trying to be supportive here. But it sounds like you think your family is better than others? Is that what they expect from you?"

She'd offended him. "I'm sorry, that's obviously not what I meant. It's just…"

She ran her fingers through her hair, getting them stuck in her ponytail.

"It's not that we're better people but we're supposed to *do* better. There are expectations. We have advantages, so we're supposed to use them."

"That sounds like the same thing."

She loosened her fingers and shook her head.

"No, not really. Being a good person isn't about success-some successful people are total jerks. I don't want to be a jerk, but I am supposed to be successful."

She risked another glance. He had a heavy frown on his face, and his hands were on his hips.

"But who decides what's successful?" He asked, quietly.

Her mouth opened, but she didn't know what to say. Surely, this was obvious. Success was being good at what you did. Being one of, if not the best. Being known and respected. Financially successful.

"Not sure I qualify as a success, Delaney. Not for Carter standards. But I know what I want, and I'm happy with what I have and that's good enough for me. Maybe you need to figure out what real success is, and what the price for a Carter success might be."

Delaney blinked back tears that were gathering in her eyes. He didn't understand. He hadn't been brought up like her. He couldn't be right, could he?

He called Ranger. "I'm going to take Ranger out, then I'm going to head upstairs. Thanks again for the meal."

Delaney watched him go, thinking something big had happened here. She just wasn't sure if she'd ended up more confused than ever.

CHAPTER ELEVEN

JORDAN LAY IN his bed, staring at the ceiling. Sleep evaded him.

He was troubled after hearing Delaney talk about success. About how Carters had to be "better".

It shouldn't surprise him. His dad had warned him about Carters all his life. He'd thought Delaney was different back in high school, and then she'd dropped him after what her brother had said to her. He'd been hurt she hadn't even tried to talk to him. He hadn't known then that his father had talked to her. Or more likely at her. But now he felt sure that without Nelson, or his dad, they still wouldn't have made it. He didn't meet the Carter's standards for success.

What had he thought? That since he and Delaney were spending time together, maybe she'd be interested in him again, now that that high school misunderstanding was cleared up? Not a chance. Maybe, back in high school, maybe then she'd have been willing to settle for someone like him. He'd never know for sure. But not now, not when her idea of success would frame a panic attack as a failure.

It wasn't just that he didn't fit her vision of success, he didn't want to. His father had spent his life trying to find that path and it had cost too much for Jordan and his mother. Maybe even his father. Jordan didn't know if the man had ever been happy.

Was Jordan?

He was content. Something his father had never learned to be. And if the choice was contentment or a life of vain searching for some peak of success to make him happy, he'd stay with content.

He would, but Delaney wouldn't. After what she'd said today, he knew she'd find some way to deal with her panic attacks and get back on her success track.

For him, success would mean owning the farm Coming home from working in the fields to someone who shared the same goal. That would never be Delaney. He just had to get through this next short period without thinking she was interested in more than she was.

In more than he was.

He punched his pillow and rolled over.

JORDAN HAD MORE deliveries to make the next day and was happy to be off on his own with Ranger. He told Delaney she was welcome to sell the trail mix, but he didn't change anything on the website. That trail mix was only lasting as long as Delaney was.

When he came in at dinnertime, another incredible smell welcoming him, she didn't say anything about the donation box, or the trail mix, though he noticed there were some bags of another mix lined up on the counter. She was quiet, asking how his deliveries went, but not offering any information about her day.

And that was his fault. He didn't need to take his disappointment out on her.

"How were things here?" He took a moment to savor the chili, today's 'experiment'.

She glanced up, her own spoon still on the table.

"Good."

"Any donations?"

A foreshadow of a smile had her eyes creasing. She reached into her pocket and pulled out some more bills.

Jordan made sure he was smiling too. "That's great Delaney. It was an excellent idea. The recipes still doing well?"

She nodded. "Someone today asked if I had

more vegetarian options, so I promised I'd get some. She's coming back next week."

That was all good. He could take that last step.

"And the trail mix?"

"I put some out as a sampler. And I sold all I had made up."

He hoped people didn't get too accustomed to it, but he didn't have to be a jerk about it. This was helping her, giving her confidence, and a chance to keep her creativity and love of food intact. He might not like that her goals were so financial, but he didn't want to hurt her.

"That's why you've got those bags lined up, for tomorrow?"

"I've tried a slightly different recipe, changed up the seasonings. I'll see what people like best."

Her fork pushed some food around on her plate. "Would you try it, let me know what you think?"

"Sure." It was just nuts and seeds, after all. He didn't need to make an issue out of it.

That brought back her full-fledged smile, and for that, he'd even make up trail mix himself.

JORDAN WAS COMING AROUND. He was accepting her ideas, giving her a chance to show him new opportunities. She had her next step planned, but she needed to mend bridges with him as well.

He was gone for the morning, and kept busy all afternoon, but she had him at her mercy at dinnertime. He didn't try to disguise how much he liked what she cooked. Once he'd had enough to take the edge off his appetite, she asked her question.

"People at the shop have talked about the corn maze. Would it be okay if I looked at it?"

Jordan paused in what had been a flatteringly eager decimation of a simple roasted chicken with garlic mashed potatoes and maple basted carrots.

"Of course. Want me to show it to you tomorrow?"

"Thanks. I'd like that."

She drew in a breath. "I also need to apologize."

This time Jordan set down his fork. "Not sure what you think you need to apologize for."

"I know you think I'm too focused on money and reputation, and because I dismissed your lack of interest in that, it sounded like I thought we were better than you."

"We being Carters?"

She felt the blush on her cheeks.

"When I describe the priorities my parents have, I know it sounds…arrogant and superficial."

Jordan leaned back in his chair. "I remember what you told me back in high school Delaney. Your parents left you in Carter's Crossing for a big project they were working on. You didn't want them to leave you behind, and they told you not to be clingy, to be more like Nelson. And he always had everything come easily, so you were always competing with him. Still are.

"I'm just not sure why you still have to do that, or how much of a threat he is working as a vet here in Cupid's Crossing."

She'd never been sure he really got it, back when they were kids. But then, she'd never understood just what his father was like till she'd talked to him that one time.

"Our parents thought healthy competition would drive us to push ourselves to be our best. And in theory, I get that. But it's difficult when you're competing with your family, not a classmate or someone you're trying to run faster than in track.

"When I told them I wanted to be a chef, I expected them to tell me that I could do better, or that they were disappointed. But instead, they just told me to make them proud. And I did."

"And that made you happy?"

She frowned. That wasn't the point.

"Peter and I finally opened our restaurant and it was great. We'd worked so hard, and things were going well. We got good reviews, and the bookings filled up so much that we had a waiting list for two months."

She could still feel that pride, when her parents came and saw just how well she'd done.

"That was just after Nelson's disastrous non-wedding to Zoey. For once, my parents were talking about me, not him. I didn't enjoy that he had gone through something like that, but I finally was the daughter they'd wanted."

Jordan had his arms crossed now, so he still wasn't getting it.

"Then Nelson was engaged to Mariah Van Dalton, and Grandmother was dating Gerald Van Dalton, and the shooting happened. My parents didn't want to talk about the restaurant and Peter and me. I know they didn't want to upset me, but it was hard to be overlooked again.

"Maybe that sounds stupid to you, but it was a good time, when the restaurant was doing so well. It was busy and stressful, but I was proud of what I'd done. And I'm glad you're happy here, and that you're getting what you want. I don't mean that in a condescending way. We grew up differently, so our goals are different. I don't want to belittle what you want in life, and I guess I just want you to understand why I want to pursue my goal."

Jordan looked at her, and finally spoke. "I know I'm messed up in a lot of ways, and my life has been different. But what I want makes me feel better. You're sure yours does?"

Delaney could feel the irritation bubbling up again. "Why would you ask that?"

Jordan stood and picked up his dishes. He headed to the sink. "When you talk about your restaurant, you talk about the number of reservations and your parents' praise, but not about the cooking, not like you do when you talk about recipes for people here. You talk about impressing your family, but not about them supporting you. I didn't have support either, but if I have a family, that's what it'll be like."

Delaney felt something under her skin when she thought about Jordan and his fictitious family, but she ignored it. Her family was supportive, weren't they? Nelson had deluged her with texts after the shooting. Her parents hadn't, but they'd helped her get into a great school in Paris. And cooking was a means to an end, not the end itself. Was farming an end in itself for Jordan?

She picked up her own plate. Didn't matter if it was or not. She needed to focus on her own life, and that meant getting back to New York. Still, despite the prickly farmer she was living with, she wasn't in a rush to leave.

DELANEY DID A lot of thinking that night. She hadn't understood how bad things had been for Jordan: too young to read between the lines back in high school. She hadn't understood how much he needed stability. But it was possible to be successful without taking on a lot of risk.

She had another idea brewing in the back of her brain. Without a restaurant to give her days focus and wanting a distraction from too much introspection relating to the panic attacks, she had discovered that the idea of helping Jordan make his farm more economically viable provided an outlet for her energy and creativity.

She'd been researching corn mazes. She'd see what Jordan's maze was like and then consider her options. She was supposed to tell people about the panic attacks, so she'd decided to start by discussing her ideas for the maze with Mariah and talking about what had happened at the Mill at the same time. She'd feel less pathetic, if she had something happening, something proactive and innovative and clever.

It wasn't that her family wouldn't be supportive of her, it's just that this would make her look weak. She'd wait to discuss the attacks with her parents until later. When she'd been in touch with Peter, so they had plans.

It was more fun to think about the corn maze.

DELANEY HAD NEVER been in a corn maze. There hadn't been one in the area when she grew up in Carter's Crossing, and afterwards she'd lived in urban centers. Somehow, though, her imagination had built up something…more.

Jordan took her over after lunch. By unspoken agreement, they'd left that last conversation unresolved. It was easy to push conflict and problems aside on a beautiful fall day. The leaves were at the peak of their color, and the hills around the farm were like a perfect postcard celebrating autumn. The parking lot was full of hiker's cars. The air was crisp enough for a sweater, but warm enough to go without a hat or gloves.

Delaney drew in a deep breath of air, trying to identify what element in the air made that the perfect fall scent. When they arrived at the maze, Jordan stopped and she stared.

She wasn't sure what she'd expected, but it was just a field of corn. The stalks whispered together, and the sun was warm, and it wasn't a bad place to be on a fall day.

Delaney looked down the outside edge, trying to imagine the size. "How big is it?"

"Eight acres."

She wasn't sure if that was large for a corn maze or not. She should check.

"Is it the same every year?"

Jordan shook his head. "Over the winter, I look at maps online and pick a different one each year."

Delaney ran a hand down a leaf from the corn stalk. It was still green and smooth. "Is this where you get the corn you sell?"

Jordan felt a leaf near him, fingers rubbing over it. "No, this isn't corn for people."

"Then it's just a waste?"

"Once the maze closes in November, I harvest it, sell it to feed cattle."

Delaney looked at the tall stalks, stretching into the distance.

"So, how does this work?"

Jordan raised his brows. "You walk in, find the center, and keep walking till you're out."

Jordan should never, ever, be in charge of marketing.

"Okay, I'm game. It's not too difficult, is it?"

Jordan shrugged. "Some people get kinda lost."

Was it a complex pattern? She wished she'd asked for a map in advance now. "You have to be around the whole time, right? So you can get people out if they get lost."

Jordan nodded.

"You do have an unfair advantage, since you know the pattern."

Jordan's hands moved to his hips.

"It's not an unfair advantage since it's not a competition. I spend hours getting this set up every year. I couldn't forget my way if I tried."

Right. Not everything was a competition, but if she was in the maze with Nelson, they'd definitely want to be the first to solve it. Maybe that was messed up. Moving on.

"How long does it take?"

"An hour or two, usually."

Delaney pulled out her phone. "Okay, I'll call you if I get stuck, but don't count on that happening."

Jordan's smile peeked out. "I won't. But I'll have the phone anyway."

Delaney needed the opportunity to explore

the maze on her own and find out what it was like, if it would work for any of her ideas. As well, she knew Jordan was busy. The man never seemed to sit down between dawn and dusk, except for meals. So that was not disappointment she felt when he left her on her own. Definitely not.

She stepped out briskly onto the path.

It was quiet. The stalks of corn rustled, and she could hear birds, but no sounds of people at all. It was peaceful, and calm. She could relax and just be.

Jordan had set up stakes at each turning, with different colors and stripes, so it was possible to make sure you didn't keep coming back to the same corner. Delaney made some wrong turns, but after three quarters of an hour, she found herself at the center and was pleased. She took a selfie, and sent it to Jordan, to let him know she'd done it.

She took time to test the maze to see if any of her ideas would work. Something could be done here, in the middle. There was space for a table and chairs, not just the bench Jordan had placed here. Then they could have a flower for each couple as a souvenir. Maybe a celebratory drink. Mariah was always looking for proposal options…it would take some work, but this could be interesting.

Delaney made some notes on her phone, and then headed out to find the exit. She made some wrong turns. It didn't bother her, the way making mistakes often did. It was a beautiful day, she was enjoying the maze, and she had ideas to keep her mind busy.

Jordan was waiting for her at the exit when she came out.

"How did you know when I'd get here? Have you been waiting long?"

He shrugged, not answering. But it gave her a warm feeling inside.

DELANEY, KEEPING AN eye on the parking lot, started some serious research.

Other farms offering corn mazes made a much bigger deal out of it. Hayrides, petting zoos…it was a whole day adventure. And they charged more for the maze as well. Those farms were family farms, with more people involved to share the labor.

Delaney had no illusions that Jordan was going to set up hayrides or a petting zoo. But they could do something to make this more appealing. Corn mazes were mentioned as being great for dates, and that was where her idea came from. An evening for couples? Mariah could help with that. One night a week, maybe, on a Saturday say. Getting lost in the maze together…could be romantic.

Friday nights could be for groups who wanted to have fun and scare each other. And could they do something related to Hallowe'en?

She texted Mariah, asked if Mariah could stop by the next day. Jordan had deliveries to make, so Delaney would be on her own. She wanted to talk to Mariah about ideas for the maze before she tried them out on Jordan. Make sure there would be demand for the events, that Mariah would help with promoting them, and that Delaney had answers prepared for any objections.

She'd have to be very careful about how she presented this. She needed to show Jordan that it was okay to try new things. They didn't have to be a crazy leap, like his dad's schemes, just a little extra and the payoff could be big.

In the morning, she helped Jordan load up the truck. He was going to open the gate as he left, flipping the sign over. Then she was on her own. He hadn't suspected anything, as far as she could tell.

It was an hour later when she heard tires and recognized Mariah's car. But it was followed by Nelson's van. She should have known. At least Jordan wasn't here.

Delaney had been working in the store. Unless she was cooking in the house, it was where she spent her time. She stepped out to meet them. She wasn't happy to see her brother, but she was impressed that Mariah had been able to keep him away this long.

"Good morning, Mariah. What a surprise, Nelson. I didn't know you were invited."

Mariah glared at Nelson, and he closed his mouth on whatever he'd been planning to say.

"I couldn't keep him away, but he's heading to work and promised he'd just make sure you were okay before going on his way."

Delaney braced herself for whatever Nelson had to say. He surprised her by walking over and pulling her into a hug. He held her till she relaxed in his arms.

"Are you okay, Dee? I've been worried."

Of course, that was when the tears had to flood her eyes. Delaney blinked them back as she returned the hug. She could be resentful, angry and annoyed with her brother, but she knew he loved her, just as she loved him.

Jordan said her family didn't sound supportive. Weren't they? Maybe she was going to find out.

She released a long breath. "I'm, well, not totally fine, but I'm okay. I'm getting there."

Nelson frowned as he examined her. "What's up? This isn't like you."

Delaney had hoped to talk about her maze ideas with Mariah and just throw in casually something about how she was seeing a therapist about her panic attacks and oh, look, she had something to do, but that plan was shot to bits.

Delaney stepped back from her brother. Mariah had probably told him this, but she needed to say it.

"I had a panic attack."

CHAPTER TWELVE

DELANEY'S BREATHING SPED up and her hands felt tingly, but she let the feelings do their thing. Her therapist said she had to feel them, experience them, and prove they weren't going to hurt her. She focused on her breathing, and the disturbing sensations started to subside.

This was just from admitting it to her brother.

"What? When? Was it something Jordan did? Where is he, anyway?"

Delaney held up her hand.

"Jordan is making a delivery, and he's done nothing. Nothing but be helpful. It happened when I went to the Mill—that's why Jordan brought me here."

Mariah gripped Nelson's arm, and he drew in a breath.

"Was that when you needed the key?"

Mariah hadn't told Nelson. That relaxed her. Mariah was her friend, not just Nelson's wife.

"Yep. Jordan found me huddling around the back of the Mill. I just…my body felt weird when I walked into the kitchen, and my head wasn't attached, and I couldn't stay there. I ran out, leaving my keys and phone inside. Jordan drove me here. I've reached out to the therapist who's been helping our employees at the restaurant."

Yep, there it was. The pity look.

Delaney uncurled her fists.

"Why didn't you call me?" Nelson looked confused. He didn't get it.

"I didn't want anyone to know. And I thought, after I knew what it was, that it wasn't anything serious. I had Jordan take me back to the Mill, and tried again, but I couldn't do it. Just couldn't work in that kitchen. We came back to the farm, and I'm helping him while I work this out in exchange for staying here."

"Why here? Why not come to us? We'd have been happy to help."

Mariah nudged him. "Maybe she didn't need more family hovering over her."

Delaney knew Mariah would be the one to get it.

Nelson looked offended. "I don't hover."

"How often were you texting her after the shooting at the restaurant?"

"But, that was, I mean, I was worried."

He had been, and he'd texted a lot. It had been

more pressure, to respond and assure him she was doing okay, even if she wasn't.

"I appreciate that. It was scary. But I think I needed time to work things out. And I'm sorry Nelson but being with you wasn't going to help me."

She didn't like the hurt look on his face, but it was the truth. She didn't know how to explain it to him without hurting him.

"Nelson, you know what I was thinking when I got to the Mill, before I had the panic attack? I thought, so this is failure."

"Why? I mean, I know you're going to get back to New York and get your restaurant going again, but that wasn't your fault. And you were helping Mariah and Grandmother."

Delaney sighed. "Do you think Mother and Dad were going to be bragging to their friends that their daughter was running the kitchen at the Mill in Cupid's Crossing? That they wouldn't have been disappointed?"

Delaney's voice broke.

"But it's just temporary." Nelson said.

"Is it? Is anyone going to want to eat in a restaurant with my name on it? Or are they going to be afraid that they'll get shot? It's not like it isn't already super competitive in the city. It doesn't take much to lose your reputation."

Nelson blinked, not familiar with anything as cutthroat as that. At least she didn't think veterinary medicine was that competitive. But he'd had his own challenges. He should be able to understand.

"How did you feel after Zoey didn't show up for your wedding? Did you want to be around family?"

His posture deflated. She didn't want to bring up his worst time, but he needed to understand. "No, but that was my fault."

"You saw Mom and Dad's faces. They were so disappointed. And this sounds so petty, but for a while, I was the golden child. Peter and I were opening the restaurant and they were bragging to their friends and that felt so good.... but then you married Mariah and the shooting at the restaurant happened and suddenly it felt like I'd never make them that proud again. That I was a failure."

Comprehension flared on his face. "I'm sorry you feel that way, Dee. What can I do?"

There it was. This was the support she needed from him.

"I just need time. I'm working with this therapist and figuring out what happened and how I can deal with it."

"But you can't do that with us?"

Delaney shook her head. "We've been rivals all our lives, Nelson."

He frowned, puzzled. "I never thought that, Dee."

"I know. You were always the one coming out on top. Mom and Dad were so proud of you—your grades, playing hockey—it was like everything you did worked. And maybe it's my fault but I always felt like I was trying to catch up.

"Right now, here, I don't feel any pressure like that. I've done some things that make me feel like I'm accomplishing something, but there's no pressure. And I need that right now."

Nelson thrust a hand through his hair. "I really wish you didn't feel that way."

"See, that's why this wouldn't work. Jordan has no expectations of me, so I can feel how I want, guilt free, and hopefully, soon be able to function properly again."

"And he's not causing any problems? Nothing I need to worry about?"

Delaney rolled her eyes. "No. He'll be the one glad to see me go."

Nelson snorted.

Mariah patted his chest. "Okay, now that you've got all that macho stuff taken care of, can you let Delaney and I talk? I told you you didn't have to come."

Delaney took a breath and decided to be the bigger person. "It was good to see you Nelson, and I appreciate that you're worried, but this is what I need right now. For a long time, I've been going non-stop, and there was so much stress with the restaurant. I was burning out anyway, before the panic attack. This is the right place for me to be."

Nelson stepped forward and pulled her into another hug. "Okay, I'll get to work. Call me if you need me, anytime."

Delaney hugged him back but didn't make any promises. She couldn't imagine calling her brother, not yet. He stepped back and dropped a kiss on Mariah's lips. "See you tonight?"

She nodded and shooed him away. They watched him get into the van and turn around, before driving away.

Mariah turned to Delaney. "He means well."

Delaney smirked. "What do they say about the road to hell?"

"I'm trying to rein him in if he gets carried away, but he is improving. Today. Well, he needed to see you."

There was a tone of censure in Mariah's voice and Delaney flinched.

Yes, she should have called. Maybe gone

to see Mariah and Nelson. But right now, the most important thing was to prioritize her own wellbeing.

"I didn't mean to upset him, but I'm dealing with a mental health issue here. I have to take care of that first."

Mariah frowned. "You couldn't have called? Your family worries about you."

"And my family is part of my problem. You knew where I was, and you would have heard if anything happened."

Mariah stared at her, and then sighed. "Okay. What was this thing you wanted to discuss?"

Delaney appreciated that Mariah was letting it go. "How romantic can a corn maze be?"

JORDAN FOUND DELANEY in the shop when he returned. She was working on her laptop and told him there were sandwiches waiting for him in the kitchen. Something seemed different with her, but a car pulled into the lot, so he went to the house where sandwiches on freshly homemade bread were on a plate under plastic wrap, and, since people were still with her once he finished, went on to the fields. The air was getting cooler, the days shorter. The leaves were a kaleidoscope of color around him, but he didn't have time to admire. He had more than enough work to keep him busy, even with Delaney's help.

When he finished what he could do for the day, he returned to the house, his footsteps rustling the leaves that were falling from the trees. Another job he'd need to get on to soon. As he stepped into the kitchen, his nose was again treated to a delightful aroma. He took off his boots and coat. Delaney turned from the stove, her cheeks flushed and a smile in her eyes.

He felt that smile, down to his core. It warmed him, relaxed him while at the same time wound up something at the base of his spine. He smiled in return, and wanted nothing more than to go to her, wrap his arms around her, bury his nose in her hair and immerse himself in her.

He couldn't do that. Instead, he stuffed his hands in his pockets, and imprinted the image into his memory for when she was gone. Someday, if he was lucky, once he had the farm settled, he could look for something like this. He'd thought he was content, just Ranger and him. Settled. Calm. Secure.

But Delaney was reminding him that there

was more. Ranger wasn't going to be enough for him, not forever. It would be a disruption, going out, meeting people, but there was an empty place inside him, and he couldn't ignore it.

For now, though, he had Delaney. And with her here, smiling at him when he came in, ready to hear what he'd done and to tell him about her day, that added immensely to his life. He would take whatever he could get with her until she was gone.

"Corn chowder and bread. Went a little simpler tonight, but it was a recipe I wanted to work out for the store."

Did she think he was complaining?

"I'll clean up quick."

Another smile saw him off for a shower.

As Jordan ran the towel over his hair (which was getting out of hand, he needed to find some time to get it cut) it occurred to him that Delaney might not want to cook every night. He should…well, he couldn't offer to cook himself, because he wasn't much good at it, and she was obviously used to good food. Not the prepared foods he often got for himself because they were easy and fast.

But would she want to go out? With him?

Maybe he should offer or ask if she wanted to take a night off to see Mariah or Nelson. He didn't like the feel of that, but he needed to get over himself and think about her.

Soup was on the table, along with bread that was still warm from the oven. She made it hard for him to even consider eating any food but hers.

Jordan sat. He searched for the right words.

Delaney jumped up to get water for them.

"Wait. I can do that."

She was already on her way back. "It's okay."

"I wanted you to know, if you want to take a night off, or a day or whatever, you can. You know that, right?"

Delaney set his glass in front of him and sat down across from him in what had become her seat.

"I could, but I don't want to."

Excellent. That made him want to grin. But did she really not want to?

"You don't get tired of cooking all the time?"

She shook her head at him. "I picked the wrong career if that's the case. I like it. I feel good when I prepare something and see people enjoy it."

This was the way she should feel about working in her restaurant, but he kept that thought to himself. "Maybe you deserve a break."

Delaney leaned back, hands dropping to her lap.

"Are you trying to tell me something Jordan? Do *you* need a break from me?"

This was coming out all wrong.

"No, it's not that. I just… I don't want to take advantage." And he didn't want her to resent him. If she did, she'd leave even sooner.

Delaney's eyes widened. "You're not, I promise. I feel like I'm taking advantage of you. I kinda forced you to let me stay here, while I work out my problems. I enjoy making our meals, I really do."

He tried to gauge the sincerity in her expression.

"You'll say if you need a break? Want to leave?" *Please don't want to leave yet.*

Delaney put her hand over his, and he felt the touch all the way up his arm.

"I'm not ready to leave yet. I'm working on that, and I can't tell you how grateful I am that you're giving me this chance to hide out from my real life."

Right. He had to remember this wasn't her real life.

"I'd be climbing the walls without something to do, and yes, cooking is my occupation, but I haven't been able to do it since—" She swallowed and he turned his hand to grip hers, to offer her reassurance like she'd done for him. "Since the shooting at the restaurant. I didn't have a kitchen to work in, and there was so much going on I didn't even try to cook at home.

"And this kind of cooking, it's different. I really am enjoying it."

He nodded, reassured. He noticed they were still holding hands and drew his back, reluctantly.

"Still, maybe we should go out sometime." That sounded like he was asking her on a date. Was he? "Go where you don't have to cook."

Delaney frowned at him. "Are you really saying you want a break from my cooking?"

Why couldn't he manage basic people skills? He shook his head. "No, I don't think I've ever had better food than what you've made here, in this little kitchen."

She smiled again.

"So, you were just trying to be nice."

Jordan felt his cheeks flushing.

"Thank you for thinking about me. But I'm good. I'm getting better and being here helps.

Let's just agree to say something if this stops working, okay?"

Jordan put a spoonful of—how could Delaney make a simple corn chowder taste this good?—soup into his mouth and nodded. He didn't think he'd be the one to want to stop their arrangement, so the agreement was easy.

Well, until his dad returned.

It was when Jordan was washing the dishes, with Delaney drying them and putting them away that she dropped the hammer.

"Mariah was here today."

The soup pot almost slipped out of Jordan's hands. "She was?"

Delaney nodded. "I asked her to come over, because I wanted to discuss something with her. Full disclosure, Nelson came by as well, but I managed to convince him everything was fine, and he left again."

Jordan closed his jaw against any comments. Delaney had handled her brother, and Jordan hadn't had to talk to him. He jerked his head in a nod. He wasn't going to lie and say he was glad Nelson had stopped by. He didn't know what kind of contact Delaney maintained with her family.

"I thought about what you'd said, about family support, and kind of surprised both Nelson and me by letting him be supportive. Not sure it'll happen with my parents, but, it's a step."

"I'm glad."

"Will you hear me out if I tell you what I talked to Mariah about?"

Jordan pulled the plug from the sink and took a breath. Delaney hadn't been talking about something personal to Mariah, it seemed. She had another idea for the farm. He didn't want her pushing her ideas on him. But she looked so happy about whatever it was, and she wasn't here for long. He leaned back against the sink, waiting to hear what she'd come up with.

"I had an idea for the corn maze."

His eye twitched, but he nodded and let her continue.

"Corn mazes are great for dates. And Cupid's Crossing is promoting romance, so I wondered about having a couple of nights with a romance theme. That's what I wanted to talk to Mariah about, and she thought it was a great idea."

Jordan didn't listen to everything she said. Talking about champagne and a non-alcoholic option and flowers and a bower. Setting up a schedule so that everyone had some private time at the heart of the maze. Special prices, for the special service. Delaney's hands were moving in the air, her excitement palpable. He let her talk, enjoy her fun, before he had to burst her bubble.

There was merit to the idea, just like all her ideas. But this was something that excited her, not him, and there was one big issue that she wasn't taking into account.

"So, what do you think?"

Jordan scratched his chin.

"It sounds like you're pretty excited about it. And you've considered a lot of details."

Delaney pursed her lips. "I hear a 'but' coming."

He kept his voice gentle. "But that's something that would take a lot of time."

"I know but you could make a lot of money from it."

He sighed. "This is my busiest time of year. I just don't have time to do anything more. The regular corn maze tours take up any free time I have. This would involve extra set up before the nights involved, someone around to keep the drinks stocked and to make sure people kept to the schedule. Then it would all need to be taken down before the regular day tours the next day."

"I know, but I could do most of that."

Jordan crossed his arms. "Are you going to be here?"

Her mouth dropped open, and then closed. "Oh."

He nodded. "There's the time it takes to get everything organized, and then to do it for a couple of weeks—that's probably at least a month-long commitment."

He wanted her to say she'd still be here, but that was more time than Delaney would be willing to be away from the city, her job, her success.

She was staring at the far side of the kitchen, thoughts whirring. He could almost see the wheels turning.

"You agree it's a good idea?"

He nodded. He could give her that.

"It would also require a cash outlay, and yes, I'd probably make it back, but what would I do with something like an arch afterwards, or signs? The other things might be reusable, but…"

He could see when she'd made her decision. Her lips firmed and her eyes narrowed.

"I'll just have to stay."

Jordan didn't want to start doing romantic maze tours. But somehow, he was smiling.

He might not want romantic maze tours, with the additional stress and hassle, but he wanted more Delaney.

She caught the smile and returned it. "That's okay? If I stay? And I can do the work. Mariah said she had a lot of props and things so we won't have to buy very much."

She was back to being happy and excited, and he loved that. But he needed to make sure. "Can you really stay that long?"

His dad wouldn't be here until November. After Thanksgiving, so the end of November. And maybe this maze plan would be the bit that put the last money he needed into the account.

Her chin lifted. "If I want to, I can. And I want to. Peter isn't ready to restart the restaurant yet."

He shouldn't be so happy to hear her say that. Another month of Delaney was only going to make it more difficult when she left. The longer she stayed, the greater the risk that somehow his father would find out.

More Delaney was enough to make him embrace risk. Like he had back in high school.

CHAPTER THIRTEEN

DELANEY DIDN'T NEED to be a mind reader to know Jordan wasn't thrilled with the idea. But he was letting her try, and she was determined to make this work. Work well enough that he could do it again another year. Hire someone to help if necessary.

She was going to make this a success for him. But she had obligations elsewhere, and she needed to let Peter, as well as her roommate, know that she wasn't going to be back in the city for several more weeks. He hadn't told her when he'd be ready to return to work yet, since he was still working through his physio, but there was a lot of planning before they could start on the concrete details.

Once Jordan had gone upstairs for the night, she sat back on the chair in the living room and pulled out her phone, hitting the contact number for Peter.

"Dee! How's it going?"

"Peter! How are *you*?" Because Peter was

the one who'd been shot, not her. He was the one in rehab, not her.

"Eh. It's coming along. Slow but sure, they say."

The bullet had hit his pelvis, and he'd been lucky it hadn't hit any major arteries. But repairing the damage had taken more than one surgery, and it would be a while before he was up to the long hours that being a chef required.

"How's the food?"

That gave Peter five minutes to monologue about issues with the food in the rehab center.

When he finally finished, she asked, "How is it really going?"

Peter sighed. "Slow. Difficult. But I'm going to do this, Dee. And you, stop right now."

"Stop what?"

"That guilty thing. I can tell by the way you're breathing that you're doing it again."

Delaney wound her hair around a finger. "How can I not feel guilty? If I hadn't fired him—"

"If you hadn't fired him, I would have."

This was not the first time they'd discussed this.

"But he might not have decided to come back with a gun if it wasn't a woman who'd fired him."

"You do understand, Dee, don't you, that if he had problems like that, this was inevitable? At some point, he'd have exploded. And still, not your fault. It's reasonable to expect that if someone doesn't do their job, you can fire them. Hiring someone isn't a lifetime commitment."

"How come you're the one consoling me, when I'm not the one who was wounded?"

"Who says you weren't hurt? Just because you didn't get hit by a bullet, doesn't mean you weren't affected."

"You're right." She told Peter about the panic attacks.

"Oh, Dee, you gotta let that go. It's not your fault."

"I'm trying to accept that. But working through this has made me realize it wasn't just the shooting. I had other problems, but I'm working on them."

"You do that."

"But, I kinda promised this farmer I'm staying with that I'd stick around for a few more weeks, help him out."

There was a pause.

"Is that what you want to do?"

"It is. This is a break for me. It was hectic, getting the restaurant up and going, and what happened was a horrible thing, but this chance to decompress for a bit, is good, I think."

"Yeah, I wouldn't recommend getting shot to anyone, but it's given me a lot of time to think as well."

"I promise I'll be back. We'll get our restaurant going somehow, I just wanted to make sure you're okay if I stay here a little longer."

"Dee, take the time you need. Look at it this way, if I came back early, and then couldn't keep things going physically, that would cause more problems, wouldn't it? Same way, you make sure you're rested and ready to go mentally before we hop back on the merry-go-round."

Delaney swallowed hard. Peter was a good person. The best. That's why she felt so badly that he'd been injured as a result of something she'd done. Sure, he'd have fired the guy if Delaney hadn't, but that didn't change the fact that Delaney was the one who had.

"I promise. I'll get myself completely healthy and be back. Are you sure I can't do anything for you?"

"I've got my family and my partner. I'm almost smothered in help. I had to shoo them all away tonight so I could watch my show."

"Am I interrupting?"

"You're always worth the interruption, Dee. Why don't you tell me about life on the farm? What's he got there—cows? Chickens?"

"The only animal on the farm is his dog, Ranger. It's an organic produce farm. But he gets milk and cheese and meat from other farmers, so the ingredients I've got to work with are fantastic."

They talked about food for a while, and then Delaney thought his voice was getting tired.

"I should let you go." She felt guilty, again.

"It was really good to talk to you. Those sparse texts you were sending were worrying me. You take care and keep in touch."

"I will, I promise."

After ending the call, Delaney stared unseeingly at the blank television set in front of her. She'd put off calling because of the guilt she felt. Peter could say it wasn't her fault, and she understood that firing someone shouldn't bring about a shooting, but at the end of the day, she was the one who had told their employee that he had to go. And he'd responded by returning with a gun.

She was going to fix it though. Once Peter was up to it, physically, they'd get back to work on their restaurant. They'd had excellent reviews, so they just needed to let the memory of the shooting fade, get a new location, change up their menu and they could do it again. They'd learned from their first go-around. This restaurant would be even better.

That was what a Carter would do, and what a friend would do.

Still, as she sat on the couch, her mind switched to a different obligation. She'd promised Jordan that she'd do this romance maze thing, and she had a month here, on the farm. The anxiety about returning to the city, starting the work for another restaurant faded into the background.

She picked up her phone and made some notes for her next talk with Mariah. They had to get word out, immediately, so they could get the bookings for this. Mariah would post info on the town website, and that would drive people to the maze. They would need signage here on the property, and they had to finalize a list of what this romance maze would include.

This felt good. It was what she needed now. This was going to be the best romantic maze tour possible.

FOR A COUPLE of days, Jordan's life continued in the new normal, with no mention of the romance maze idea. He didn't fool himself that Delaney would have let it go.

Then the signs showed up. When he went to close the gate for the day, there was a sign on the ground, propped beneath the farm sign. He now knew the times, and where to sign up for one of the scheduled slots to have a Romantic Maze Date. No prices were listed.

Tension tightened his shoulders, and he felt his mouth pulling down. But he reminded himself that he'd agreed to this. It was helping Delaney, so she felt like she was accomplishing something. If he was lucky, he'd mostly be able to avoid the whole thing and forget it was happening.

He looked at the sign. Forgetting was probably pushing it. Focus on the additional cash instead.

Since Delaney was still handling the store, he didn't run into many people and thought he was safe from questions. But he learned how far the news about the romance maze was travelling when the sous chef at the restaurant in Oak Hill asked him about it on his next delivery run.

"So what's up with this Romance Maze Date?" Gayle asked.

Jordan passed her a crate of potatoes. "I'm not exactly sure."

Her brow creased. "But it's your corn maze, right? On your farm?"

Jordan went back to the truck to pick up a bin with onions. "It is, but I'm not involved in that part of it. I'm doing my best to stay out of it."

She didn't ask why, but she knew he wasn't very sociable.

"Is Mariah taking care of it?"

Jordan had mostly tried to ignore the romance initiative in Cupid's Crossing, only involving himself as much as was needed to promote the farm. When the transformation of the Mill and town had started, Mariah hadn't been directly connected to the Carters, but now that she'd married Nelson, his dad would insist they have nothing to do with her or the romance-themed maze if he found out. But Mariah was not easy to ignore. Even Gayle knew what was going on in Cupid's Crossing, and she was new to Oak Hill.

"She's involved." Delaney had mentioned talking to her, so that was the truth, right?

"I was thinking of signing up, I just wanted more information."

Jordan put the last bin down. He dusted his hands on his jeans.

"It's not something I care much about, so I've stayed out of it."

Gayle made a notation that everything was received. Jordan was ready to leave, when she asked another question.

"Did I hear you're giving out recipes at your farm now?"

"Uh...yes?"

The card forms had arrived, and Delaney had printed her recipes on them. He didn't know exactly how many she'd given out, or how many different recipes she'd come up with.

"I didn't know you cooked."

"I don't. Uh, a...friend is staying with me for a bit. She's the one doing the maze and the recipes."

"A friend huh?"

He could feel his cheeks warming.

"Who is she?"

He could just leave. He didn't have to answer. But with the way word was getting out, about the maze and the recipes and who knew what else, Delaney's presence would soon be known as well. Since his father didn't talk to people in the area when he visited, surely he wouldn't hear about this. Gayle had never met him.

"Delaney Carter."

"One of the Carter's Crossing Carters?"

He didn't want the reminder of the Carter name, in case this woman had heard about the Everton's feud with them.

"It's been Cupid's Crossing for a year or so now."

"Right but…oh wait, is she the one with the restaurant in New York? Where they had the shooting? Oh, that was terrible. Is she okay?"

Jordan nodded and left as quickly as he could. On his way home, the conversation replayed in his head. He didn't know what recipes were being given out at his store, and he didn't know what was up with Romantic Maze Dates. It wasn't something he wanted to be part of, so he'd stepped aside.

But this was his farm, and his business. He should know what was going on. Burying his head in the sand was a good way to find himself in financial trouble. How could he have forgotten that he needed to stay on top of things before they spun out of control?

He pulled into the farm, partly pleased, partly annoyed at the number of cars in the lot. It was stupid to be upset with more business. But he'd been doing fine before Delaney Carter showed up and wanted to take over. To try to make Everton Farms into a Carter-style success.

He needed to get control back. Because in a month, Delaney would be gone, and it would be all on him again.

JORDAN WAS READY to talk to Delaney right away. But there were people in the shop, and he needed to get more produce off the field for his delivery tomorrow. He vented his frustration on some weeds and finished with his harvest for the day not long before sundown. He drove the tractor and wagon back and unloaded the produce into the storage room.

The parking lot was empty, so he whistled to Ranger, and walked down the drive to shut the gate and turn the closed sign over.

The Romantic Maze Date sign was still there, and he grunted. He needed to hang on to that irritation, but it was hard when, like ___ night now, once he went through the back door a delicious meal was waiting.

Delaney was stirring something at the stove. She turned to smile at him.

"Coq au vin. You like mushrooms, right?"

He nodded. "I'll clean up and be back." Just like he said every night.

He reminded himself that Delaney had asked, about the recipes, the trail mix, the donation box, and the romantic maze tour. He'd stepped back, thinking he could ignore it till she went away. But ignoring it was stressing him.

If things went wrong, Delaney would return to her life in the city, while he'd face losing the farm.

A plate of savory smelling chicken was waiting. There were roasted carrots, Brussel sprouts and potatoes in a glaze, and more home-made bread.

He should wait until after dinner to talk to her. It would be a shame to disrupt the meal.

Turned out he didn't have to talk much. Delaney told him what produce had sold, how many hikers came by-the number had increased as the leaves put on their best show. She asked what deliveries he had to make the next day and it was warm and familiar and cozy, and it wasn't going to last, so he couldn't get used to it.

He picked up his empty plate to take over to the sink. "Someone at the restaurant asked about your recipes."

Delaney followed behind him, carrying her own plate. "Really? Did they like them?"

"She didn't say. Just asked if I was doing a lot of cooking now, since she'd heard I was giving out recipes."

Delaney crossed her arms. "She did, did she?"

Jordan ran water and poured in some dish soap.

"Made me realize I don't even know what recipes you're giving out. Or how many."

"Oh." Delaney was still behind him. "I've done about a dozen. I can show you. I was going to try this one tomorrow, the coq au vin. Is that okay?"

Jordan sighed. She thought he was questioning her recipes?

"I don't mind, I just hadn't paid attention. And I should."

"I have them all in the shop, so you can see them any time. I'm not trying to take over, Jordan. I just want to help."

But she was also helping herself, even if she didn't get that. He wasn't sure that what he needed and what she was offering as help were in sync.

"And I should know more about the romance maze. When Gayle asked about that, I didn't have any answers either."

"Gayle? Did Gayle want to go with you?" Did Delaney's voice sound...hurt?

Jordan turned to look at her, but she didn't meet his gaze.

"I don't think so. I just felt…like I was letting things get away from me."

Delaney bit her lip. "I bet you felt that way a lot with your dad."

"I know you want to help, but at the end of the day, I need to say no if it gets out of hand."

Delaney's brow furrowed as she looked at him. He wanted to squirm.

"I do tend to step in and take over. And I don't want to make you feel the way your dad did. So ask me any questions, and tell me to step back if you need to."

Jordan's anger and frustration softened and began to slip away. She was right, and it felt good to have someone understand before he had to explained. "Thanks. I will."

Delaney looked up at him and there was a new expression on her face. Her chin was up and her eyes creased. "Want to go see what we're doing with the maze? The romantic experience we're going to give people?"

Jordan glanced out the window. "It's dark."

"That's when the tours will be. You have flashlights, right?"

Jordan never bothered going into the maze for fun. He'd never thought of it as a romantic place. But with Delany challenging him, and the thought of the two of them alone in the

pathways, with only the glow of a flashlight…
he began to think he'd been missing things. A
lot of them. And now, he determined to live
in the moment and enjoy what was right in
front of him.

"You'll need a warm jacket."

"I'll be fine. You get your own coat and those
flashlights."

DELANEY GRABBED HER JACKET. The jacket might
not be quite as warm as Jordan was thinking,
but it was what she had. She'd forgotten what
the weather was like outside of the city, where
you'd experience the elements for longer than
it took to run from the subway to the door of
a building.

She didn't want Jordan to feel left out of
what was happening on his own farm. He'd
seemed so uncomfortable with the whole idea
of creating a date night in the maze, that she'd
avoided bringing it up.

This would be the best way to show him
how it would work. She'd done some research.
She knew Jordan didn't have a GPS enabled
mower to take care of making the paths in the
corn. Jordan would be doing it with a regular
mower and he had the rest of the farm to deal
with as well. He'd be working like a dog to get

it all done. But not like Ranger. Ranger had a much easier life.

If she was going to show him the magic in the maze, she'd need the dark, and quiet and a good sales pitch. At least she'd had a chance to practice selling people on her ideas while getting the restaurant up and going.

Jordan met her wearing a puffy jacket that looked incredibly warm. He eyed her light-weight car coat but didn't say anything. He just pulled a scarf out of a basket in the mud room and wrapped it around her neck. He paused for a moment, hands on the scarf, a hint of the old Jordan in his expression.

She smiled, tempted to lean in closer. For a moment…but then he dropped the ends of the scarf and passed her a flashlight. She slipped it in her pocket while he held open the door.

He led the way to the maze. The air was crisp, and their breaths puffed in the night air. There was almost no moon, but Jordan didn't bother with a flashlight yet, familiar with every foot of the farm. Delaney wouldn't be surprised if he could walk through the whole maze in the dark and had only brought the flashlights for her.

They reached the entrance and Delaney

reached forward to grab his hand, pulling him to a stop.

"Wait. You can't just march through."

"I can't?" Jordan's voice was light and teasing. She hadn't heard him sound like that since they were back in high school, when they'd met in secret, and he'd set aside his burdens for the time they could claim together.

She nudged her shoulder against him. It didn't budge him, but he didn't push back.

"You need to use your imagination."

"I don't know how much imagination I have."

"Try. Imagine you and I are a couple. Maybe we haven't been dating very long, maybe we haven't even kissed. And we've scheduled a maze date."

"I think I could come up with something better than that."

Delaney ignored him. He didn't get it yet.

"So, we're here. The start times for the dates are staggered fifteen minutes apart, so we're not totally alone, but we'll be almost alone. We won't have flashlights—Mariah has sourced artificial candles. Couples will carry them, and we'll have some on the paths."

She felt him stiffen. "No flame, I know, but we wanted something romantic. We each have a candle, in case one dies. And when it's our turn, we go into the maze, holding hands, our path lit only by a flickering candle. *Fake* candle."

Delaney wondered if Jordan had the experience of many romantic dates. If he'd looked at someone over the flickering light of a candle and stared into her eyes, nothing else existing in that moment. The idea gave her a strange, longing feeling, so she shook it off.

Jordan was already leading her inside the maze, holding her mittened hand.

"Okay, we're holding hands, we'll have to pretend about candles." He flicked on one of the flashlights, pointing at the path ahead of them. When they came to the first fork, Jordan turned right without hesitation. Delaney tugged his hand.

"This couple doesn't know the maze off by heart."

He tugged her back. "How do you know I'm going the right way? Maybe I'm purposely taking you down the wrong path."

"I've been through this maze at least five times in the last couple of days. I know it now too. Where you have stakes to help people keep track in case they're lost, we're going to have ribbons tied on. Mariah has the stuff ready to go, so we'll just walk through putting things in place before hand and taking them down the next morning."

Jordan nodded. Then he tugged her to the left. It caught her off guard, and she almost fell into him.

"Why did you change your mind?" she asked.

She could see his raised eyebrow in the light of their flashlight. The light wasn't soft and sympathetic, like the candles would be, but she had no problem imagining Jordan as a romantic figure.

He leaned down to whisper in her ear. "I'm lost, remember? I don't know the maze."

She'd been playing with him, when she asked why he'd taken the correct path. Really, she just wanted to show him the possibilities of the maze for a date. But somehow, the maze had already done some magic, because this was a different Jordan.

Instead of reminding him they were here for work, not fun, she let him lead her down the wrong path. He pretended surprise when they hit a dead end and had to return. At the next fork, he took the wrong path again.

It was deliberate. And she loved it. It made it seem like a real date. Like they were a real couple.

At the fifth dead end, she couldn't hold back a laugh. "You're terrible at mazes."

She saw a smile tugging the corner of his mouth. "I told you this wasn't a good date idea."

"I guess that depends on what your goal is for a date."

His eyes fastened on hers.

"The goal isn't to solve the maze?"

She shook her head, never breaking their gaze.

He took a step closer. "What is the goal, then, Delaney?"

CHAPTER FOURTEEN

DELANEY'S BREATH STUTTERED.

"If it was fifteen-year-old me, I'd just want to find a place we could be alone."

Jordan was right in front of her. Had he moved, or had she?

"We're alone, Delaney. What would we do?" His voice was low and husky, and it sent shivers down her spine.

Her hands clutched his jacket, and she stood on tiptoe. "This." And she pressed her lips to his.

Right now, she was fifteen-year-old Delaney, and all she wanted was to be with Jordan, to kiss him the way she dreamed of in her room. And Jordan was right there with her, kissing her back, hands moving around her waist, holding her close.

She didn't have to worry about someone seeing them. She didn't have to keep an eye on the time, to be sure she got back home before someone realized she was missing. She could just stand here, wrapped in Jordan's arms, kissing him.

There were other differences as well. He was bigger, taller and stronger, and his beard tickled her face. He wasn't tentative, unsure like he'd been. He was kissing her as a man would. Not a boy.

And she was so up for it.

Then the kiss ended. They pulled apart, and reality threatened to break in. Delaney had had enough of reality and dealing with adult problems. She wanted to escape a little longer.

She tugged his hand, leading him back to the last fork, and this time they ran forward. Sometimes they took the correct fork, sometimes not, forgetting where they were while they kissed and ran through the maze which was magical even in the harsh beams of their flashlights. With Jordan holding her hand, the rustling of the corn stalks wasn't scary, it was the promise of privacy. Delaney scarcely felt the hard packed earth beneath her shoes, caught up in the crisp fall air, smelling corn and earth and Jordan. When they arrived in the center of the maze, her cheeks and nose were chilled and pink, and her toes were tingling.

She didn't care. Her lips were tingling too, and that was what she focused on.

Arms wrapped around Jordan's neck, his forehead resting on hers, she whispered. "We made it to the middle."

"So now what happens?" he whispered back.

"Now…now there's champagne and sparkling water, and chocolate covered strawberries and roses, and an arch for pictures. We can have a photo to keep as a souvenir."

"I don't need a photo." And he drew her in for another kiss.

It was Ranger who brought them back to reality. Cold and bored, he bumped against their legs and Delaney lost her balance, breaking their kiss and their trance.

She saw Jordan aging before her eyes, changing from the pretend seventeen-year-old she'd fallen in love with when she was in high school. The lighthearted expression froze and hardened. He stepped back, leaving her cold and alone.

Reality hit her as well. What was she doing? She wasn't here to kiss Jordan. She had issues on top of issues to work on before returning to the city. She wasn't ready to go yet, and he was going to tell her to leave. If he thought she was feeling something for him, he wouldn't want her to stay. She was still a Carter, his dad still owned the farm, and she had to be gone before Thanksgiving anyway.

Drawing on whatever reserves she had left, she forced a smile to her lips. "Did it work? Have I convinced you that the maze can be romantic?"

He stared at her, with that closed expression and rigid stance.

"You put on a good show. I don't know about romantic, but it's good for making out."

His voice was cold and distant and the words-they hurt. They shouldn't. She'd been desperate to make this seem like something fun, easy, meaningless. But it hadn't been, not for her. She hadn't been pretending. Instead, those old feelings had surfaced, ones that she'd thought were long gone.

But she couldn't flinch. Couldn't give in to that hurt feeling.

She turned around, as if seeing the center of the maze in the dark was giving her ideas instead of just the opportunity to fight back tears unobserved.

"Glad I convinced you. We've already got people signed up, so it's going to be a success. I'll make sure of that. In fact, I should get back to write my notes before I forget."

Lie. She had her phone with her and could

note down her ideas if she actually had any. The only one from this ill-fated expedition was that there was still something about Jordan Everton that pulled at her, and made her want to help him, and kiss him. To spend as much time with him as she could.

Just like at fifteen. But whereas fifteen-year-old Delaney had left because of a misunderstanding, adult Delaney had obligations and a life somewhere else. So those feelings needed to be cut off as soon as possible.

They were quiet as they finished the maze, taking every turn correctly.

JORDAN STARED AT the ceiling through the darkness. Again. This was what Delaney Carter did to him.

He tried to make sense out of what had happened in the maze.

When Delaney mentioned her teenage self, the one he'd fallen so hard for, he'd felt like he was that boy again. As if the weight of taking on the farm and the heartbreak from high school had never happened. His seventeen-year-old self had enjoyed playing and kissing in the maze. There'd been a freedom they'd never had when they'd been together back then.

But when Ranger had interrupted them, he'd

remembered, all too well. The maze, something his dad had started and abandoned, and that Jordan had had to take over and maintain. Delaney, no longer that fifteen-year-old now, with her firmer, curvier body and shadowed eyes. They weren't those high school kids.

Indulging in closeness like that was going to make it all the more difficult when Delaney left, and she would leave. She was staying for the maze, making it a success to feed that Carter drive until she got a grip on her panic attacks. She wasn't doing it for him. Not because she had any of those feelings for him, not now.

She'd been revisiting the past when they'd kissed in the maze, and he was afraid it had been real for him and firmly grounded in the present. He'd braced himself for her response, knowing he couldn't hope that she'd want him, and this farm. And he was right. She'd only wanted to convince him that the maze could be romantic.

It should be marked as dangerously romantic. And he hadn't even had the full treatment.

He'd said goodnight as soon as they got back to the farmhouse, so that he could lie in bed, staring at his ceiling, reminding himself that if Delaney had feelings for him, if she'd found something in his grumpy self to love, she'd still never want to be with him. She wanted, or more accurately, needed to be the success her family wanted from her.

That would never happen on his farm, unless it changed to be a place he no longer felt secure or at home.

Even if something happened, and he wasn't on this farm, his skills with growing things would be useless in a city. There was no future where they worked together.

The farm was all he had, and it wasn't what a Carter would settle for, so he needed to push those feelings back into the past, because they would only lead to heartbreak in the future.

It took a long time to fall asleep, but once he'd determined that there could be no more kisses, or touching, but only the semi-professional relationship they'd had, he finally drifted into a restless sleep.

DELANEY WAS TAKING care of the store and all the extra things involved in the romantic maze adventures, but Jordan had plenty to keep him busy, with harvest, deliveries, and the regular maze tours beginning on the weekend.

Customers had heard about the romance part, and at least now he could talk about what was happening. The interest in the romantic maze event surprised him, but maybe it just spoke to how few opportunities there were for dates in the area.

He couldn't deny its appeal, not after that night with Delaney. He almost felt like it should come with a warning.

Danger! Feelings may get out of hand in this place!

But he didn't tell anyone because they didn't need to know he'd been stupid.

The first weekend of regular maze tours went as expected. There were some differences: since Jordan was on maze duty, he normally had to close the store while he was watching over the tours. This time, Delaney kept the shop going. They ran out of corn and beans. Delaney might think he hadn't noticed, but she'd raised the prices on the stock they were getting low on.

Financially, this time with Delaney was going to be profitable. He might end the year with a bruised heart, but a healthier bank balance.

The next weekend was going to have the first romantic maze event. Delaney asked if it would be okay if Mariah came by one evening to go over the last-minute arrangements.

Jordan wasn't sure if Delaney had asked her to come to the farm so they could check out the maze or if Delaney was still wary of leaving the farm. In the weeks she'd been here, she hadn't gone anywhere but the grocery store in Oak Hill.

She had her car, so she was free to go if she wanted, but she didn't. He wondered if he should push her or not, but he didn't want to cause any problems for her, so he left the decision to her. She was still meeting online with the therapist, so he had to trust she knew what she was doing.

He wouldn't refuse to let Mariah come to the farm. He had no problems with her, outside of her poor taste in men, and she promoted the farm on the town website. He was, somewhat reluctantly, a part of the Cupid's Crossing romance initiative. He could pretend Nelson didn't exist.

Jordan was in the shop in the evening, after dinner, packaging produce for deliveries the next day when he heard a vehicle come in the drive. He assumed it was Mariah and didn't bother looking out. Then the car drove away again, so he must have been mistaken. Someone lost, perhaps? But when he returned to the house, Mariah and Delaney were sitting at the table, a teapot and a plate of Delaney's scones set in the midst of their laptops and notepads.

Mariah looked up and smiled at him. "Jordan! Come see how well we're going to do your maze this weekend!"

Delaney looked up and gave him a careful smile. Things had been awkward between them since that night in the maze. Jordan would rather have plucked his beard out with tweezers than talk about it, so he'd tried to act in a way that let her know he wasn't making any presumptions about what had happened and wouldn't try to repeat it, all without mentioning kissing, feelings, or even the maze if he could help it. They'd settled into an uneasy partnership.

He'd loved those kisses, but he wasn't sure they were worth the loss of the easy friendship they'd developed.

"Delaney told me about it." Mariah shot him a look. "I didn't realize you were here already." He'd lingered as long as he could prepping his deliveries. He was spending as much time as possible away from the house.

"Nelson dropped me off."

He stiffened. Did Nelson think he had a free pass to come here anytime he wanted now?

Mariah watched him. "If that's a problem,

I'll drive myself in future. He was heading in to play darts at the Goat, so we thought we'd save gas."

Jordan clenched his jaw. He'd like to say Nelson shouldn't come back, ever. But that also made it sound like he was stuck in the past. Maybe he was. But he didn't need to tell everyone. It was best for him to move on, from his anger at Nelson and his feelings about Delaney.

"Not a problem." He almost felt his nose to see if it had grown.

Mariah looked ready to call him out on it, but let it pass.

"What time are the regular customers out of the maze?"

"I usually stop letting anyone in about four. They can be an hour or two."

Mariah tapped her pen on the table. "We need about an hour to set up for the romance tours. And the first of those are at seven."

"Then I can stop them at 3? 3:30?"

"That would help."

"Your tours are making me more money, so sure. Whatever works. I can close up the regular tours and take over the shop so Delaney can be free."

Delaney nodded without looking at him. Mariah alternated between watching Delaney and him, a frown on her face. They were awkward around each other. He should do something about that. Unfortunately, it would involve talking and he'd really prefer to avoid that.

But if Delaney wasn't comfortable, maybe she'd leave sooner than she planned. Something inside lurched at the thought. He would miss her when she left. He didn't want her to leave, not yet. Which meant…talking soon. *Sigh*.

Mariah turned back to Delaney. "That should cover most of it. I'll bring over the stuff we're putting in the maze on Thursday, and I'll be here on Friday to help you get it set up. Friday night is completely booked, and there are only a couple of slots open on Saturday."

Mariah started to gather her papers together. She put her fingers on her laptop touch pad, ready to close it, but something caught her attention. She moved her fingers on the keyboard and paused for a moment.

"Jordan." She had a different note in her voice when she said his name.

"Yes?" He had the feeling he might not like what was coming up next.

"Would you consider letting someone use the maze for a proposal?"

Mariah lifted her head and locked eyes with him. He stood, frozen. Why would anyone— but a memory of Delaney at the center of the maze crossed his mind, and the question was answered.

"If you'd open it up next Sunday, they'd pay you more than we charge for all the tours for one night. We can take some video, photos, and post it on our website. It could promote your maze. Maybe not a lot more traffic this season, since there's only a few weeks left, but for next year..."

Jordan breathed in and out, carefully.

He had to agree. The money was good. He'd lost some produce to frost, and there were fewer hikers as the weather cooled. But it meant he almost *had* to do this again, next year. When Delaney wasn't here. Would he be able to afford someone to help? Or maybe go without sleep? Harvest crops in the dark by flashlight? Could he not just run the farm the way he wanted?

He shoved his hands in his pockets. He longed for the day he didn't have to try to pinch every penny to buy the farm, and balance that against what his father would say or do if he knew about how involved he was getting with Cupid's Crossing. Today was not that day. He had to risk it.

"Of course. Excuse me, I'm just gonna—"

He turned and walked out.

He headed out to the parking lot, and down the drive to the gate. He couldn't shut it, though the sign was flipped to closed. Nelson was coming to pick up Mariah.

He couldn't even shut his own gate when he wanted to. He stood beside it, tempted to close it, lock it, and walk away until everyone left.

Delaney was setting things up that would continue after she left. Things that weren't his idea, but he was going to have to deal with the fallout if they didn't work out.

He stood there long enough to feel the cold seep through his jacket and his boots, but he stayed. He didn't want to face anyone right now. He didn't know the best thing to do, and he needed to get that straight in his mind.

A passing vehicle slowed, and then the headlights swept over him as they turned into the drive.

Jordan's first instinct was to tell the driver they'd made a wrong turn. The farm was closed. Then he recognized Nelson.

Right. Another thing that had happened with Delaney's arrival. Nelson, on his farm.

He stood still, prepared for Nelson to drive by, pick up his wife and leave. Then Jordan could lock up the gate, and for a few hours, things would be the way he wanted them to be.

Nelson pulled the car to a stop.

Jordan looked away. He didn't need this now.

Nelson turned the car off and stepped out.

"Jordan?"

He didn't think he needed to answer that question.

"Can we talk for a minute? Just us?"

Jordan still didn't answer.

Nelson leaned against the fence beside him.

"I owe you an apology."

Jordan shot him a glance, but the shadows from the headlights hid Nelson's expression.

"It took me a while to understand how I treated other people. Grandmother is great, but my parents were very driven people, and they expected the same from Delaney and me. My life wasn't perfect, growing up, but from the outside it would have looked that way.

"School, sports, everything came easily. And my parents encouraged me to take the lead in everything. I thought I knew a lot more than I did."

He stopped for a moment, and Jordan considered his words. They confirmed what Delaney had said, about Carters and success.

"I'm sorry for what I did back in high school.

I wanted to solve Grandmother's problems and show my parents how well I was doing, and I was insensitive and arrogant. It wasn't the first time, and I'm sure I'll do it again, but I'm trying to do better.

"Being here with you has been good for Delaney. You've been more than kind considering how we've treated you. Thank you. If sometime I can do something for you, just ask."

Jordan frowned as he considered the words from the man beside him.

He'd never expected an apology. It was unsettling. As much as he didn't want to get wrapped up in his father's vendetta, he'd absorbed his opinions on the Carters. An apology and an admission of blame wasn't how it was supposed to play out.

If Nelson Carter could change, perhaps Jordan could as well. Enough to offer a bridge, a meeting place.

"Thank you. And I'm sorry for how my father hurt your family."

Nelson shrugged. "Who knows what all went down between them? I'd just like to bury the hatchet. I think Mariah and Delaney have plans for your farm and I don't want to be what gets in the way."

"They do have plans. I'm just not sure they're the right ones."

Nelson grunted. "I won't offer to step in, even though a part of me wants to. But I'll remind Mariah that she needs to step back sometimes."

Jordan nodded.

He should be the one to step up and say no if he didn't want something. But he realized it was important for Delaney to make a success of something, so that she didn't think she was a failure. She couldn't get back to a restaurant kitchen until she worked through the panic attacks, but maybe what she was doing on the farm was filling that need for her at the moment.

Maybe he should start saying yes to what he wanted, as well. Right now, the farm was taking all of his time and energy, but Delaney brought something extra to his life. Something he wanted, longed for. Maybe he could have it all, just for a little while, to help him get through. Risk the hurt that would come.

Maybe he could have kisses and smiles, to tide him over until she left.

CHAPTER FIFTEEN

DELANEY COULD ALMOST feel the questions in Mariah's head, but she didn't ask. Delaney was grateful.

Things with Jordan had been awkward since the kisses in the maze. She'd been afraid to talk about it. She'd treasured those kisses the way she had the ones in high school, until Nelson and Jordan's father had convinced her that it was all fake and she shoved the memories away. They'd been spoiled, her first kisses, her first love.

Jordan hadn't been using her, though, and those kisses the other night had dug up memories of the high school ones, rubbing off the tarnish and making them shine again. But the kisses in the maze had been even better, less hesitant, less pressured, less innocent.

They certainly topped any kisses she'd had since Jordan's in high school.

But he had drawn back, and she'd been mortified. She'd been the first to kiss him. Had he kissed her back just to make it seem like they were on a date in the maze? Had he enjoyed the kisses—she was sure he had—but they hadn't meant anything? She was afraid to know what he'd thought. She'd given him all the space she could, trying to show him without having to say anything that she wouldn't pressure him by asking him to explain what had happened in the maze.

He'd agreed to the romance maze tours, but still didn't seem to be onboard, so in a way she was pressuring him on that too. She wanted to help him but felt like she kept making things worse. Her refuge here was beginning to feel more like another problem. At least, her therapy was progressing, but she wasn't ready to leave yet.

She didn't feel that she could talk about it with Mariah. And if she wanted answers, the person to talk to was Jordan.

She'd wait till the Maze tours were over though, because she'd promised to stay, and a talk like that might make it impossible to do so.

She and Mariah were waiting by the front door, since Nelson texted he was on his way. Delaney was more than a little surprised to see Jordan step out of Nelson's car. She couldn't imagine him getting in Nelson's vehicle unless he was forced.

Mariah had already put on her coat and walked toward the car. Nelson crossed and kissed her, and that made Delaney uncomfortably aware of the kisses that she couldn't talk about with Jordan.

They said their goodnights, Jordan standing beside her on the porch as the car drove away. Delaney moved to return inside, when Jordan put his hand on her arm. "Would you take a walk with me?"

Delaney felt the heat of his touch moving up her arm. Was he asking her to go back to the maze? Something inside her leapt.

"I talk better outside, when I'm moving. If you wouldn't mind getting your coat and coming with me."

And the leaping thing dropped. She was apprehensive but nodded and went back in to get her jacket. She felt her breathing speed up and reminded herself that her body was just reacting to her anxiety. But the anxiety wasn't about something that was happening, just something that might, so her body didn't need to react yet. It might not ever need to. She focused on her breaths, taking a few necessary moments to let the anxiety subside.

Jordan and Ranger were waiting for her outside the back door. Jordan led the way, not to the maze, but towards the fields.

The night was crisp and still. They didn't have flashlights this time, but the moon was waxing, and Jordan knew the way, probably blindfolded. There was room for the two of them to walk side by side, which they did, without touching. Ranger ran ahead of them, sniffing and peeing on bushes.

"I don't like talking about things." Jordan broke the silence.

Did he think this was news? "I believe you."

"I had to talk to Nelson, when he drove in. I was at the gate."

"Really?" She'd have expected fireworks from a meeting between the two men.

"He apologized. Told me why he'd behaved like he did, said he was trying to do better."

Delaney's heart warmed with pride for her brother. She knew it wouldn't have been easy for Nelson. And not for Jordan either. "I know he is. I'm glad he apologized."

"Kind of expected something crazy to happen, with a Carter and an Everton getting along. Like a meteor hitting the earth, or zombies or something."

Delaney paused. She understood what he

was saying, but… "You and I have been getting along."

His gloved hand rubbed his beard. "Yeah. I think we have to talk about what happened in the maze. Because we're thinking about it."

He was right about that.

"I want you to know I liked it." Delaney almost tripped when Jordan admitted that. She'd been pretty sure he did. That wasn't the problem part. But if he could admit it, so could she.

"I did too."

He nodded. "I also know you're leaving soon. And you'll be going back to New York."

She would. And once she worked out her anxiety issues, she'd be excited about it.

"I don't want us to be awkward around each other. But I can't pretend I'm not attracted to you, Delaney."

Her throat was thick, and she couldn't swallow.

"I know you'll never stay here, and I'll never be in the city. But maybe, for the little while you're here, we can pretend we're getting a do-over from high school. Like we were in the maze."

She forced herself to swallow. She had to make sounds.

"If you don't want to, that's okay as well.

You're still welcome to stay, and I won't embarrass you. But since we were already tiptoeing around each other, I thought I'd put it out there."

Delaney finally managed to squeak a word out. "Yes."

Jordan came to a stop, turning toward her. "Yes?"

"Yes." She nodded. "That's kind of what I thought, about that night in the maze."

He was watching her, but she didn't know what he could see in the faint light. "We both know this is just temporary. It can't go anywhere. And maybe we shouldn't tell anyone, so they don't fuss about it after."

She nodded again. She didn't want to discuss this with Nelson, or anyone else in her family. She shuddered at the thought.

Jordan reached his hand out for hers and she gripped his in return. They headed back towards the house.

"Do you know when you're going?"

Because that would be the end date. When they said goodbye and moved on to their separate worlds.

"I'll have to talk to Peter—see when he's ready to start planning again. And I should go back to the Mill as a test. See if the things

I've been working on with my therapist have helped. But it'll be soon. Before your father comes back."

"Okay." He didn't pressure her, just accepted she'd let him know. And he'd be happy to have her stay on the farm as long as she wanted or needed to. Until his dad returned.

This was why she was here. She needed that sense of freedom while she worked through her problems. No pressure, no demands.

She was trying to help him, find ways to make the farm work financially so he wouldn't be worse off for helping her. But as sweet as it was that they had this time, it wouldn't do to prolong it. Her feelings for Jordan were growing from the innocent love she'd felt in high school into serious, and possibly permanent adult feelings.

She had trained and worked hard to be more than someone selling produce in a stand and creating simple recipes for people to make at home. She had the skills and talent to be a successful chef at her own restaurant, to see the pride on her parents' faces.

She couldn't waste that.

And there was Peter. Her actions, though unintentional, had cost him his dream as well as hers. She owed him. She had to go back and give him that chance again.

"Do you know when exactly your dad is coming?

"He calls when he's leaving, but he's normally here a day or two after Thanksgiving. He celebrates with his brother, then comes up."

"I'll stay till then. Maybe we can have a Carter/Everton family dinner, early, just to really upset the universe. Then I'll have to get back to the city."

Jordan stopped walking, and Delaney turned to him.

"I'll make sure Mariah and Nelson don't say anything about me being here."

He nodded. "I don't see many people, so that shouldn't be a problem."

It was depressing, talking about how they were keeping the information that she'd even been on the farm a secret. Limited time, no future. Just a chance to revisit their first love and take make some new memories.

Delaney didn't want to dwell on that. They had a few weeks and she wanted to make the most of them. She moved her hand from his cheek to the back of his neck and pulled him down into a kiss.

There was a rumble in his throat, and he soon had her wrapped tightly against him. Like the night in the maze, she forgot where she was, or the cold, caught up in his kiss. And again, it was Ranger who reminded them that there was more to their lives than kissing.

They had weeks to kiss. Delaney planned to take full advantage.

JORDAN WOKE WITH a happy, light feeling in his chest. It was still dark out, but he was accustomed to getting up before the sun at this time of year. He needed to get his deliveries done. There was work to do on the maze, and vegetables to harvest.

And Delaney.

Memories of last night filled his head. Kissing. Holding her. And he could do that, for the next few weeks. Jordan was smiling. He didn't start a day like that, didn't smile that often. He didn't often have Delaney.

The knowledge that he wouldn't have her for much longer dampened his mood, but he pushed those thoughts aside. He had this, this brief interlude, and he would make the most of it.

He shoved back the covers on his bed, ignoring the chill in the room. He could already smell coffee, knew Delaney must be up, and was eager to see her. He'd been eager to see her every day, if he was honest, but now he didn't have to hide it.

He dressed quickly and made his way down the stairs. Delaney was making something on the stove, Ranger watching closely, when he entered the kitchen. She turned her head and smiled. He crossed the room, and wrapped his arms around her waist, loosely, not sure if this was part of what they were doing now.

She leaned back against him, and he drew her closer.

"Morning." His voice was rough, unused.

"It is. And you have an early delivery. I've made an omelet for you."

"Thank you." He kissed her temple.

It would be good he knew. Better than good. But holding her like this was the best.

He had work to do, so he released her, and she slid the omelet onto a plate, adding some slices of her homemade bread toasted. He wished this was his future, for more than just a few weeks. But he pushed that thought down. He'd had a lot of wishes over the years and was used to them going unfulfilled. Still, when he went out into the cold morning air, he felt happier than he could remember being. He was getting his wish. He'd just forgotten to ask for longer.

CHAPTER SIXTEEN

HIS DAY WENT QUICKLY. Deliveries, lunch with Delaney, then more crops to bring in from the field. He could see the end of the season coming. His fall plantings, broccoli, cabbage and beets, would soon be ready to harvest, and with the way Delaney was selling the produce he'd already gathered, he needed to check stock. There was a certain amount he kept for himself, and for planting next season. He had some promised deliveries, including another two to the Mill. He might have to stop selling some items in the store.

That didn't happen often.

He headed out of the storage room to let Delaney know and found her discussing pumpkin recipes with a customer.

"If you like the pumpkin in pie, but want to level it up, why not add some maple syrup?"

The woman's eyes widened. "Oh, that sounds yummy."

Delaney nodded. "I've been adding maple

syrup to vegetable glazes, and I'm working on a pie recipe with syrup in it. Sign up on the website and I'll forward it to you once it's ready."

The woman left clutching a pumpkin for carving, as well as a sugar pumpkin for baking. Jordan let his smile show. "You're good at this."

Delaney smiled back at him. "I'm good at food—at least, with what I can do after you've grown it. And I like sharing that with people."

He crossed his arms, sorry to tell her that she was going to have less food to share.

"What's wrong?" Her eyes widened. He hadn't wanted to upset her, so he released his arms to pick up one of her hands in his. "Nothing wrong, at least, not from my side. But once you sell the beans you've got here, that's it."

She looked at the almost empty bin. "Really?"

He nodded. "The rest are all promised."

Her smile returned. "You've sold all you have. That's great. Why is that a problem?"

"Well, you can't share them with people anymore."

Her laugh rang out. "That's not a problem. I've got more in my repertoire. But thanks for letting me know. Anything else you're selling out of?"

Jordan took her into the storage room, showing her which items were spoken for.

"This is for the Mill tomorrow."

She stilled beside him, and he wondered if he shouldn't have mentioned that. She seemed so confident and relaxed here, that he sometimes forgot she was still working on the panic attacks. He waited to see what she'd do or say to guide him for what to do next.

"Can I go with you?"

Her voice was small. He wanted to hold her in his arms and promise everything would be okay, but he knew better. Things weren't always okay.

"You want to? Really? You don't have to prove anything."

"No, I don't really want to. But I think I should. I've been working with the therapist, and I have some strategies I've been using. Maybe I'll just stay in the truck for starters and see how it goes."

Jordan pulled her close to him.

"If there's a problem, we can turn around anytime, okay?"

He felt her nod against his chest, and he wanted to keep her there, protect her. But this was in her head, and he had no power over that. All he could do was offer her a refuge. He hoped things went well for her, but part of him liked that she needed him, his place, his shelter. Selfish thoughts, but he wanted her here. Wanted someone here for him. This might be all he got.

He pulled back, determined to show her that he had confidence in her, even if he wished she needed him more.

She drew a shaky breath. "What time? Mariah needs to come by with the things for the maze tomorrow." She looked at him. "Nelson offered to help, since there's a lot to carry."

She was leaving it up to him. She didn't know if he'd be comfortable with Nelson here. His knee jerk reaction was to say no. But Nelson had apologized, and Jordan was tired of carrying on the Everton feud. He liked one Carter so much that maybe it was time to build a bridge to the others as well.

"Anytime after noon should be fine. And Nelson is welcome." Words that surprised him to hear coming from his mouth. "Invite them for dinner if you want."

He'd have been happy for Delaney to say no, because he enjoyed the dinners the two of them shared. But her being happy and getting healthy was more important than that.

Her face lit up. "That would be great. I'll let Mariah know and figure out what to serve. Oh, I can test out that pie on everyone."

She's leaving, he reminded himself. He needed to prepare himself for a time when he didn't have dinner with her. When he'd be making his own meals, stuck with his own cooking and with only Ranger for company.

But now he was more determined than ever to expand his circle and find someone, someone for whom he'd be enough. Once he'd secured the farm. He left Delaney with her plans while he walked down the drive to close the farm for the day.

DELANEY WAS NERVOUS as the truck got closer to the Mill. She knew what she needed to do. It was brain versus emotions. She could let the emotions do their thing and use her brain to remember that feeling something didn't mean it was true.

There was no threat at the Mill. The problem was her anxiety, and she'd been working on that.

She'd done a lot of hard work with the therapist, figuring out why she was so anxious. It wasn't just the shooting. That obviously was part of it, but she hadn't had a panic attack in the city. It was things like family pressure and her constant drive to be successful that were triggers. It was time to test whether she was ready to challenge herself.

Jordan reached over and rested a hand on her knee. She felt that warmth, and her tense muscles relaxed. She wasn't alone. If things got bad, Jordan would take her away.

The Mill wasn't empty today. There were cars in the lot, both at the back where she'd parked the first day she'd been here, and at the front, the public part. It looked like they were getting ready for an event.

The tension built again.

Jordan stopped the truck, put it in Park.

"Are you good?"

She took a long breath. Then she nodded. Maybe not good, but good enough.

He turned off the truck and waited again.

"Go." She could at least sit in the cab and do nothing.

He took a moment to check on her, and then said *Stay* to Ranger. He moved around to the back and took out the bins of produce to deliver. She closed her eyes, hearing his footsteps walking away. The door opening, the sounds of a busy kitchen hitting her ears.

Her breathing grew shallow. She clenched Ranger's fur with trembling hands. The hands felt like they belonged to someone else. Her stomach twisted.

Her body was preparing to fight or flee. Moving oxygen to the large muscle groups, away from her digestive system. Amping up her breathing for cardio exertion. Her anxiety told her body she was in danger.

She closed her eyes and went through her mantra. *This is my anxiety. I'm not in danger.*

Her body shivered, and she realized she'd drawn herself up into a ball. Breathing. She needed to do her breathing. She was wrapped around Ranger, trembling and nauseated. She drew in air and started counting.

She didn't know how much time passed before her body felt like her own again. She sat up, releasing Ranger, who shook himself out. She looked around. People moved in and out of the Mill. No one paid attention to her. She was fine.

It felt horrible, going through the attack, but nothing had happened. She was okay.

Jordan was standing outside the truck, beside the passenger door. She didn't know how long he'd been there. He kept his distance, like she'd asked, and she nodded to reassure him.

She reached for the door handle and pushed the door open. Jordan caught it.

"You sure about this?"

Not completely. But she slid off the seat and stood beside the truck. Her legs held her up.

She walked towards the kitchen door, nervously assessing how her body reacted. She was tense, but she didn't know if that was an attack, or just her fear of an attack. She checked on how she was breathing. She headed to the door of the kitchen, one deliberate step at a time.

She was at the door. She gripped the handle and pulled it toward her.

Inside was a busy kitchen. They did have an event going on. This was her familiar, her version of Jordan's farm. But it didn't feel the same. Didn't feel like her life. Maybe because it wasn't her kitchen? She trembled, but watched for a minute, till someone looked up.

"Hey, Jordan, did we forget something?"

Jordan stood behind her, offering silent support.

"No, just taking a look."

The prep chef seemed surprised but shrugged and kept going.

"How are you?" His voice was next to her ear, calm and supportive.

Delaney turned and gave him a wobbly smile. "I'm good. Not perfect, but good."

THE REST OF the day was even better. Delaney was flying high on the feeling of having made progress. She'd had a panic attack, true, but she'd got through it, and managed to open the door to the kitchen. She was going to get there, she knew it.

But right now, she was too busy to worry about it.

While Jordan worked out in the fields, she shuttled between the kitchen of the farmhouse and the shop. Word was getting out, and hikers were now stopping by to buy the trail mix and energy bars she'd made, and often some of the water and sports drinks Jordan stocked. She had recipes ready that didn't require the veggies that were in low supply, so she'd been able to share those with the people wanting Jordan's organic produce.

She made chicken pot pies; a meal she knew Nelson loved. Nelson and Mariah had agreed to come over, and she was determined the meal would be perfect. Some of the extra steps she went through might not make any difference to the people she was feeding, but she was keeping her hand in, making sure she hadn't lost her skills.

Well, as much as she could with the tools she had available. There was no point in asking Jordan to get utensils he'd never use after she left. And since she was focusing on direct farm to table fare, keeping it simple made her recipes workable for people who had limited kitchens. Regular people, not chefs.

Jordan was back to clean up before Nelson and Mariah arrived. Delaney had twenty dollars from the donation box: they'd passed peak leaf season, so there were fewer hikers.

Jordan returned to the kitchen in khakis and a button-down shirt. A non-flannel one.

"Don't you look good." She teased. She'd dressed up too, but her outfit was covered by an apron.

Jordan gave her a shy smile and crossed to kiss her.

"Mhmmm." She smiled back at him as he stepped away.

"This looks and smells great."

She'd taken some extra care with the table, set for four. She bent to check the pies in the oven.

"They should be here soon, and the pies are

almost ready." She stood back up and Jordan turned toward the front of the house.

"Sounds like them." She heard it then, the sound of tires.

They moved to the front door together, as if they were a couple. Delaney took a moment to imagine it. She and Jordan here on the farm. Working together, dinner, having guests over. It was a nice picture. It tugged at her, the possibility.

But it wasn't going to happen. She owed Peter, to go back and do the restaurant again. To show everyone she was still at the top of her game. Even if she and Jordan didn't have the distance thing, even if somehow his farm was close to the city, her days were long and late. Restaurant hours were brutal on relationships.

Would Jordan even want a relationship with someone who was out six nights out of seven, coming home only a few hours before he had to get up and deal with the farm? Why was she thinking about this?

This was just temporary.

She pushed those thoughts to the back of her mind as she prepared to greet her brother and his wife.

Neither Nelson nor Mariah commented on the two of them standing cozily beside each other. Jordan helped Nelson unload the props they'd brought over for the maze while Mariah went into the kitchen with Delaney. When the guys returned Delaney invited them to sit.

The pies had come out a few minutes previously. She'd made individual servings, with a creamy, chicken and vegetable filling, and a mushroom sauce to pour over the top.

"This is my absolute favorite meal." Nelson had barely waited until everyone was served before digging in. "I loved the ones Grandmother served, but these are even better. Good job, Dee."

Jordan squinted at him. "She *is* a chef."

Nelson paused, eyes wide. "Sorry, sis, I forgot. I didn't mean to sound patronizing."

Delaney knew Nelson hadn't meant anything by it, but his comment had irked. Having Jordan point out that Nelson wasn't being respectful was probably due in large part to his still fractious reaction to Nelson, but she'd take it as support. Jordan nudged her with his knee, and she nudged back. Maybe it was more supportive than anything to do with Nelson.

Mariah interrupted.

"If you're sure about being open Sunday night for a proposal, the client is totally on board. I've warned him about the time parameters, and details like no smoking, no flame, no going off the paths. Can we do the paperwork?"

For a moment, Delaney thought Jordan was going to say no. Something about that idea bothered him, but she didn't know what. Instead, he jerked his head in a nod. "As long as you take care of it. I don't even care what the farm's cut is, I just don't want to be involved."

That left a moment of uneasy silence, but Mariah got over it first.

"Absolutely. That's my job. The customer has requested some special props, and I'll deal with all that. You can stay in the house, or leave the property, whatever you feel more comfortable with. He'd just like a guarantee of privacy."

Jordan nodded. Conversation moved on. The maple pumpkin pie was a spectacular success.

Yet, she felt somehow deflated when she was back in her room, alone and unable to sleep. Why?

She'd made a concrete step towards returning to her own life, by going to the Mill and surviving a panic attack. Two Carters had eaten at the Everton house, and there was no sign of the apocalypse. They had everything ready for the maze tomorrow, and it was going great. And what should have been the cherry on a perfect sundae of a day was Jordan's kisses. She could still feel them.

It wasn't enough. Somehow, the day made her feel her life was lacking.

No, it was just the aftermath of an emotional day. That was all it could be.

MARIAH WAS BACK to organize the maze for the first night. Delaney and Mariah staged everything they needed for the tour. Jordan hauled the heavy things and left the fine tuning to the two of them. Delaney could make a table setting look good, but Mariah had skills beyond that.

Delaney knew this was going to be a success. Just look what had happened with Jordan and her that night in the maze—and that was before Mariah had done her magic. The proposal would be a success as well.

Gentle battery-operated candles were scattered along the paths, making the whole maze glow. The sky was clear, stars shining brightly. The candles for customers to hold were wrapped in gold and cream ribbons. Mariah had even wrapped ribbons and fairy lights around the wooden entrance to the maze.

Delaney and Mariah were seated in chairs at the entrance when the first couple showed up. They looked to be high school students, a little nervous, a lot excited. Mariah ticked them off her list, showing Delaney how the online checklist worked. The next couple arrived soon after, waiting on additional chairs for their turn.

Once the requisite fifteen minutes was over, Mariah let them into the maze.

"It's pretty straightforward, unless someone has a problem—like if they trip or the candles both burn out."

"How many slots are still open?"

Mariah grinned. "None. It's sold out now. This was a great idea. I didn't think Jordan would go for something like this. He's been a little resistant to some of the suggestions I've made."

Delaney considered. "Maybe he just needs someone to nudge him. Or push him a bit."

Mariah considered. "That's not my place. Being with your brother has made me more aware of how easy it is to feel like you know what's best for someone, but you can be wrong. I don't want to push my plans for what will make Cupid's Crossing a success onto anyone who may have good reason to have contrary interests."

Delaney blinked at her. "Did I do that with Jordan?"

Mariah shrugged as the next couple walked up to the maze. "How would I know?"

Delaney looked towards the farmhouse. What did Jordan want? A wildly successful farm, or a safe retreat?

THE NIGHT WAS a success, exactly as predicted. Mariah stayed to make sure everyone was safely out, since the last two couples didn't want to leave despite the dropping temperatures. When Delaney got back into the house, she couldn't find Jordan or Ranger anywhere.

Mariah's words made her think about what she'd been doing with Jordan. Had she been pushing? She'd only wanted to help. He needed the farm to stand on its feet financially, and he wanted to make enough to buy it from his father. So, these had all been good suggestions, right?

But Jordan hadn't been thrilled. And now that they were acknowledging feelings between them, albeit with a time limit, she wondered if he was agreeing because of the benefit to the farm, or for her. Would he do that for her? She thought of the ways he'd been protective of her and taken care of her. He might.

She didn't want another mostly sleepless night dealing with uncomfortable feelings she couldn't resolve. She kept on her jacket and went to find him.

He wasn't at the store or storage barn. He wasn't at the maze. She could have wandered around the outskirts of the maze or the fields, but she would have spent a long time and probably still missed him. She didn't know this part of the farm.

She followed the driveway and found him hanging over the farm gate. He must have closed it after Mariah left and made sure the sign was flipped over. He didn't turn when she drew close and Ranger came to greet her, so she leaned on the gate beside him.

There was silence for a few minutes.

"The night was a success. All the slots are sold out."

Jordan nodded. "That's what Mariah said."

"That's more money for the farm, right? The hiking donation box, the recipes, the romance maze…this is all helping, right?"

He nodded again. But she could sense his tension. This was all good…but somehow, it wasn't making him happy.

Delaney sighed, and reached for Ranger, finding comfort in stroking his head. "I know I've done something wrong. I thought all this would improve things for you. The farm making money, paying your dad off sooner…so where did I go wrong?"

Jordan turned to look at her then. "Why do you think you did something wrong?"

He was asking her *why* she thought that. Not saying that she was wrong. Deflection?

"Because you're not happy."

He shrugged. "I'm not usually happy. But I'm not unhappy."

"No?"

She knew he liked her making meals, helping with the store, kissing. But he wasn't joyful.

He turned away again. "It's not you."

"What is it? I don't mean to pry, but I don't want to do something you don't like." Her hand tensed on Ranger, and the dog pulled away.

Jordan rubbed his hands over the fence rail. "Delaney, I get how you're looking at this. You want this farm to be the Carter version of a farm. Busy, prosperous—maybe written up in some magazine or paper, right?"

"Yeah. It has a lot of potential."

Jordan sighed. "This has been a family farm for generations. Some things have changed. Used to be cattle, mixed animals, now produce."

He nodded his head at the signs for the farm, mostly invisible in the light available.

"Now, we've got people coming to hike. Go through the corn maze. Kiss in the maze and propose.

"What's next? Hayrides? Petting zoo?"

Yes, Delaney thought. Those were all good ideas. He could also get other farms to come with tables of their produce to sell on the weekends. Stoney Creek would become a destination, a place people wanted to come, all summer and fall. But Jordan didn't sound like this was what he wanted.

"You're not here much longer. So, to do all that stuff after you're gone, I either have to clone myself, or I have to hire people. Manage schedules and taxes."

That was all true. Delaney was familiar with the administration required from the restaurant. "And that's not what you want? If you were making enough money, you could hire people to take care of those things and do more of the work."

Jordan turned to her again. "Do I look like the kind of person who wants to be in the middle of a circus? Spend all day with people running around, asking for things, taking over the place?"

Suddenly, the pieces dropped into place. Jordan was right. He wasn't that person.

He'd been alone here on the farm for years. Even back in high school, he'd hung around with Dave and Nelson, and for a while her, but he'd never been someone to look for the limelight. He didn't want to be part of a crowd.

Her stomach fell as the realization hit. She hadn't been listening or paying attention. His father had started the maze, and Jordan had been forced to keep it going so as not to lose money that one year.

The hiking trails. He didn't have to deal with anyone for that. He'd resisted charging for parking, since that would involve his time and energy in something he didn't want.

And she'd pushed him into doing this romantic corn maze thing, which people would want him to repeat next year, based on how successful it already was. And Jordan was at his busiest at this time of year, so he'd have to hire help.

Delaney closed her eyes. She hadn't paid attention. She'd pushed, and run roughshod over his objections, just like Nelson would do. No wonder the Evertons weren't fond of the Carters. Who knew, maybe the Carters had been doing this for generations.

"Why didn't you say anything? Why did

you let me go ahead with all this stuff? I didn't need to."

"Didn't you?" His voice was gentle. Tears pricked her eyes.

"What do you mean?"

The silence stretched, and Delaney knew he didn't want to answer. But something told her this answer was important.

"Carters have to be successful, right? That's what you said. Because of all the privileges you grew up with. You have to do something with it."

Yes, she'd been the idiot who said that.

"I thought, well, right now you're not feeling like you're making a success of anything, and if you did some things here, helped with the farm, you'd feel better. It's not as good as your restaurant in the city, but it was something."

While she thought she'd been helping him, he'd been helping *her*. He'd let her take over, so that she'd feel useful. It was a sacrifice for someone who'd had so little control over his life growing up.

"I'm sorry. I was taking control away from you, wasn't I?"

He shrugged. "I probably need to get over that, anyway. What my dad does, doesn't really affect me anymore, as long as he lets me buy the farm. Once I own it, I can be free."

"Has he tried to do something else with it? Have you stopped him?" That had puzzled her. The land was a valuable asset, even if it wasn't farmed.

"There's some kind of legal thing, that he can't mortgage the farm. I don't know the details since Dad has all the paperwork. The only money comes from what revenue the farm can produce. I'm doing all the producing, so we have an agreement. He tried a few things here that didn't work, so now I do the labor, and use most of the profits to buy the place. We set up a bank account in Oak Hill for that – all the rest of the admin stuff is in Florida now."

"It doesn't sound fair. Or right."

Jordan sounded resigned. "As long as I can have the farm, I don't care."

"You love it here that much?"

"It's mine. It's something that's mine."

Delaney had grown up with lots of things that were hers. But now, she realized Jordan hadn't told her, or probably anyone, exactly what life had been like, growing up with a man obsessed with making the next big fortune. It was like a gambling addiction, only with ideas, not cards or dice or slot machines.

She wondered how much he'd lost, how many things he'd thought were his that were taken from him or left behind. She wanted to yell at his dad. Make him see what he'd done. But she wasn't sure she really had the higher moral ground here.

What she could do was stop pushing. Stop using the farm for her own needs. He was right, she had pushed, wanted to show she knew how to make the farm a success, like she'd been trying to do with everything.

For Jordan, success was not measured with money or outside validation. He just wanted this place, a place that was his. Where he could do the things he enjoyed. Being outside, being mostly on his own, making things grow. Maybe he had more potential, just like the farm did, but he didn't have to take advantage of it all. It was his life, his choice, and it wasn't her place to make him feel that his idea of success, what made him happy, wasn't enough.

Was that why he wasn't happy? She wanted to push, to know why he was content to just not be unhappy, but there'd been more than enough pushy Cartering in his life.

"I'm sorry. And thank you. But the burden of my need to be successful on my terms doesn't have to lie on you. Oh no." She covered her face in her hand.

"What is it?" Jordan still was concerned about her.

"Your dad. When he sees all the changes, he might think there's something for him to exploit here."

"He promised me he wouldn't, and my uncle heard him. He wants the money to buy a boat, so he'll take that over farmland he doesn't want to work. I'm counting on that. As long as he never knows I've had a Carter living on the farm, I'm good."

"Jordan, thank you. Thanks for risking your future to help me. And I promise, I'll stop pushing you and let you enjoy your farm your way."

Jordan laid a hand on her cheek. "It's had its compensations." And he kissed her.

CHAPTER SEVENTEEN

JORDAN WASN'T SURE how things would be the next morning, after that talk. When he came down to the kitchen, she had coffee and breakfast ready, circles under her eyes as if she'd also had difficulty sleeping. He wanted to make those go away.

"I thought it would be good to have breakfast ready, since we need to change out the maze before we open up."

She didn't meet his eyes, but he mostly avoided hers as well. And when they got to the maze, there wasn't much opportunity to be awkward. There was a lot to do. Another reason why he couldn't do date mazes on his own.

Lunch was warmed up leftovers from the night before. And whether or not it was because of the buzz the Romantic Maze Dates were generating, there was a steady flow of people all afternoon. They wandered through the maze, hiked or bought produce. and then it was time to set up the maze for the date nights again.

This was the second night for the romantic maze. Two nights next weekend, and the proposal, and it was over. Back to the regular maze until the end of October, and then he'd harvest the whole thing.

After a busy day Saturday, they were both tired and ready for a quiet evening. Sunday they would be able to relax, without a maze to set up. Jordan felt restless and decided to take a walk. Delaney asked to go with him. She hadn't done that before, and he tensed. Why did she want to walk? Was it going to be another talk, something to make them even more awkward around each other?

But he didn't say no.

He walked out to the fields. There was little left to harvest—some plant material he'd turn over with the rotor tiller. The mounds of upturned dirt were shades of grey in the moonlight. The hills were mottled black and white, and the stars shone bright in the still air.

Jordan wanted space. Maybe room to run if Delaney wanted to talk about something difficult. He wished they could go back to the days where they'd kissed and kept things light. Now, he was unsettled, restless, wanting more of something he couldn't have.

"I've been thinking a lot about what you said." Her breath was cloudy in the cold air.

Jordan kept walking, eyes on the ground ahead.

"I said a few things."

"About success. It made me wonder what I considered a success and why. It ties in a lot with what I've been talking about with my therapist."

"Oh." Jordan didn't know what else to say. *Good for thinking about it? Glad I could help? Did I?*

"Having a popular restaurant, making my family proud—that was one of the ways I defined success. When I reached the end of my life, I could look back and say it was a life worth living."

Jordan kept quiet. He'd like the farm to still be operating when he took his final breaths, but then what? He hadn't worried about leaving any kind of legacy.

"The problem, what the panic attacks have made me realize, is that the life I'm living to get there isn't making me happy. It's making me unhappy."

Which was not acceptable. Delaney deserved to be happy.

"I'm trying to work out what *would* make

me happy. Both now, and when I look back on my life. And something else you said is haunting me."

"I didn't say anything that remarkable."

"You said you weren't happy, but you weren't unhappy. The things I was trying to do to help weren't making you happy—they were pushing you toward unhappy. I wondered, what would make you happy, Jordan? I think you really deserve that. And maybe, since the Carter family has done so much to fight against your happiness, I could help. If you wanted me to. If I could."

Jordan's lungs stopped working, while his heart speeded up as if it had to make up for them.

Delaney made him happy.

He couldn't tell her that. Couldn't expose himself further. Not when she was leaving. Not when telling her that would put even more pressure on her slender shoulders.

But he had to give her something, if for no other reason than to divert her from his truth.

"You've helped me, just by being here. I've made myself a hermit. I don't want to be around people all the time, but I shouldn't cut myself off completely.

"When you're gone." And how the thought

hurt. "I'll make an effort. Maybe meet up with some of the other farmers I've been dealing with online."

It wasn't a big step, and probably long overdue, but he could handle that. Even if Delaney never knew how he felt about her, he wanted to be as honest with her as he could.

He glanced down and saw a big smile on her face.

"That sounds like a good plan, Jordan. I'm not going to pressure you, but I hope you do that. I'd like you to be happy."

He stopped and she halted in front of him. He couldn't resist. He ran the finger of his gloved hand over her cheek.

"This makes me happy." And he kissed her.

IT WAS TIME for another delivery to the Mill, the final one booked for the season. Delaney was with him again. She'd insisted she was ready to try another step.

The last few days had been good. Delaney was still handling the store and making meals and talking to her therapist. She seemed at least content. He would find her, sitting with a notebook and pen, staring into space, but she smiled when she saw him, and they were touching and kissing again.

She didn't frown those times. He thought she was working on her definition of happiness, and he hoped she found it. He wished he was part of it, but even if he was, he couldn't imagine a way they'd make it work.

Getting a handle on her panic attacks was definitely part of the plan, so they were pulling into the lot of the Mill now. She was tense, but not wound to the point of vibrating, like she'd been the other times he'd come here with her.

He opened his door, told Ranger to stay, and moved to the back of the truck. He dropped the tailgate and pulled the first bin towards him. Delaney appeared at his elbow.

"I'm going to help you take the stuff in."

Jordan wanted to tell her she didn't need to. Or that he'd help her if she found it more than she could do. But she knew all that. He passed her a small basket instead and followed her in with his own larger bin.

She stood for a moment, eyes closed, breathing the long ins and outs he'd seen her do before. She opened her eyes and pressed the buzzer by the door, and her hand trembled. Just for a moment, and then she had it under control. She could be starting to panic, or just be worried that she was going to.

The door opened, a young man in a chef's

coat answering the ring. "Oh, the veggies. This way."

Delaney hesitated, just long enough that he was about to drop his bin to reach for her, and then she took a deep breath and a step forward. And another.

Then they were in the cooler.

Back at the truck, her eyes were sparkling. "I did it."

He nodded.

"Let's get this finished." She picked up another bin and took off. This time her steps were quick, and he had to hustle to keep up with her.

Time was getting away on her.

When she'd told Jordan she'd stay for the maze, and then, till almost Thanksgiving, it had seemed like a big commitment. But she was almost out of time.

The romantic maze tours had been a big hit. Even without that addition, the maze was popular, especially as they neared the end of October and Hallowe'en. Delaney knew, after research, that there was a lot they could do to make the maze scary and even more fun for the holiday, but she didn't mention her ideas to Jordan or try to push him. That wasn't what he enjoyed, and she'd pushed him enough.

Now he was harvesting the corn, before cutting the whole thing down.

It was silly to think that was the end of her reprieve, before she had to get back to her plans in New York. She still had time. There was the last of the produce to sell in the store. Now the focus was on Thanksgiving: root vegetables and squashes. Jordan was pleased with the amount sold. And surprised, she could tell. She had made a difference here.

Her phone buzzed. She was in the shop. It had become a pleasant place to work, in spite of the lack of a proper desk setup. She didn't have to bundle up to race from the house when someone came to buy a pumpkin and some potatoes and being near the food inspired her.

She was working out recipes for next season for Jordan. If she printed them out for him, and all he had to do was leave them by the cash register in the shop here, then it wouldn't be pushing him into something he didn't want to do. It would be good promotion for him. He grew an impressive variety of crops, and once she found out what was available and when, she'd group the recipes by months to match availability.

She'd also been working on the assignments

her therapist gave her. They didn't take up a tremendous amount of time, but required a lot of thinking. She had to piece out what she really wanted and was fulfilled by, versus what other people had put on her.

The call was from Peter.

"Peter! It's so great to hear from you. How are you?"

She listened, keeping an eye out for a car coming in.

"That's really great to hear. Yeah, I'm doing better too. I think I was overdue for a break." Delaney hadn't told him about the panic attacks. She didn't want to worry him, since his rehab was a lot to worry about already.

A car pulled in, but it was hikers. The leaves were mostly gone, but there was still beauty to be seen here.

"You're right. Absolutely. We need to meet and talk. I—"

She'd been about to say she'd be back after Thanksgiving. But that was still a couple of weeks away. She was staying at the farm until then, but that didn't mean she didn't need to start preparing to leave. She had been putting it off.

Peter wanted to talk as soon as possible. Delaney knew she should make a trip back to the city. Her roommate had been enjoying the apartment to herself, but Delaney could air her room out, and maybe do some laundry. Stock up with the tea and coffee she liked and have a plan in place for when she moved back permanently.

Putting her return off wasn't going to make it any easier. With a feeling of dread, she said "My schedule is flexible. When would you like me to come?"

JORDAN HAD BEEN quiet when she told him at dinner that she was driving to New York next Wednesday.

"It's just for a couple of days. Peter wants to talk. I'll be back for the weekend."

He stared over her shoulder at the kitchen door.

"Take as long as you need. Things are quieter here."

She heard what he wasn't saying. He didn't need her now. Still, she stubbornly insisted she'd be back. She wanted to soak up every minute she could in this happy place so she could remember it when things got hectic in the city.

"Mariah invited me to go to the Goat with her tomorrow night."

Jordan nodded, still not looking at her.

"Come with me."

That got his attention. His shocked gaze met hers.

"What?"

"Come to the Goat. The Goat and Barley."

He frowned. "I know what the Goat is."

Did he go there, sometimes, when he didn't have her staying on the farm?

"Have you been staying home because of me? Would you normally go there?"

Jordan shook his head. "No, Delaney, you haven't cut into my busy social life. Yeah, I know the Goat, but I haven't been there for years."

"Would you come with me?" She rushed on before the refusal she could see coming made it out of his mouth.

"You said you'd like to start getting out to see people. And I know it's difficult to go someplace on your own. If we went together, maybe you'd run into someone you know or meet someone new, and it would be easier to go the next time."

He didn't say anything, so she rushed on. "You can say no. It's an idea, but it's entirely up to you. Just a chance to take the first step with someone else along with you. I mean, I don't know the people who are going to be there either."

She had one other argument, one she knew would have him agree to come in a flash, but was it too manipulative? Was she pushing him again? But no, this was something he said he wanted. Something difficult for him, and she could help.

"And then, if the crowds are a little too much for me—"

He sighed and nodded. "You're right. It would be easier to go with you the first time. I'll drive. If anything gets to you, we can leave."

JORDAN WOULD MUCH rather have stayed in the following night. He'd avoided everyone from Cupid's Crossing, worried that the damage his father had inflicted on the Everton name would make him a pariah. But staying in was better when Delaney was there too.

He didn't want to miss the dwindling number of evenings he had with her, and he wanted to be around if something made her anxious while she was in the crowd. Mariah and Nelson would be there, but Delaney had shared things with Jordan that he didn't think she had with anyone else. He'd be the best to support her if things became too much for her.

His wardrobe left a lot to be desired. He didn't spend money on clothes, so what he had was all for work. The best option he found was his cleanest jeans, and a button-down shirt he wore to meet new customers. It was a little formal, so he rolled up the sleeves.

His hair and beard were past due for a trim. He never had time during harvest season, but if he was going to be social, he should take care of that sooner than later. It wouldn't help for tonight. He shook his head. If he was going to be harassed for being an Everton, the way he looked wouldn't change anything.

Delaney wasn't down yet, so he pulled on his parka and gloves, ready to warm up the truck.

"Sorry, Ranger, you're not on this trip."

After giving him sad eyes, the dog curled up on his dog bed. Jordan didn't think he really minded staying in on a cold evening.

The dog had the right idea, but Jordan had said he'd go out with Delaney, so he grabbed his keys and headed out into the night.

THE PARKING LOT at the Goat and Barley was crowded, and on his own, Jordan would have promptly turned around and driven home. But Delaney was with him, so he found a spot in the back corner and pulled to a stop. He glanced at her, wondering if the crowd was going to be a problem for her.

"You good? We can always go back." He hoped his voice didn't express just how much he hoped she'd go for that option.

She ran a hand over her hair, pushing it back. She'd left it down instead of pulling it back into her usual ponytail. "No, I don't feel anxious at all. It's kind of surprising. I don't think crowds are a problem—there was no one at the Mill when the first attack happened. And if it bothers me, I'll just slow down and do the breathing."

Right. No more excuses.

Delaney led the way to the front of the busy pub. Once they were in the door, the noise and warmth spilled over them. Delaney pushed on tiptoe to look around for Mariah and Nelson.

Jordan pulled in a breath, counted like Delaney did. He wasn't having a panic attack, but he was nervous and stressed.

Since he'd been back, he hadn't done more than drive through Carter's Crossing. That hadn't changed when the name became Cupid's Crossing. The Mill was the only business he dealt with there. It was outside of the town proper, and even that delivery had just started this harvest season. He drove to Oak Hill for his other clients and did his shopping and any other business there.

The Goat and Barley was about halfway between the two towns, but he'd avoided it, since he knew people from the Crossing, whichever one they called it, hung out here. He'd assumed he and his father would still not be welcome.

No one in the crowd recognized him, and no one stopped to ask him how he dared show his face in the place. People jostled them as they made their way through, and then they arrived at a table full of people that he mostly didn't recognize.

Mariah stood up and hugged Delaney. "I'm so glad you made it, Delaney."

Behind her, Nelson stood as well. "Dee, Jordan." He nodded at them.

Jordan nodded back.

The man who'd been seated next to Nelson looked up. It had been years, but Jordan recognized his former friend, Dave Davenport. Dave stood, pushing past Nelson, and grabbed Jordan's hand, pulling him into a bro-hug.

"Jordan, it's so good to see you. And I owe you a big apology. Nelson said you guys worked it out, and I'm really sorry for my part."

Jordan didn't have words. He hadn't expected this. He hadn't expected to meet some-one he knew and be welcomed and offered an apology. He nodded and tried to put on a wel-coming smile.

There was a pretty woman beside Dave. She stared at him, mouth dropping open.

"Jordan? Jordan Everton? Is that you hiding behind all that—" her hand circled her own face, obviously meaning his hair and beard. "It's been years, I wouldn't have recognized you. How are you? Come on, sit down."

Jordan found himself seated at the table be-side her. The woman was Jaycee, now mar-ried to Dave. He was introduced to others, new faces he didn't know.

Most surprising to him though, was that no one said anything about his father, or what had happened at the mill. There'd been a few ques-tions about the corn maze, but most of the con-versation centered on darts. Apparently, that's what Tuesday nights were about.

Once Jordan confirmed that he didn't play, no one bothered him about it. People came and went. After one beer, Jordan stuck to water. He didn't drink much, and he had to drive Delaney home after.

He wasn't the life of the party, but that seemed okay with these people.

Dave shifted to sit by him when everyone else had gone up to watch Mariah play. He'd been told she was the best player in the group, even though she didn't show up every Tuesday night. Tonight she'd been issued a challenge, or Nelson had.

"I really am sorry." Dave was speaking low enough that no one else could overhear. "Nelson and I were totally out of line. I think part of it, for me, was ego. Delaney hadn't really been into me. When I found out about the two of you, I was upset when I had no cause to be.

"Not that I was really interested in her like that, but my mom thought it was a great idea, and I was a kid and thought I was something else. What we did wasn't right, especially now that I know the whole story. I hope you can forgive us, and maybe we can hang out. Jaycee swears we're doing the maze next year."

"Sure." Jordan didn't know what else to say. He was here because he needed to expand his social horizons. And until the blow up, Dave had been a good friend.

He'd assumed any social life he found would be in Oak Hill, because no one would want anything to do with him in Cupid's Crossing. He was wrong about that. He didn't know how much of what he'd assumed about the town came from his dad, and it was time he started thinking for himself.

"THANKS." JORDAN TOLD Delaney as they drove back to the farm.

He could see her head turn towards him in his peripheral vision. "What for?"

He let a smile form. Just a little one. She probably couldn't see it, what with the beard and the dark, but he felt good and let it show. This time.

"For taking me with you tonight."

"You had fun?" She was smiling too. He could hear it in her voice.

He thought over the evening. Was it fun? It wasn't a perfect evening, and not what he'd have chosen for himself, but it got him off the farm and out with people. It hadn't been completely comfortable, but it also hadn't been as difficult as he'd expected.

"Fun-adjacent. It broke the ice. I'd never wanted to go into Cupid's Crossing, because of everything that had happened with my dad. But I spent the evening with people from the Crossing, and they didn't care about that. I wouldn't have done that on my own, so thank you."

A glance confirmed she was smiling.

"I'm really glad, Jordan. So, you'll do it again?"

"Maybe not darts night. But yeah, I'll get out again."

"That's good." It was. Because when Delaney was gone, the farm was going to be lonely.

CHAPTER EIGHTEEN

HAD IT ALWAYS been this noisy?

Delaney didn't normally drive in the city, but she'd driven herself back from Cupid's Crossing since she was only staying in New York a couple of days. The parking would cost a fortune, but she hadn't been spending much while she was at Jordan's.

The contrast between the quiet of his farm and this onslaught of sound was jarring. Being back was going to take some adjusting. She paid to have her grandmother's car taken care of at a nearby garage until she was ready to leave and headed for her apartment with her carryon bag rolling behind her.

Such a difference since she'd left for Cupid's Crossing. She'd hated leaving New York, and resented the position offered by her grandmother because it had felt like failure.

A lot had happened in a couple of months, and she felt like a different Delaney. Like she was trying to fit herself back inside the person she'd been but wasn't any longer.

It would take some getting used to.

Her roommate was at work this time of day, so the apartment was relatively quiet. Delaney went to her room to change from the jeans and sweatshirt she'd worn for the drive up. Her room smelled musty and felt smaller. Bland.

Delaney shook her head. Not the time for musings. She quickly changed into slacks and a cashmere sweater, added jewelry, some makeup. She tied her hair back and put her laptop in a leather briefcase. If she was meeting Peter, they might as well start on planning their next steps. She'd like to incorporate the farm to table ideas that she'd been working on at Jordan's, but in a more refined way. She wasn't sure whether that would interest Peter, but it would make a change, show that their new restaurant wasn't the same as the last one. She wanted to keep some part of the farm with her, if she could.

If he didn't like the idea, that was okay as well. She could keep preparing the kind of food they'd been doing. It was expected. It had been successful before, and it should be again.

A wave of fatigue swept over her. The drive

must have taken more out of her than she thought. But she needed to get going.

She left the apartment and headed for the subway.

PETER WAS WALKING NOW, and it was a relief to see him on his feet. She gripped him in a hug. And held on. Her eyes filled with tears, and she blinked them back.

"It is so good to see you again, Peter." She released him, once she had herself under control again.

Peter was blinking his own eyes. "It's good to see you too, Dee. How's the country been treating you? Looks like it's done you good."

Delaney sniffed. And ran her fingers under her eyes to pick up mascara smudges.

"Yes, it has."

Peter smiled and fidgeted with his cane.

"There's a place down the hall where we can talk. Is that Luciano's coffee you have with you?"

"Nothing but."

Delaney walked beside him, slowing her steps to match his pace. He glanced at her, smiling, but still nervous. "I love you for it. The coffee here...well, let's not call it coffee."

Delaney laughed and followed him to a small room, with a couple of chairs and a TV.

Peter collapsed on a chair with a sigh.

"How's it going? For real." Delaney asked as she set the coffee and scones out.

"Slow. Difficult. Boring." He shook his head at her. "Don't even start."

"But—"

"No, Delaney, you didn't do this to me. Just drop that before we go any further."

Delaney drew a deep breath and sat down.

"Okay. I'll pretend."

"No pretending—it's not your fault. Full Stop. End."

Her shoulders slumped. "I'm working on it, I promise. In any case, it's not why you wanted to talk to me. So, thinking of what we'll do now? I had some ideas—I've been working on the farm to table concept, since I've been on a farm, and I've been inspired. Does that have any appeal to you?"

Peter didn't respond immediately.

"Peter?"

He closed his eyes. Delaney checked out his expression.

"What is it? Are you in pain?"

A shake of his head.

"Are you not going to get all your mobility

back? Is there something else wrong?" Delaney gripped her hands; not sure she could handle Peter being permanently disabled.

He opened his eyes and held up his hand.

"Slow down, Delaney. Nothing like that."

Delaney glared at him. "You scared me, Peter. Whatever it is, spill. I know your bad news face."

He gave her a lopsided grin. "Yeah, I guess you do. I told you it was boring here, didn't I?"

She nodded.

He rubbed his hands on his thighs. Delaney pinched her lips together, determined to let him have his say. It was bad news, whatever it was.

"Okay. I've had a lot of time to think. This—" He waved at his hip. "Was a wake-up call. For a minute there, I really thought that might be it for me."

Chills rippled over her skin at the thought. She was about to apologize again when he held up his hand and shook his head.

"We're not doing that. But I've been thinking about my life, what I want, where it's going, and I've realized something. I don't want to start another restaurant."

Peter stopped then, and Delaney processed

what he'd said. "Start another restaurant ever? Or with me?"

Peter leaned forward and held her hands. "It's not you, Dee. You were a great partner. You are a great partner. But I want to spend more time with my life partner. I still want to cook, but I want to do my job and then be free to enjoy the rest of my time. Owning the restaurant—that demands so much of your life."

Delaney was still struggling to understand. "You don't want to open another restaurant."

He shook his head. "If you do, I'd be thrilled to work for you. I mean that. But when I leave the place, I don't want to have to worry about staffing and scheduling and supplier problems or if the rent is going up. Not anymore.

"I'll help you all I can, but as a friend, not a partner. I hope that doesn't upset you. I love you, Dee, but my priorities have changed."

Delaney squeezed his hands.

"Peter, please, that's fine. You're entitled to put what you want first. I'm not upset, I promise. I just… I guess I need to see how my priorities line up now."

"You still want a restaurant, don't you?"

She shrugged. "I don't even know. I just knew that was the next step. We'd start over. But if it's just me, well…"

Peter squeezed her hands. "Delaney Carter, were you going to do this just for me?"

His hands gripped hers tightly, and she could see that the idea upset him. "Maybe? I don't know."

Peter sighed. "I don't recommend getting shot in the pelvis to anyone. But the good thing that came out of it was time to evaluate my life and what I wanted. You should do the same. I'm feeling optimistic about my future now, and I want that for you."

Delaney's smile was a little wobbly. "I know, Peter, I know. And I will."

"You think about what you want for you, not me or anyone else. Find what makes you happy."

Delaney frowned. "Don't you dare make me cry, Peter."

Peter let her hands go and leaned back in his chair. "I'll try not to. Let's leave the serious stuff aside for now. Instead, tell me what's been going on with you, because did I mention it's been boring here? Tell me about this farm to table stuff."

THE HOUSE WAS QUIET.

That was normal. But for the past several weeks, it hadn't been this quiet. There'd been the sounds of Delaney in the kitchen, making something delicious. Asking about corn or potatoes or telling him about the hikers. Footsteps and the sounds of water running.

And the kissing.

Now it was just him and Ranger. Ranger was not a good cook. And Jordan had no desire to kiss him, though he loved the dog.

Delaney had left a fridge full of leftovers he could reheat for meals, and he knew they'd be good. He was almost done harvesting, and the interruptions by customers weren't a problem. But he was restless and on edge.

He should get used to it, because Delaney wasn't here much longer. Thanksgiving was just over a week away.

He could go out. Leave the house and go somewhere to find company. Before, that hadn't been a real option. After going to the Goat with Delaney, he knew he could do it again. If he went back to the Goat, he might meet new people. Or he could reach out to Dave or Nelson.

He remembered Jaycee's words, about not recognizing him with his shaggy hair and beard. He needed a haircut and trim.

There. That's what he ould do. Anyone desperate for potatoes could just wait. He'd get his hair cut in Oak Hill, at the barber he visited too infrequently. After, maybe he'd stop some-where. Grab a drink or a meal.

The farm had been his refuge for so long. Now, it wasn't the same. It felt more like a cage.

FRIDAY AFTERNOON. Delaney was due back sometime soon. She'd planned to leave the city about an hour or so ago, so it was going to take a while yet, but Jordan had prepared.

He'd cleaned the house. During harvest, that tended to be a task he let go, but he had the time now, and he thought it would be nice for Delaney. He'd changed the sheets on her bed and aired out the room, doing his best to stay on the hotel maid side of the room-intruder line, and not cross into snooping. The bath-room shone, and she still had products in the shower. That reassured him. She was coming back.

The downstairs was dusted and vacuumed, and he'd mopped the kitchen floor. Washed all the dishcloths and tea towels. There was one of her casseroles in the oven, waiting to be warmed up.

He'd showered and shaved as well. Looking in the mirror he saw a different person than he was used to. He ran a hand over his chin. It was strange to be without the beard, but he'd been hiding behind it. He wanted to show Delaney that he'd be okay after she left. She didn't need to worry about the farm and him. He'd miss her, but she'd changed him, and he was better for it.

He heard tires on the gravel. It was late in the day for hikers, so it must be someone for the store. He had limited stock, but that didn't mean he'd turn down a customer. He grabbed his jacket, prepared to jog over.

He might close up early today. He didn't want to be distracted from Delaney.

He came around from the back, expecting to see a vehicle outside the store. Instead, he found a familiar car parked in front of the house. A tall, lean man with iron gray hair was standing beside the truck, staring around the lot.

He blinked. "Dad?"

What was his dad doing here now, early and unannounced?

His father swung his gaze over to him. He was frowning, brows down. "What's this I hear about you and the Carters?"

He felt a lurch in his stomach. This was going to be bad. Maybe lose the deal to buy the farm bad.

"What did you hear?"

He didn't know what his dad knew. Was it about doing business with the Mill? Jordan had set up OPD just to keep his father in the dark about that, but had he found something with the name of the Mill in the bank records?

That would be bad enough, but Delaney was on her way here, and her things were in the house. He didn't want to think about how his father would respond to that. He had to do something, find a way to make sure this didn't blow up. Abigail Carter didn't live here anymore, so his dad couldn't protest in front of her house, but Nelson had his vet clinic and lived on the Abbot's old farm, not too far away.

Why had his father driven up early without telling him?

"It's on the internet."

Jordan frowned. He hadn't put anything connected to the Mill or the Carter family on their website. "What is?"

"Pictures of that Carter girl here, at the store."

Jordan was sure Delaney hadn't posted any pictures, but maybe customers had.

Still, all his father could know from those pictures was that Delaney had been at the store. That was better than knowing she was staying here. Though unless he could convince his dad everything was good and get him out of here, Delaney was going to show up soon and then the truth would be out.

He'd best try to explain in a way that his father could handle. He hoped.

"Delaney helped with the store and wrote up some recipes to help sell the crop."

Not like his father wouldn't find that out if he asked around. Maybe if Jordan admitted that he could convince him…what? To turn around and drive back to Florida? No, that wasn't going to happen.

He could text Delaney, ask her to stay at her brother's. He could pack up her stuff. But how could he get his dad out of the way while he did that? She had things all over the house—including a freezer full of food.

Okay, next plan, get his dad away for a bit, and ask Delaney to get her stuff while they were gone. Yeah, that might be doable.

"Why was a Carter here on our land? *My* land?"

His father's arms were crossed, expression set in anger. Why couldn't his dad let this go? Everyone else had. The feud had done nothing but harm the Evertons so far.

Until now. How would Delaney handle his father, when she was still coping with panic attacks? Last time she'd seen him, she'd left Carter's Crossing for boarding school.

"Let's go out for dinner, and I'll explain it all. You must be hungry after driving, so we'll grab a bite, and I'll tell you what happened."

Yeah, and maybe in public his dad couldn't flip out as much.

His dad's eyes narrowed, and then Jordan heard tires on the drive.

Another customer? Hiker? Someone to distract his father?

Lead settled in his stomach as he recognized Delaney's car.

CHAPTER NINETEEN

JORDAN WATCHED DELANEY approach with the inevitability of a car crash. She pulled up beside his father's car and stepped out.

"Jordan?" She wouldn't recognize his father, would she? It had been a long time.

"This is her, the Carter girl. Something rotten's going on here."

Delaney turned to his father and took a step back. Jordan wasn't surprised—his father was furious.

"Delaney, you remember my father?"

"Mr. Everton, hello. Maybe I should go, Jordan?"

"You should go and never come back. Never set foot on this property again. Stay away from me and my son and tell your family that whatever they've been planning, it's not going to work. You might be able to fool him, but not me."

Delaney drew back, as if the words had struck her. Jordan stepped forward, putting himself between them.

"That's enough, Dad. This whole feud is more than enough. It's over. You need to move on."

His father turned on him, his face ugly and cruel.

"Move on? I'll move on when those murderous, thieving, treacherous—"

"Stop!" Jordan wasn't sure he'd ever raised his voice to his father before. "Whatever happened in the past, Delaney has nothing to do with it. You're getting worse about this. The Carters have never and will never be out to get us!"

"Oh, she's already worked on you, has she? Seducing you, whispering her lies…did she sleep with you? In my house?"

Jordan found himself moving, hands pushing against his father, desperate to get him to stop. The older man slipped, fell down.

"Stop it! You can't talk like that about her!"

His father stared up at him. "And how do you think you can stop me? Gonna hit me? Knock me down again? I can call the cops, get you arrested for assault."

Jordan stepped back. He was trembling with the effort it took to control his temper.

"I won't stay here and listen to that garbage you keep spouting. You need help."

Everton pushed himself to his feet. "I don't need help from you or anyone else. And you don't have to stay here and listen to anything. Go. Go off with your Carter witch. But if you go, don't come back."

Jordan rubbed his hands over his eyes. This was—it was a disaster.

"It's okay, Jordan. I'll get my stuff and go to Nelson's." Delaney's hand was soft on his arm, comforting.

Everton turned to her, snarl on his face. "Yeah, you'd like to get whatever you want from here, wouldn't you?"

Jordan pushed between them again. "She's been staying here for weeks. If she wanted something, she already found it."

Delaney turned her eyes toward him, hurt showing. Jordan reached for her hand.

"But she hasn't found anything, because there's nothing here she wants, Dad. The Carters don't care about this feud you keep obsessing over. It's just you, no one else."

"She got you, didn't she? Probably found everything she needs, and you were too stupid to see it. What a worthless, useless thing you are. Thank goodness you're not really my blood."

The silence stretched. Jordan blinked, unsure of what he had heard. Not his blood? What was he talking about? How could he not be an Everton? The old man must just be flailing, trying to hurt him. His father was smiling, a nasty glint in his eye.

"Guess you don't know as much as you thought, do you? Your mother was pregnant when I met her. I'm not your father, and I'm glad of it."

That hurt. The man had been a terrible father, but at least he'd been one, nominally.

"Go on!" The man swung his arms. "Get out of here! You're not mine and I don't want you."

Jordan wasn't sure there was any feeling in his limbs. He didn't know if he could move. Suddenly Delaney was back beside him, holding him up.

"Fine, Mr. Everton. We'll go. But we're taking our things now, and Jordan will come back for anything he's forgotten."

Her voice was cold, her disdain evident. "Watch me if you want. But the only thing of value here is this man, and you're throwing him out. That makes you the worthless one."

Then she was moving him, into the house, and up the stairs. She led him into his room, the room that had been his but wasn't now, and let him drop on the bed. He watched, eyes unfocussed, as she gathered things up and put them in a couple of duffle bags.

Then she crossed the hallway to the room that she'd stayed in. She took a moment in the bathroom to gather the things in there.

"Jordan."

Gentle fingers ran over his cheeks. She was wiping away the tears he hadn't even known were falling.

"I didn't get a chance to tell you. I like the new look."

He nodded. Then shook his head.

"Do you want me to carry those bags?"

He shrugged. Wait. He had to do something.

He rose to his feet and picked them up. Okay. One thing at a time. Carry the bags. That he could do. He stood outside the door of the bedroom, unsure where to go. Delaney came out with her bag, ran a hand over his arm.

"Just follow me."

Down the familiar stairs. He heard his father—no, not his father, Mr. Everton, in the kitchen. He should warn him Delaney made the food in the oven. Or he could wait till the old man had eaten and tell him then. What would he do after he discovered he'd eaten Delaney's food?

He almost laughed, but he couldn't do it.

Delaney gently pushed him out the door, and to his truck. He threw his bags into the back, but now what? What was he supposed to do, where was he supposed to go?

Delaney opened the passenger door and Ranger jumped in. She gave him another gentle push and he got in the truck. He was vaguely aware of someone else there—who was it? Oh, Dave, and he'd driven over Mariah. Delaney must have called. How long had they been upstairs? Mariah got into Delaney's car. Then Delaney was in the driver's seat of the truck, pulling it forward.

"Where are we going?" He didn't really care, but he should probably know.

"Nelson's. Don't worry about it—I told them we needed to stay at their place. No one is going to bother you."

Huh. Maybe she should explain to him what had just happened, because he had no idea. But he no longer had a chance of owning the farm. He had…nothing.

DELANEY WAS WORRIED about Jordan. He'd been surprisingly docile as she drove to Nelson and Mariah's farm. Hadn't complained. Saturday he'd gone out of the house with Ranger, walked somewhere and only returned as the sun set.

The next day she'd given him a backpack with water, a thermos of coffee and some sandwiches when he left to do the same.

It was Monday, and she couldn't let him pace Nelson's farm for another day, so she waited at the door until he came down from the bedroom. She didn't trust Everton and didn't know if they could believe anything he'd said, especially about Jordan's birth. They had to find out what was truth, and what was spite and what was going to happen to Jordan's future on the farm. She didn't know what her future was, not after talking to Peter, but she needed to make sure Jordan had his farm. She'd do the work for him, but she had to get his permission and find out what he knew for her to start.

He came down the stairs with that same blank expression on his face. He hadn't shaved since the confrontation with his father, notfather, whatever the man was. She was pretty sure he had on the same clothes he'd been wearing since they left the farm. He ducked his head when he saw her, as if hiding.

No. She'd had a chance to work some things out, and Jordan hiding from her was not part of her plan.

She pulled on her hat and zipped up her jacket. "Let's go."

"Where?"

"I have no idea. Wherever you've been going these last couple of days. I've got water, coffee and sandwiches. Also, some cookies." And a notepad and pen, but that was phase two. Phase one was getting him to accept her company.

"Why?"

Why had a lot of answers, and she didn't think he was ready for some of them. "Because we need to take action. Or at least, someone does. I'll do it if you don't want to, but then I need information from you."

He shrugged. "Nothing to be done." He stomped off the porch and Delaney followed him.

When she was still behind him once he was past the barn, he turned to face her. "What are you doing?"

"Following you." That was obvious.

"Don't."

She shook her head. "I gave you two days to mope. Now it's time to do something."

He looked past her, hands on his hips. "What, Delaney? What exactly am I supposed to do? I don't have a father, I don't have a farm, I don't have a home or a job."

Exactly. "We need to figure it out."

"What *we*?"

"You and me. I'm with you on this."

"Why? You don't owe me anything. Just go, back to the city, to your life."

He was finally looking at her, and she could see the pain in his eyes. No, she wasn't leaving.

"I promised I was here till Thanksgiving. Still got a few days."

He waved an arm. "I release you from your promise."

"Sorry, that doesn't work."

He turned around again and stomped on. Delaney tagged along. He hadn't told her not to.

They travelled like this for about ten minutes. Delaney didn't know her brother's farm, but Jordan must after two days of tromping around.

"I can't stay here." He growled. Tension left her body. He was talking, finally.

"Of course not. That's why we have to start doing things."

He stopped, staring over the bare trees. He released a long, shuddering breath. "I don't know what to do."

It wasn't hard to see how much that hurt him. Again, something she could lay at his father's door. She hadn't known what to do either after the talk with Peter, but she'd worked at it. She didn't have to process the shock that Jordan did.

"First, I think we need to figure out if Mr. Everton was lying."

Jordan whipped around. "Lying? Why would he lie?"

Delaney shrugged. "I don't know. Anger? Spite? Revenge? He doesn't seem like a very nice man. Would he do that? Lie just to hurt someone?"

Jordan stared over the field behind them. "Possibly."

"So, I thought that was step one. The answer to that might bring up some legal issues."

Jordan looked at her. His eyes were clearer now, more alert.

"How would we do that? Force him to take a paternity test?"

"That's an option. But it would involve lawyers, and it's going to take a while. I wondered if you had any documents, knew anything about your mother's family, things like that to start."

He shook his head. "Da-he wouldn't talk about her after she died. And before that, we never talked about her family. I think they cut her off."

"What about those papers in the envelope in your closet?"

His brow creased. "What…oh. That was some stuff my mom saved. He was going to throw it out, back before we moved to Florida. I saved it, tossed it in the closet before we left and kinda forgot about it."

He ran his hand over the stubble on his chin. "Wait, how do you know about that?"

"I packed your bags Friday. I was grabbing things from your closet, and there was an envelope with your mom's name on it. I thought it might be important and threw it in with your clothes."

He sighed. "Go ahead and look if you want. I don't think it's going to help you."

"Us."

"Us?"

"It's not to help you, it's to help us." She smiled at him.

"There's no us, Delaney. You're leaving, remember?"

"That's kind of up in the air right now, but let's deal with that another time."

He shrugged. Then started walking again. Delaney followed. They came to a stream, with a fallen log beside it. The leaves on the deciduous trees were gone, only evergreens still providing color. It was stark, but beautiful in its own way.

Jordan sat on the log. Delaney sat down beside him and shrugged off the backpack. She pulled out two thermoses, and the sandwiches. She shoved one thermos at him, relieved when he took it and unscrewed the lid. She watched him pour out the coffee, sweetened the way he liked it. He took a sip.

"Thank you."

"For the food?"

Jordan nodded. "And for taking care of me the last couple of days. I don't know why this has thrown me like this. I never really cared for him."

Delaney shifted closer to Jordan. "But he was part of your identity. And you love the farm—it was your safe place. He pulled the foundations of your life apart. That was cruel. I just hope there's something we can do about it."

Jordan turned the thermos cap in his hands, watching the coffee swirl. "I'll need to find a job, and a place to stay. Probably won't be able to do anything until after the holiday."

Good. He was starting to think ahead.

"I know Nelson and Mariah will let you stay

here as long as you need." They'd already told Delaney she could stay.

The corner of his mouth pulled, not quite in a smile. "The Carters are going to save me. If I'm not really an Everton, that makes sense."

Delaney put a hand on his arm. "I don't care if you're an Everton or not. You're Jordan, and that's all that's important."

THEY WENT BACK to the house after lunching on sandwiches and cookies. Nelson was at the vet clinic, and Mariah was busy running the town, which was what she seemed to do most days. Jordan went to take a shower and told Delaney to go ahead and look at the papers. He asked her to destroy anything she thought he wouldn't want to see.

Delaney went down to the big country kitchen, thinking very uncharitable thoughts about Everton senior. She set the envelope down on the kitchen island. It was a size larger than a legal envelope and was stuffed full. On it was a name, Martha Callahan, with Everton added in a different colored ink. Callahan must be his mother's maiden name. Delaney had only known her as Martha Everton.

The seal was old and opened easily. Delaney drew the contents out carefully. There were some old photos, and other envelopes, two from legal firms. Delaney had a strong feeling that there were things in here that were going to blow up Jordan's life all over again. She hesitated, not sure she should do this. This was private, for Jordan, and maybe he needed time before he received any more shocks.

But he'd asked her. He trusted her. If there was anything too bad, she could wait to tell him. She just desperately hoped for some way to salvage his safe place for him, and this was the only immediate option. She didn't trust Everton senior and they needed to move quickly. What if the man sold the farm before Jordan had his chance?

She carefully checked out each item. A couple of times, she reread the paperwork, just to clarify the contents. She made notes and stacked the paperwork up carefully in piles. Then she made some more coffee and waited for Jordan. This was going to shock him. But it was going to be good, she hoped.

She heard his footsteps coming down the stairs and got up to pour him a mug of coffee.

"Thanks." His hair was damp, and his face freshly shaven again. His expression was determined, the blankness gone from his eyes.

Delaney hoped this new information wouldn't bring it back.

"You ready?"

He searched her face. "Do I want to see this?"

She put a hand up to his cheek. "I think so."

He closed his eyes, leaning into her touch. "Then let's get it over with."

At the table, she sat across from him.

"There are some photos. I think you'll like them." She passed the pictures over, and he picked them up carefully. There were only a few. One she thought was his mother and Everton on their wedding day. If you suspected it, you might think the dress his mother was wearing was covering a baby bump.

Then three with Jordan and his mother, baby, toddler and maybe a first day of school photo?

That was all. Everton was only in the one picture.

Jordan ran a finger over one of the photos. "I'd almost forgotten what she looked like."

Delaney swallowed a lump in her throat.

He blinked rapidly, and then looked up. "What else?"

"There's a copy of your birth certificate, no

name given as father. And a copy of adoption papers. Everton legally adopted you."

Jordan pushed his mug out of the way.

"So, he was right. He's not my father."

"Legally, he is. Your adopted father. But probably not your biological father."

He leaned back in the chair. "In a way, that's a relief. It explains a lot."

Delaney wasn't sure she wanted to know all that lay behind his remark. "There's nothing in here to indicate who that man was, your biological father."

Jordan shrugged. "I wonder why Everton married her. If he knew she was pregnant, or maybe she tricked him."

"In any case, he adopted you when you were about two."

Jordan ran a hand over his face. "I don't even know what to do with all this information."

"There's something more you need to know. It's good news, I think. But it means we're going to need a lawyer."

Delaney pulled forward the oldest of the papers she'd found, and also the biggest.

"I'm not a lawyer, so I did my best to understand what this was really saying. I've read a few contracts while we were getting the restaurant up. This is… I guess some kind of trust? It's about the farm."

Jordan stared at the envelope. "I didn't know there was any kind of trust connected to the farm."

Delaney had suspected as much. "It's also in the same of Callahan."

Jordan looked up, puzzled. "That was Mom's name."

"I guessed. The farm was her family's, not your dad's."

Jordan didn't move.

For a moment, Delaney wondered if she hadn't said the words out loud. She opened her mouth to repeat them when Jordan spoke.

"But I thought it was the Everton's farm. I mean…" He shoved his hand through his shorter hair. "I'm trying to remember when we first moved there. I'd never been before, and I didn't even think about which family it had belonged to. I was just glad to have a place we could stay."

Delaney didn't doubt that Everton had carefully kept this information from Jordan after his mother died.

"Best I can tell, this trust is in effect until both the current owner or guardian and heir agree to dissolve it, and that hadn't happened yet, as far as this paperwork goes. Your mother inherited it under these terms, so unless you signed something, after you reached the age of majority, it's yours, once you turn thirty-five or get married."

Jordan was frowning at the table, fingers still rubbing on the top.

"I'm pretty sure I'd remember anything like that."

She hoped he would. She had no faith that Everton wouldn't have tried to find a way to use the farm for his own benefit.

"If the farm belonged to my mother, and I don't get it till I'm thirty-five." He paused, and Delaney noted that he passed right by the married option. "Who owns it now?"

Then he looked at her, something bright in his eyes. "It'll be mine?"

Delaney tapped the papers in front of her. "If I'm reading this right. I'd guess your father—your adopted father—is the guardian of it till then."

Jordan flinched. "This is a mess."

"Rachel Slade works for a lawyer. You might remember her as Pastor Lowther's daughter? She was in your class. Want me to see if she can get you in to check this over?"

"Oh yeah. I want to know what's up." He

looked up at her. "Is it possible to see someone this close to Thanksgiving?"

Delaney had been itching to call but held
back. She wasn't going to push on this—it was
Jordan's decision. "I'll contact her. See if it's
possible."

Jordan pushed to his feet. "I need to talk to
him. Make sure he doesn't do something to
mess up the farm. If he scatters pesticide on
the fields…"

Delaney grabbed his arm. "Why don't you
let me talk to Rachel first. Make sure I'm right
about what I'm saying. I'm not a lawyer."

Delaney could feel the tension running
through his arm. "I need to do something. I
can't just sit."

"Let's go shopping."

Jordan stared at her like she'd asked him to
go skinny dipping.

"I'm making Thanksgiving dinner. I'll call
Rachel, and then I need to get a turkey."

She wasn't sure if he'd agree, but with a
shake of his head, he said, "Sure. I'm going to
go stir crazy just sitting here waiting. Let's go."

She took some photos on her phone of what
seemed like the most important parts of the
trust document, and sent it in an email to Rachel, asking if there was anything she could

help them with, so they understood what was going on as soon as possible. Then she grabbed her shopping bags, and they got in Jordan's truck.

Rachel called Delaney as she was weighing the merits of two smaller turkeys versus one large one. Delaney stepped aside in a quiet corner of the store to answer her. She thanked Rachel and looked up at Jordan. "Rachel says if we come right now, we can talk to the new lawyer, Deacon Standish, for a few minutes.

Jordan nodded.

CHAPTER TWENTY

THE MEETING WAS SHORT. There was only so much Deacon could tell them after one reading of the document, but Rachel had managed to check that no changes to the trust had been recorded. Therefore, the farm was Jordan's in another two years. Unless he got married. Deacon wasn't sure if Everton could keep Jordan off the farm until either of those events occurred. They thanked Rachel and Deacon for fitting them in. Deacon promised to work on the issue as soon as he could.

Outside, they paused by Jordan's truck.

"I need to go to the farm." It was the one thing he was sure of.

Delaney paused at the passenger door. "Do you think that's wise?"

"I don't know. I need to know if he's there, or if he's gone again and what he plans to do." Jordan needed to know if he could make plans. If he had a home.

"When do you want to go?"

"Now."

Delaney stepped back. "Would you rather go alone? I can stop at the diner or find Mariah. He won't be happy to see me."

Jordan checked her expression. He couldn't imagine anyone wanting to be around for this meeting with his father, but he wanted her there. And maybe it was okay to ask for that. Even if there were only a few more days before she was gone.

"You don't have to come." Did she understand he was giving her an out, but he'd like her to come?

"I will." A tentative smile crossed her face. "I'll see what he's done to my store."

He liked that she was possessive about the store. He wanted her to be possessive about him too.

They didn't speak on the drive. Jordan was anxious, determined to find out what was going on. Needing to know what his next two years would be like. Because he wouldn't marry just anyone to get his farm, and the only person he could think of marrying now was Delaney. But she was leaving.

He found himself counting his breaths, like Delaney had learned to do.

The gate to the farm was shut, and the sign

was turned to Closed. Jordan opened the gate and drove through. He pulled up in the lot, in front of the house. The car his father had arrived in was there, but there was no sign of the man himself.

They got out of the truck, and stood, looking around, unsure of what to do and where to go. There was no sign of any changes.

The front door slammed open.

"What are you doing here? I told you to leave. I'll call the cops."

Jordan didn't think he would. The closest police would come from Cupid's Crossing, and his father refused to deal with anyone from there.

"I came for my things. And to find out what you're going to do with the farm for the next two years until it's mine."

The man stepped back. "What are you talking about?"

"The trust. Do you really think the lawyers wouldn't reach out to me??"

The man's lips twitched. "How did they find you?" Anger rose. The man had deliberately kept him in the dark about this and had manipulated things to keep Jordan from knowing who really owned the farm.

Jordan had planned to pay him for property that was his own. How twisted was that?

"They didn't. I found the paperwork when Delaney packed up the stuff in my room."

"Interfering Carters." Anger flushed the man's face.

Jordan took a step forward, putting himself between Delaney and his father.

"Why didn't you tell me?"

"Why would I?"

Obviously ethical and moral considerations had no value to this man. He was a stranger to Jordan now, not the man he'd known all his life. "If you hate me so much, why did you bother adopting me?"

The man's eyes flashed. "Been doing a lot of snooping, have you?"

"It's not snooping when it's my life."

Another pause. Then, "I told your mother I'd adopt you. We'd get the farm when her father died, and I'd marry her and adopt her kid. Her family had kicked her out when she got knocked up."

Jordan didn't follow. The farm wasn't enough to tempt his father to agree to a marriage.

"She was supposed to break the trust when you were of legal age, but she died. And now, the place is mine for two more years. If you want to stay here, you have to do exactly what I say. And that means no Carters."

Jordan didn't believe him. The man would be vindictive. He wouldn't keep to his side of any bargain, not if there was a chance to make money, or get back at the Carters.

He was done with depending on this undependable man.

"I'm not staying here as your unpaid labor, not now that I know you've lied to me. In two years, the place is mine."

"What's left of it."

Jordan took a step forward, then stopped. He couldn't give the man any ammunition, any excuse to destroy the farm out of spite.

"I don't know what's twisted you up so much, but I won't risk being like you. I'll get my stuff and be gone. You'll hear from my lawyer." He hoped Deacon could do something to protect the farm.

The man laughed, nastily, and Jordan tensed as he passed him to enter the house. He wasn't sure Everton wouldn't turn violent.

Jordan could only take what was his. The laptop, the files, those all belonged to the farm. He took the stairs two at a time and stopped in the doorway of his room. Not his anymore. Would the house even be here in two years?

He could hear his father's raised voice, and knew he was talking to Delaney. He shouldn't have left her there without any protection, but he wouldn't have been able to bring her in the house this time. He should have just left the rest of his belongings. He could replace them.

He crossed to the window, slipping the pane up so he could tell Delaney to get in the truck, lock it, and ignore the man yelling at her.

"It's none of your business, Carter girl. I don't owe him anything. And I've got two years to destroy this place, just like the Carters destroyed us."

His logic made no sense. He never used to be this bad. Jordan hadn't seen him much over the past few years and hadn't realized. He was so twisted with hate and envy that all he wanted to do was hurt people. Jordan didn't want to leave his father alone on the farm and have to rebuild it again, but he couldn't spend two years around Everton. It would be bad enough living his life without Delaney, let alone listening to this poison.

"Don't get too comfortable. You won't be here long." Delaney's voice was strong and confident.

"I've got two years. Oh wait, two years and three months, till his 35th birthday."

She crossed her arms, holding her ground. "Unless he gets married."

Jordan had thought of that. But he only wanted Delaney. He wouldn't use someone else just to get his inheritance, not like this man had used his mother.

"He's not going to get married." But the man's voice was less confident.

"He is if I have anything to do with it."

Jordan gripped the window. What was she saying?

"A Carter stoop to marry an Everton? Not likely. You don't need the farm. Or is this part of some new plan your grandmother has? What do you want to do with this land?"

Delaney was talking about marrying him to scare his father. That's all she could be doing. She had a future in New York, and she didn't care about him. Not the way he did for her.

"I don't care about the farm. I care about Jordan. I love him. And I'd marry him today if he wanted. So maybe you want to be a little nicer. Work something out."

"You're bluffing." Everton said. "Trying to manipulate me."

She smiled. "I'm not the one with the vendetta. I just want to make him happy. Hmmm.

Maybe tomorrow would be a good day to shop for a ring."

Jordan finally came to his senses and gently slid the window back down.

Did Delaney mean that? Could she love him? How could it possibly work? If he didn't have the farm, then, maybe he could follow her to New York, but no, if they got married, he'd have the farm.

Would Delaney consider staying here?

It didn't seem possible, but in any case, it wasn't fair to leave her to more of Everton's hate. He stuffed more clothing in a bag to justify the trip and looked around the room. There was nothing else of value here. But maybe he could change that.

JORDAN WAS DESPERATE to talk to Delaney, but he was nervous. Had he read too much into her conversation with Everton? Had she just been giving him a bad time?

When they'd returned to Nelson's place later on Monday, Mariah and Nelson had returned. He'd given Delaney permission to tell them what they'd learned. Nelson wanted to take immediate action, and Mariah had given him a speculative look. Jordan had taken Ranger for a walk, and when he returned, found Delaney and Mariah in the middle of a conversation they stopped as soon as he appeared.

Delaney was sitting at the table, working over a list when he came back from a morning walk with Ranger on Tuesday. He didn't like to let the dog loose with the horses, not until he was sure how both the horses and Ranger would behave. They had no animals on the farm, so this was new for the dog.

"What are you planning?"

Delaney smiled up at him. "Thanksgiving dinner. Grandmother and Gerry are going to be here, so I need to up my game. I'm going to the store again once I've got my list done."

Gerry was the multi-millionaire Delaney's grandmother was dating, and Mariah's grandfather. "They're that demanding?"

Delaney shook her head. "Not really, but now I need to add a couple more dishes. And I want them to be perfect."

Of course she did. "They will be. Would you like me to get what you need, save you some time?"

He could put off talking for a couple of hours, help her get ready for the big dinner. The results were always worth it.

He drove into Oak Hill, stopping at the bank. When Everton and he had set up the arrangement to transfer the farm, they'd opened a bank account in Oak Hill, separate from the farm's other accounts. He could deposit money, and transfer funds to the Florida account.

Now he knew it was a further step to ensure Jordan didn't find the truth. He checked to see if his father had done anything to empty that bank account. Assured that his signature would be required on any withdrawals, he did a few errands for himself as well as getting the items Delaney had listed. When he returned the house was full of the delectable odors that meant Delaney was cooking. She looked up when he came in and smiled, and he took a risk, crossing over to put the bags down and kiss her. Her smile grew bigger.

"Thank you."

"It's my pleasure. Really. Because what you make with this is amazing. Want any help?"

"That would be great. I've got pasta for tonight, and a lighter, vegetarian soup for tomorrow night so we're not too stuffed for the big turkey dinner on Thursday, so there's lots of chopping."

That was fine with him. It would give them a chance to talk.

Delaney dropped a cutting board and knife

in front of him, and then a row of onions. "This okay?"

"Okay." He agreed.

She marked something off on her notebook and went back to the stove.

"So, your grandmother is coming?"

"Umhmm. They were supposed to be in Europe, but they came back last night."

"Where do they normally live?" He wasn't used to a jet setting lifestyle, where travelling to and from Europe wasn't a big deal.

"Gerry's got a big place in New York, and that's where his businesses are. He's stepping back, but he still keeps his hand in."

"And they're coming up here for Thanksgiving?"

"They'll be here tomorrow night."

"Are you going back to New York with them after the holiday?"

Was his voice even? He was trying. If she was going back to New York, then he could ignore what she'd told his father.

"Actually.... No. I'm not."

Jordan stopped his chopping. Delaney met his gaze, her hands moving restlessly on the counter.

"You're going later? On your own?"

"I'm not sure I'm going. At all."

Something inside his chest was tripping up, making it harder to breathe.

"That was your plan, right?"

She drew in a long, slow breath and huffed it out. "Plans are changing. Peter—you remember Peter?"

"Your partner in the restaurant?"

She nodded. "He doesn't want to start up another restaurant."

That's what Delaney had talked about. Starting up another restaurant with Peter. But didn't she want that anyway? He had total confidence that she could manage it without any partners.

"You don't want to do that on your own?"

Delaney shrugged. "I could. Peter said he'd be happy to work for me, but he didn't want the extra responsibilities of being the owner. After the shooting, he re-evaluated his priorities."

Jordan didn't know anything about managing a restaurant. Maybe it was too much work to do solo. "Is a restaurant too much for you on your own?"

"It depends."

He waited.

"I could do it, but I'd have to give up a lot."

What was she not willing to give up? This was her thing—being a Carter success in her field. Why was she making him drag this out of her? "What would you have to give up?"

She wiped her apron. "Free time. Friends. Dating. Marriage and family. At least, to do it the way I'd planned to."

He pressed his hands against the counter to hide their trembling, but he couldn't hide the husk in his voice.

"And you want that?"

A glance at him before more fussing with the apron. "The time away from it all these last couple of months, yeah, I realized there were things I wanted that weren't all about a restaurant."

Was there any chance that he was one of the things she wanted?

"What are you going to do instead?"

Delaney waved her hands. "I have a few ideas."

"Did you mean what you said to my father? Everton?"

Her eyes widened, and her cheeks flushed. "Mean what?"

"I heard you. I opened the window when I heard him yelling. You said—"

It was hard to get this out. Hard to say it like there was any possibility at all that she'd been serious.

"I said…." She echoed.

"That you would marry me. That you love me and would marry me." He knew his cheeks were flushing, and he no longer had the protection of his beard and long hair to hide behind.

Delaney laid down her spoon. "And if I did?"

"Would you be okay staying here, in Cupid's Crossing? Would that be enough? We could do some of those things you wanted on the farm, or you could find another restaurant."

Delaney looked at him, and it wasn't a happy face.

"I love you, Delaney. It's not about the farm."

Delaney held up her hand. "No, no, you can't do this."

The bottom fell out of his stomach. Everything inside him dropped, leaving him empty and hurting. He looked at the onions, picked up the knife. This would cover the stinging tears in his eyes.

"No, I get it."

She'd been helping, like she'd been doing all fall. Helping him get the farm and making it a success. How could he possibly have imagined she'd really care for him?

Suddenly Delaney was right in front of him. She took the knife out of his hand and set it down. Then she wove her fingers through his, grabbing his other hand to do the same.

"Jordan."

He shifted his feet, refusing to meet her eyes.

"Jordan." She squeezed his hands. "Jordan, could you please look at me?"

He didn't want to. He was all kinds of stupid, and this was embarrassing, and he never wanted to have her look at him again.

But she'd said please, so he raised his head, meeting her gaze.

He didn't see pity, or embarrassment. She looked happy. Glowing. He was about to step back, get away from whatever this was, when she reached up and kissed him.

Like a fool, he kissed her back. This time the smell of something on the stove made Delaney break the embrace and turn off the burner. She looked back at him, with a finger raised.

"This conversation isn't going any further, okay? Because I talked to Mariah and she's planning a whole proposal thing for when everyone is here. And you're going to act surprised when it happens, and hopefully say yes?"

She...she'd planned to propose to him? The breath rushed out of his lungs. But that bit of question on the end killed him.

"I'll say yes to anything you ask me, Delaney."

She bit her lip. "A petting zoo?"

He nodded.

"Hayrides?"

He nodded again.

"And a wedding right away?"

"Especially that."

TWO DAYS LATER, at the end of a spectacular meal, Delaney stood up with a glass of champagne.

"I'd like to propose a toast to an amazing man who took me in when I was struggling." Nelson gave Jordan a side eye, but Mariah had a big smile on her face.

"He gave me so much of himself. Even though it made him uncomfortable, and he even though he risked his future, he never said no."

Jordan's cheeks were warm, but he held Delaney's gaze.

"Now I have a question to ask him, and I hope he still can't say no."

Jordan could feel the smile on his face growing.

"Jordan Callahan Everton, would you do me the honor of marrying me?"

He stood to his feet.

"Anytime. I'd be honored."

Around them he heard sounds, surprised and happy. But Jordan set his glass down, eyes focused on Delaney and made his way around the table. Something glittery was falling from the ceiling, and music was playing, but he didn't care about any of that.

Delaney had set her own glass down, and he wrapped his arms around her. Hers slid up to cling to the back of his neck.

"Can I kiss you now?" He asked.

"Anytime. I'd be honored."

So he did.

EPILOGUE

JORDAN TUCKED DELANEY into the curve of his arm as they snuggled on Nelson's couch.

"Leftovers are almost better than the original meal." It was Saturday evening, and there was still food in the fridge from Delaney's Thanksgiving feast.

"Mhhmm." Delaney's eyes were closed as she rested her head on his chest.

"Thanks for coming to the farm again with me."

She shrugged. "You're mine now." Jordan loved the sound of that.

"Do you think it's really the end? With Everton?"

"I don't know. But I think the only pain he can inflict now is what you let him."

Abigail had driven to the farm with the two of them yesterday, after the dinner and proposal on Thanksgiving, and a detailed discussion about Jordan's next steps. The three of them had faced his father. His adopted father.

He'd been drunk and belligerent, but Abigail was unfazed.

She'd offered him the settlement money for his wife's death that he'd refused before, if he would leave the farm before doing any damage. Once Jordan announced his engagement, the clock was ticking down anyway. Everton agreed to take the money.

Abigail insisted on a notarized signature before she gave him the cheque.

The man hadn't shown any interest in Jordan or expressed any remorse for how he'd tried to basically embezzle money from his son to purchase a property that was already Jordan's. Jordan told him he was going to be living on the farm, with Delaney and that he was only welcome back if he was sober and respectful and willing to apologize for what he'd done.

Jordan didn't think he'd see the man again. It had been painful. Everton had been the only family he had left.

But he'd returned from that visit with Delaney and Abigail, and was greeted with a warm welcome from Nelson, Mariah, and the rather intimidating Gerald Van Dalton. He had a new family, one who showed more care for him than his adopted father ever had.

Now, Gerald and Abigail had retired, and

Mariah went out to the barn with Nelson to check on his rescue horses. They took Ranger with them to get the dog and horses familiar with each other. Jordan would rather not return to the farm until his father was gone, so he would be staying for a couple more days.

Delaney was curled into his side, and Jordan didn't think he'd ever been happier.

"We were talking, me and Mariah and Grandmother this aft, while you and Ranger were out."

Jordan ran his fingers through her hair.

"You were, were you?"

He felt her head nodding against his chest.

"I was trying out ideas about what I was going to do, things I could do here, not in New York City."

He stilled. "If you need to go back—"

This time her head was shaking no against him.

"I need some downtime. Make sure I have a handle on the panic attacks, and also take time to figure out what I really want to do. I'm going to keep seeing my therapist, making sure I can tell the difference between what I really want and what I'm just doing to try to impress my family."

Jordan took a breath and forced himself to

be honest. "I think maybe I should—" This was almost painful to say out loud and commit to. "Talk to someone like that too."

Delaney twisted to look at his face. "Really?"

He nodded. "What happened to my dad—Everton?" He didn't think he wanted to call him dad anymore, which was something he needed to work through. "I don't ever want to get like that. And I don't know how much he might have influenced me."

Delaney brushed a hand over his jaw. "I don't think you're anything like him, but I can see where he might have messed you up in other ways."

She poked his ribs. "You do realize that means you're going to have to do a lot of talking."

He grunted.

"I'm proud of you, Jordan. And would you like to hear what I think I should do for the next several months?"

"Yeah." He didn't have the words to express how important that was to him, but he knew she could tell.

"I'd like to spend the winter working on recipes. Simple ones. Maybe for a cookbook—I have some connections if I wanted to do that. But I just want to be in the kitchen, doing something for me. Maybe it could end up as a cookbook, or things I could use in a restaurant, but I'll figure that out when the time is right."

"How about we figure it out together?"

Delaney wrapped her arm around his waist. "I like the sound of that."

He rubbed his chin against her hair. Hard to believe a few days ago he thought he'd lost everything. Now he had more than he could have thought of asking for.

"I have some money I was saving for a new restaurant. I thought maybe I could use that to update the appliances at the farm?"

She wanted to be on the farm. He felt his cheeks lift with his smile.

"I've got the money I was saving up to buy out the farm. We can use that."

Delaney leaned up, away from him. "No, I want you to use that on the farm. Make sure you get some help so you're not exhausted all the time."

Jordan thought he could argue the fact that the kitchen on the farm was technically the farm, but they could work that out later. Right now, it was enough to know that Delaney was planning a future with him. She wanted to marry him, even though his dad was leaving the farm and he didn't need to get married to protect it.

He could tell her that. But he was a firm believer that actions spoke louder than words. So instead, he put a finger on her chin, and leaned down to kiss her.

* * * * *

Get 4 FREE REWARDS!

We'll send you 2 FREE Books plus 2 FREE Mystery Gifts.

FREE Value Over **$20**

Both the **Love Inspired**® and **Love Inspired**® Suspense series feature compelling novels filled with inspirational romance, faith, forgiveness and hope.

YES! Please send me 2 FREE novels from the Love Inspired or Love Inspired Suspense series and my 2 FREE gifts (gifts are worth about $10 retail). After receiving them, if I don't wish to receive any more books, I can return the shipping statement marked "cancel." If I don't cancel, I will receive 6 brand-new Love Inspired Larger-Print books or Love Inspired Suspense Larger-Print books every month and be billed just $6.49 each in the U.S. or $6.74 each in Canada. That is a savings of at least 16% off the cover price. It's quite a bargain! Shipping and handling is just 50¢ per book in the U.S. and $1.25 per book in Canada.* I understand that accepting the 2 free books and gifts places me under no obligation to buy anything. I can always return a shipment and cancel at any time by calling the number below. The free books and gifts are mine to keep no matter what I decide.

Choose one: ☐ **Love Inspired**
Larger-Print
(122/322 IDN GRHK)

☐ **Love Inspired Suspense**
Larger-Print
(107/307 IDN GRHK)

Name (please print)

Address   Apt. #

City   State/Province   Zip/Postal Code

Email: Please check this box ☐ if you would like to receive newsletters and promotional emails from Harlequin Enterprises ULC and its affiliates. You can unsubscribe anytime.

Mail to the Harlequin Reader Service:
IN U.S.A.: P.O. Box 1341, Buffalo, NY 14240-8531
IN CANADA: P.O. Box 603, Fort Erie, Ontario L2A 5X3

Want to try 2 free books from another series! Call 1-800-873-8635 or visit www.ReaderService.com.

LIRLIS22R3

Get 4 FREE REWARDS!

We'll send you 2 FREE Books plus 2 FREE Mystery Gifts.

FREE
Value Over
$20

Both the **Harlequin® Special Edition** and **Harlequin® Heartwarming™** series feature compelling novels filled with stories of love and strength where the bonds of friendship, family and community unite.

YES! Please send me 2 FREE novels from the Harlequin Special Edition or Harlequin Heartwarming series and my 2 FREE gifts (gifts are worth about $10 retail). After receiving them, if I don't wish to receive any more books, I can return the shipping statement marked "cancel." If I don't cancel, I will receive 6 brand-new Harlequin Special Edition books every month and be billed just $5.49 each in the U.S. or $6.24 each in Canada, a savings of at least 12% off the cover price, or 4 brand-new Harlequin Heartwarming Larger-Print books every month and be billed just $6.24 each in the U.S. or $6.74 each in Canada, a savings of at least 19% off the cover price. It's quite a bargain! Shipping and handling is just 50¢ per book in the U.S. and $1.25 per book in Canada.* I understand that accepting the 2 free books and gifts places me under no obligation to buy anything. I can always return a shipment and cancel at any time by calling the number below. The free books and gifts are mine to keep no matter what I decide.

Choose one: ☐ **Harlequin Special Edition** ☐ **Harlequin Heartwarming**
(235/335 HDN GRJV)   **Larger-Print**
(161/361 HDN GRJV)

Name (please print)

Address _____ Apt. #

City _____ State/Province _____ Zip/Postal Code

Email: Please check this box ☐ if you would like to receive newsletters and promotional emails from Harlequin Enterprises ULC and its affiliates. You can unsubscribe anytime.

Mail to the **Harlequin Reader Service:**
IN U.S.A.: P.O. Box 1341, Buffalo, NY 14240-8531
IN CANADA: P.O. Box 603, Fort Erie, Ontario L2A 5X3

Want to try 2 free books from another series? Call 1-800-873-8635 or visit www.ReaderService.com.

COUNTRY LEGACY COLLECTION

19 FREE BOOKS IN ALL!

EMMETT
Diana Palmer

COURTED BY THE COWBOY

THE RANCHER AND THE BABY

Cowboys, adventure and romance await you in this new collection! Enjoy superb reading all year long with books by bestselling authors like Diana Palmer, Sasha Summers and Marie Ferrarella!

YES! Please send me the **Country Legacy Collection!** This collection begins with 3 FREE books and 2 FREE gifts in the first shipment. Along with my 3 free books, I'll also get 3 more books from the **Country Legacy Collection**, which I may either return and owe nothing or keep for the low price of $24.60 U.S./$28.12 CDN each plus $2.99 U.S./$7.49 CDN for shipping and handling per shipment*. If I decide to continue, about once a month for 8 months, I will get 6 or 7 more books but will only pay for 4. That means 2 or 3 books in every shipment will be FREE! If I decide to keep the entire collection, I'll have paid for only 32 books because 19 are FREE! I understand that accepting the 3 free books and gifts places me under no obligation to buy anything. I can always return a shipment and cancel at any time. My free books and gifts are mine to keep no matter what I decide.

☐ 275 HCK 1939   ☐ 475 HCK 1939

Name (please print)

Address   Apt. #

City   State/Province   Zip/Postal Code

Mail to the Harlequin Reader Service:
IN U.S.A.: P.O. Box 1341, Buffalo, NY 14240-8571
IN CANADA: P.O. Box 603, Fort Erie, Ontario L2A 5X3